VINTAGE
VERONICA

VINTAGE
VERONICA

by
Erica S. Perl

Alfred A. Knopf

New York

Library of Congress Cataloging-in-Publication Data
Perl, Erica S.
Vintage Veronica / by Erica S. Perl. — 1st ed.
p. cm.
Summary: After getting a job at a vintage clothing shop and quickly bonding with two older girls, fifteen-year-old Veronica finds herself making bad decisions in order to keep their friendship.
ISBN 978-0-375-85923-6 (trade) — ISBN 978-0-375-95923-3 (lib. bdg.) —
ISBN 978-0-375-89554-8 (e-book)
[1. Friendship—Fiction. 2. Vintage clothing—Fiction. 3. Overweight persons—Fiction.· 4. Summer employment—Fiction. 5. Work—Fiction.] I. Title.
PZ7.P3163Vi 2010   [Fic]—dc22   2009005280

The text of this book is set in 13-point Galena.

Printed in the United States of America
March 2010
10 9 8 7 6 5 4 3 2 1
First Edition

To Mike,
Franny, and
Bougie

PREFACE

I'm sure you don't know me.

But you've probably seen me around.

I'm that fat girl. You know, the one who dresses funny. The one who wears those ridiculous poufy skirts from the fifties that look like she hacked off the top of an old prom dress (because actually, I did). The one who wears them with the vintage guayabera shirts and the men's bowling shoes and the cat's-eye sunglasses and the whole nine yards. The one who always wears her hair in two stumpy pigtails and cuts her own bangs because it doesn't look good anyway, so why bother?

Maybe you've made fun of her. I mean, me.

If not, I'm sure you've thought about it.

If you haven't, then I guess you probably haven't seen me around after all.

Don't feel bad.

I'm used to it by now.

Have you ever played that game "I Never"? It's where you sit in a circle and one kid says "I never . . . ," and every kid who has done it has to stand up.

Do you see where this is going?

Yeah? Well, I didn't.

Then again, I was ten at the time.

Anyway, I was over at this girl's house—for a party, I think, one of those invite-the-whole-class numbers. And someone started the game, so everyone had to play.

At first it was funny. "I never slept in a tent." "I never threw up." Then Shawn McKinney said, "I never wore a bra" and all the girls that did had to stand up while the boys laughed and laughed.

Now, I was one of those chubby girls who was saddled with a bra at about the same time I learned to ride a bike. But for once I almost didn't mind, because some of the pretty girls had to stand up, too. It was almost like we were all in a club together for a minute there.

But there was this one pretty girl, Spencer Royce, who must have hated having me standing up there with her. She glared at me and went next. "I never ate an entire box of Thin Mints all at once." She knew because she had seen me do it. We had been in the same Brownie troop.

At first I didn't stand up. I looked away, hoping someone else would jump up and her turn would pass.

But before I knew it, Spencer and her friends had grabbed me by the arms and dragged me onto my feet. Then they plunked themselves down and fell into each other's laps, laughing their heads off.

I stood there, blinking back dumb, fat tears, thinking
I'm NEVER
playing with girls ever again

playing with boys ever again
wearing this stupid bra ever again
trusting anyone ever again
ever.

And until this summer, except for the bra part, I never have.

But this summer—well, this summer changed everything.

CHAPTER ONE

F riday is seventy-five-cents day at Dollar-a-Pound. Today is Friday, so when I get to the store a few minutes after nine, the line of Pickers is around the block. To make matters worse, it's one of those steamy July days that start out hot and miserable and clearly intend to get hotter and miserabler by the minute.

"Crap," I say, stopping in my tracks at the sight of the line and wiping the sweat from my brow.

Why I come to work on Fridays is beyond me.

The Pickers are the Dollar-a-Pound regulars. They show up extra early, grumbling and jockeying for position, each and every Friday morning to await the doors opening at the largest vintage clothing store in the Northeast: THE CLOTHING BONANZA

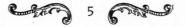

(HOME OF THE ORIGINAL DOLLAR-A-POUND!), otherwise known as THE STORE CAUGHT IN A TIME WARP!, according to the big neon-pink and black sandwich board sign out front. Whoever made the store signs a million years ago was a big fan of exclamation marks.

Dollar-a-Pound takes up the entire first floor of the store. It is exactly like it sounds: a huge, towering heap of used clothes (known to those of us who work at the store simply as The Pile), spilling like a giant stain over most of the painted wood floor.

This hippie guy named Bill runs Dollar-a-Pound. He claims that the Friday discount draws the most aggressive Pickers. He also says that sometimes he has to break up Pile fights. Apparently, what happens is that overeager Pickers claim opposite ends of the same thing—usually something long, like a pair of overalls. Then it's like some dumb cartoon: they discover they're connected and start scrapping and yelling. Elbows swinging, feet flailing, lots of shuffling, and the inevitable sound of fabric ripping.

Bill keeps a bottle of seltzer under the counter at all times. Once I asked him if he had it to spray on Pile fights, like I saw my neighbor do with regular water when his dog got into a fight.

"Nah, man," he said, deadpan. "I just like seltzer."

I stand there, confronting the line and suppressing the tidal-wave urge to run in the opposite direction.

I don't do crowds.

Too much potential for anonymous heckling. I mean, look at me. My unruly hair, bunched into two lopsided pigtails. My

cat's-eye sunglasses and, of course, my clothes. Today I'm wearing my second-favorite skirt, which is a white 1950s circle style with bright red appliquéd slices of cherry pie on the pockets and a hemline border of cherries playing tag. On top, I'm wearing one of my many bowling shirts, which has the words *Valley Vending* stitched in cursive on the back.

And if my ensemble isn't enough to bring out the guffaws of the masses, there's always my size. Big girls like me know it's never a good idea to have a bunch of people standing behind you. This past school year, my freshman year, brought this point home more than ever.

To state the obvious: high school is a lousy place to be a fat girl. Of course, the good news is, if you ARE a fat girl, you're not really risking much socially to become The Fat Girl Who Dresses Weird. So once the eye-rolling subsided, my freshman year was basically defined by my being almost universally ignored.

As the crowd of Pickers rumbles restlessly, I turn slowly on the heels of my shoes. The tulle layers of the big bubble-gum-pink vintage crinoline I'm wearing under my cherry pie skirt whisper uneasily to each other.

I smooth my crinoline absently, distracted by a different siren song. It is the sultry voice of an iced mocha smoothie and it comes from the Mookie's Donut Shop, next door to The Clothing Bonanza. *Veronicaaaa! Come get me! It's soooo hot outside, and I'm soooo cold and refreshing!* The donuts chime in, too, harmonizing. *Us, too! Don't forget about us!* They're those chocolate-glazed ones, I can tell.

Of course, I also hear another voice. My mother, chiding,

One moment on the lips, Veronica! I smile to myself, imagining her here right now, witnessing my premeditated act of debauched gluttony (*Donuts? AND a milkshake? At nine in the morning???*). My mother, the dance diva, the plié princess, the prima pain-in-the-ass-a. It's a good thing she thinks my summer job is halfway across town, at some animal shelter run by one of her former dance students. I picture her barricading the door to Mookie's Donuts with her skinny little spandex-clad body, having a cow and a half over my inability to live by her beloved Weight Watchers point system.

In my mind, I swing the door open, knocking her out of the way. *Sorry, lady. Some days, you just need a donut.*

In my town, Mookie's Donut Shops are everywhere. People call them "Mooks" and give directions by them, like "Go down a couple of blocks and turn right at the Mooks."

The Mooks next door to The Clothing Bonanza is like the one that time forgot. The counters and stools are pink vinyl and chrome, like in an old diner, even though the Mookie's Donuts corporate colors are yellow and orange. It's sort of fitting that the only Mooks in town that missed out on being renovated is the one next door to The Store Caught in a Time Warp! Of course, this Mooks doesn't take the retro theme any further than the stools and counters. The employees all wear Mookie's Donuts pee-and-cheddar-cheese-striped polo shirts, which you'd think would be an equal opportunity fashion disaster, but which look particularly hideous on girls built like me. Not that I'd ever consider working there under any circumstances.

The Clothing Bonanza, thank God, has no dress code

except *No New Clothing!* The Florons, which is what my boss, Claire, calls everyone who works on the main retail floor, wear a pretty wide variety of vintage clothes, often mixed with more modern touches like blue hair dye, tats, and piercings. Mod is very popular with the Florons—monochromatic polyester minidresses and the like—as are Glam, Goth, and what I like to think of as Gloth, which is a look that's kind of both. And kind of neither.

My own look is a little hard to define, or at least I like to think it is. I'm all about individual pieces. If they speak to me, I buy them, even if they don't fit. Back when my mom didn't cringe at the sight of me quite so much, we used to do all sorts of dumb, crunchy activities together. So I actually know how to sew pretty well, which helps if you want to wear a dress that is a couple of sizes too big or, as is more often the case for me, too small.

Most of what I buy and what I wear is stuff from the fifties, although occasionally I'll venture out of my decade for the right piece. The only thing I skip is the shoes—fifties girls' shoes are death. I stick with men's stuff like two-tone creepers and bricks, good clompy shoes that go with everything. I also have a pair of Chuck Taylors, and a pair of bowling shoes that I only wear in the winter. But from the ankles up, I like girly stuff. Tulle crinolines, full circle skirts, bolero jackets, silk dressing gown jackets, beaded cardigans. Especially beaded cardigans. I'm also a sucker for anything with fruit on it. Cherries, pineapples, lemons . . . I even have a watermelon dress. The fifties were all about fruit.

Today, under a ridiculous number of layers of pink tulle,

I'm wearing my (men's size eight-and-a-half wide) black-and-white two-tone creepers, which are uncomfortably hot but not as bad as bowling shoes. When I swish on over to the Mooks, there's a line out the door there, too. It's not Pickers, of course. In fact, it seems to be a lot of the Florons. I recognize two of them, Zoe and Ginger, right off the bat. They are in line a few people up from me, but they're very noticeable because Zoe's like a full head taller than anybody else and Ginger's got bright pink hair and a squeaky laugh you can hear about a mile away. They seem like they're probably about nineteen or so—enough older than me that I'm simply not on their radar, even though they've been on mine since day one.

Zoe and Ginger are pretty much always together. With the exception of their shared appreciation for thick black eyeliner, they look about as dissimilar as any two girls possibly could. Zoe's look is over-the-top Gloth. She's also, as I mentioned, an Amazon. She's got a jet-black Cleopatra hairdo and these va-va-voom black outfits that a drag queen would envy. Ginger, on the other hand, is short and skinny. She's got a long horsy face, big eyes that shift from side to side like one of those fifties cat clocks, and long, stringy hair that changes color practically every week. She dresses mostly in shapeless sixties shifts and white go-go boots. She's also fond of Hello Kitty baby barrettes.

I get in line several people behind them and wait. Bill is there, so I give him a noncommittal nod. Bill is an old guy, maybe twenty-five, with a long, straggly ponytail. He sounds even older when he opens his mouth, because he calls everyone "man" and says things like "heavy" to mean that something sucks. He's also the closest thing I have to a friend at work. Unfortunately, he seems to think he's my ex, because at the beginning of the summer, when I first started working at the store, I went over to his apartment after work a couple of times to watch movies and eat nachos. I guess he thinks that meant something. I think it didn't. When I stopped coming over, I told him that it wasn't him, it was the goddamned Weight Watchers. Nachos are just plain not worth the points.

Plus, he's boring, but I didn't tell him that.

It turns out Bill isn't in line. He's just standing there, holding a Mooks bag and smoking a cigarette. When I nod in his direction, he comes right over.

"Hey, Veronica. What's up?"

"Nothing. You?"

"Not a lot."

We both nod and look away for a while.

"You walking back after?" he asks finally.

"Looks that way."

"Cool. I'll hang." He shuffles forward with me as the line inches along. We watch some fire ants attacking a half-eaten cruller. Bill pokes it with his sneaker and one of the fire ants rears up, waving angry legs.

"Is anyone watching Dollar-a-Pound?" I ask.

"Yeah, I got Zoe to cover for me, why?"

I point in her direction. Bill rolls his eyes.

"Christ," he says, taking a last drag. "Later, man."

"Aren't you going to give her shit or anything?"

Bill raises one eyebrow at me. "I'm a lover, not a fighter," he tells me.

"Good to know," I say, turning my attention back to the ants.

After Bill leaves, the line crawls into the Mooks. The service there is uniformly lousy, which I find comforting in its predictability. I also enjoy the fact that after going there about twice a day for the entire summer I've been working at The Clothing Bonanza, no one has ever remembered my order. It's not a particularly complicated one, either: one extra-large iced mocha smoothie, which they insist on calling (and I refuse to call) a "s'Mookie."

From where I'm standing, I can see that Zoe and Ginger have almost made it to the counter. Then someone in front of me steps out of line, so there are only two customers between me and them. I hear Zoe say, "Well, whaddaya know? They have a new assistant manager this week."

"Why should this week be any different?" replies Ginger, giggling.

The counter girl narrows her eyes and takes a deep breath as Zoe and Ginger close in on her. She looks like one of those animals that try to make themselves appear larger when predators approach. She has thick glasses, the standard-issue Mookie's uniform, and these ginormous boobs. Clearly, it's not her lucky day—the water parts and Zoe and Ginger step forward to become her next customers.

"Welcome-to-Mookie's-I'm-Carla-can-I-take-your-order?"

"Mmmmmm, I'll bet you are," says Zoe, reaching out and tweaking the orange and yellow advertising button (which reads MMM . . . S'MOOKIE-LICIOUS!) that perches on the girl's polo shirt like a goat on a mountain range.

"I'm . . . sorry?" The girl steps back, clutching herself protectively.

"Could you please try not being such a bitch all the time?" says Zoe brightly. Since I'm behind her, I can't see her face, but I can tell from her tone of voice that she's grinning like a barracuda.

The counter girl blinks repeatedly.

"What?" she asks.

"I *said*," says Zoe, sounding impatient, "could I please try the sausage bagel sandwich this time?"

The counter girl storms off. Some sort of huddle takes place behind the counter. Meanwhile, the two people ahead of me get served at another register. I shuffle toward the counter, where Zoe and Ginger are still standing.

"Hello? Ec-squeeze me?" calls Zoe, leaning over the counter and waving. Turning to Ginger, she gripes, "Who do you have to blow around here to get a sausage bagel?"

Just then Ginger looks my way. "Hey," she says. It is the first word she's ever spoken to me.

"Hey, what's up?" I ask, trying to sound casual.

"Oh, nothing. Same old, same old."

A short Indian-looking man with a mustache breaks away from the huddle and comes to the counter.

"Well, *hello*," simpers Zoe, putting both elbows on the counter and leaning on them so her cleavage is even more unavoidable than usual. "You must be the assistant manager."

"I am Mr. Singh. Is there a problem?"

"Well, I don't know. I haven't been able to get my order filled. Do you think you could *fill my order*? I asked for a hot sausage in my buns . . . ooh, I mean my bagel."

The man's darkish face begins to look purple.

"I think you should leave," he says in kind of a clipped way.

"YOU WANT TO GO OUT WITH ME?" asks Zoe, loud and incredulous.

"No, I think you should leave. Before I call the police."

"Are you threatening me?"

"Zo?" Ginger pipes up. "Let's bounce."

"NO," says Zoe firmly. "I will not step down in the face of SEXUAL HARASSMENT. I will take back the night, as will all my sisters. This is not about donuts. This is about OP-PRESSION."

Every eye in the Mooks is on her.

"And I will not be silenced. Before I am through, everyone will know that *that* man said that GIRLS LIKE ME DON'T DE-SERVE TO BE TREATED FAIRLY."

"Now wait just a minute, Miss," says Mr. Singh. It comes out *mees*.

"AND SOMEDAY," Zoe continues, "I hope he will learn that ALL PEOPLE SHOULD BE TREATED EQUALLY, WITH COURTESY AND RESPECT. And then and only then will I say, HALLELUJAH."

"Hallelujah," says someone in line behind me.

"Amen," chimes in someone else.

I turn around. The entire store is glaring at Mr. Singh. He leans forward and says something quietly to Zoe.

"Okay," she says.

Then he leaves the counter and comes back with a large Mookie's bag. He hands it to Zoe, and she and Ginger practically skip out of the store.

Without missing a beat, the counter girl with the huge boobs looks at me and says, "Welcome-to-Mookie's-I'm-Carla-can-I-take-your-order?"

No wonder Claire's first piece of advice to me was: Never talk to the Florons if you can help it.

CHAPTER TWO

I don't end up ordering a donut after all.

After Zoe and Ginger leave, I just want to get the hell out of the Mooks as fast as I can. Donning my sunglasses, I clutch my purse and my iced mocha smoothie tightly to my chest and march straight from the Mooks to The Clothing Bonanza.

I brush past the line of Pickers, trying to look as officious and disinterested as possible so none of them will launch into an angry tirade about "cutters" or start riffing on my look. Luckily, Bill sees me struggling with the front door and opens it for me.

"Must be a full moon or something," he says, glaring over my shoulder at the teeming masses as I cross the threshold.

"Or something," I say.

Bill shrugs at me, like *What are you gonna do?* He must be pretty used to the Pickers by now. After all, he's been working at Dollar-a-Pound since the earth cooled. On a positive note, this has given him an unrivaled collection of vintage iron-on T-shirts. Today he's wearing a baseball-style shirt that says I'VE GOT A MAGIC STICK! and has a picture of a caveman on it.

About every hour or so, Bill reassembles The Pile with a garden rake and yells "Clear!" On cue, the Pickers shuffle out of The Pile. Then Bill presses a button and a torrent of additional garments rains down from a hole in the ceiling. It's a loud process, kind of like a subway train running through the store.

From what I can tell, the common denominator among the Pickers is being very cheap. Or very poor, maybe. Some Pickers are insatiable and root around in The Pile all day long. Some are only interested in one kind of item, like this guy who collects hats. Sometimes I see him sitting at the Mookie's Donuts next door, drinking a coffee, with a stack of eight or ten hats piled on top of his head. He looks like this picture in a book I had when I was little. And he's one of the more normal ones.

The Pickers never go upstairs to the store's main retail floor, which is called The Real Deal. It's also a resale shop, but there's no scale. Clothing is priced by the piece and is organized in a variety of ways: by decade, by color, by theme (there's a big rack of army surplus, for example, and another one of marching band uniforms), by type of piece (the silk smoking jackets live together, as do the leather biker jackets). Never by size. Since the Pickers never venture upstairs, they probably don't know that there's other stuff for sale on The Real Deal, too: jewelry, makeup, shoes, wigs, and costume props like swords and tiaras. It's a huge store, and there's stuff everywhere: feathered boas form a wall of curtains, sequined ball gowns shimmer from the rafters, and rows upon rows of false eyelashes wink at you from their perches above the jewelry counter mirrors.

The decor of Dollar-a-Pound is pretty much like The Real Deal's, only messier and more worn-out. For example, there's an old vintage motorcycle hanging from the ceiling of The Real Deal, and there's an even older Volkswagen Beetle (unnecessarily labeled THIS RIDE'S NOT FOR SALE!) parked on Dollar-a-Pound, right next to The Pile.

The sign on the Volkswagen, like all the store signs, is painted in screaming neon pink and black. The Clothing Bonanza's front door has this weird drawing of a neon-pink cat holding a huge black barbell above his head. One side of the barbell says, VINTAGE, PRACTICAL, AND CONTEMPORARY CLOTHING! The other side says SOMETHING FOR EVERYONE! On the cat's T-shirt it says OL' RAGS. Apparently, Rags's shirt was not deemed worthy of an exclamation mark.

Rags is actually the name of one of the store cats, although he's like Rags the Seventeenth or something. There are four or five other store cats and they all have names, but since I can't tell them apart I think of them all as Rags. The store rules are also painted on pink and black signs, one by the cash registers on The Real Deal and one by Bill's cash register on Dollar-a-Pound. Rule number seven is PLEASE DO NOT HARASS THE CATS! Rags spends a lot of time sleeping on or in The Pile, where he is as likely to get harassed as he is anywhere else. Today, however, I don't see him. Maybe he doesn't like Fridays either.

In case you're wondering how I can work at Dollar-a-Pound when I hate it so much, let me set you straight:

I don't.

I work in the Consignment Corner, which is on the floor two flights up from Dollar-a-Pound. This floor is known as Employees Only!, which is for EMPLOYEES ONLY!, as the pink and black sign on the door leading upstairs emphatically states. Employees Only! and Dollar-a-Pound are not only two flights of stairs apart, they're pretty much a whole world apart. They are connected, however, by a long metal chute. The chute starts at a metal bin near my desk and runs vertically through the store, cutting through ceilings and floors, and ending at the hole in the ceiling directly above The Pile. It is my job to weed through the clothing that people bring in and decide what should go to the good racks on The Real Deal and what should get dumped down the chute to The Pile. In effect, it is my job to keep The Pile well fed.

My boss, Claire, calls banishing something down the chute "depping" it. When she first said it, I gave her a confused look.

"Dep. Stands for Dollar-a-Pound," she explained.

"Not 'dap'?" I asked. Claire furrowed her brow and considered this.

"No, it's dep," she finally said. "Like, now I'm gonna dep this skanky old shirt." She took a ratty T-shirt and threw it in the direction of the chute to demonstrate.

Because my job is in the Consignment Corner, I don't have to do any "floor time" in retail land on either of the lower floors. In fact, I barely have to interact with anyone, which suits me just fine. I just deal with the clothes, which is great because I'm all about the clothes. I'll take clothes over people any day of the week.

The truth is, I have a serious vintage clothing problem. I've been crawling around vintage stores, tag sales, and flea markets since I was a kid. Sometime shortly after my dad moved out, trolling them together became our standing Saturday morning activity. He'd pick me up with a tray of cinnamon buns and a folded section of the newspaper marked up with red pen. "Hey, Ronnie," he'd always say, "let's go to the fleas." At first I thought it was boring, but I didn't complain because it was nice to see my dad and it got me out of having to play soccer.

Then I got hooked, big-time.

My dad is a serious collector. All serious collectors specialize, and his specialty is musical theater, especially all things Broadway. Mostly memorabilia, but he also buys vinyl recordings. My dad and I share a passion for the hunt, but our differences as collectors are clearly defined. He's a total bug about condition. If a *Playbill* cover is ripped, or even bent a little, he'll pass. Me, I'm more about the piece itself. My specialty is vintage clothes and quirky stuff from the fifties, and my crusade is for diamonds in the rough. Unfortunately, this means I sometimes fall for things that I only realize later are mostly rough and very little diamond. My dad claims this is unavoidable. "That's show biz," is what he says.

I spent a lot of time with my dad when I was a kid. Hanging out with him was a welcome alternative to hanging out with other kids, who basically turned on me once they got old enough to figure out my place in the social hierarchy. My parents got a whiff of this when I was in grade school and thought they could dodge this particular bullet by sending me to one of those crunchy schools.

Boy, were they wrong.

Journey back with me to where I went from third grade through eighth. A hundred and twenty kids behind a pair of double doors painted with a big yellow smiling sun and the school slogan: THE SUNSHINE SCHOOL, WHERE THE SUN SHINES ON EVERYONE. They took that crap seriously, too. If you were having a problem with another kid, the school rule was that you were supposed to say, "Stop, I really mean it." Those five magic words were treated with reverence and squirreled away as last resorts. Each classroom was also equipped with a "friendship table" where adults could perch on tiny chairs to help kids overanalyze their playground squabbles.

Everything was great for a while. Meaning: third and fourth grades. Kids in my class asked me to their birthday parties and picked me as their folk-dancing partner and filled my red-construction-paper-covered shoebox with drugstore valentines each February.

But then I started fifth grade. I felt the tide turn that year. It happened little by little, like brown leaves dropping off a tree one by one until you suddenly look up and, boom, you can't remember a time when it wasn't fall. One afternoon, probably about a month before the fateful "I Never" party, I was playing on the swings with a girl named Tanya. A girl I thought of at the time as my best friend. We were lying face-down and running forward to take off and feel the swings catch us like we were flying. I was a bird, flapping my wings, taking off and being caught, swinging back, again and again, soaring and feeling so free.

Then something hit the back of my leg. Hard.

"Bull's-eye!" I heard someone say, followed by loud, rough guffaws.

I landed and looked over my shoulder at a bunch of older boys with a huge pile of horse chestnuts. You know, the ones that have those thick yellow-green peels that make them look like prickly tennis balls? They were using my butt for target practice.

My eyes welled up with tears, from pain as well as humiliation. I turned to Tanya for help. To my surprise, she was doubled over, laughing.

"Stop, Tanya," I said, evoking the magic incantation as I had been taught. "I really mean it."

The next thing I knew, she had run off and was letting the boys catch her and pin her down. When our teacher called us back inside, I marched Tanya over to the friendship table and gave her my indignant side of things. Tanya listened politely. I think she even apologized. I had the nagging sense that it seemed too easy, but I allowed myself to ignore it and feel better, to hug her and smile.

When recess time came the next day and Tanya ran off with the boys again, the nagging feeling came back and I was unable to escape the realization that something had changed forever.

I cried to my mother, who, to her credit, rubbed my back and just listened for a while. Back then, she still wore clothes she made herself sometimes, but increasingly she wore leotards. She was studying to be a dance teacher and seemed to be busy a lot with rehearsals and master classes in the evenings. She also seemed perpetually distracted, staring off into the distance like the music in her head had started up and she didn't want to miss her cue. And she got really into posture all of a sudden. Sometimes she would straighten up and she'd look like a swan or something. I'd try to copy her, straining unsuccessfully.

She held me for maybe a minute, minute and a half. Then she took hold of my shoulders and kind of faced off with me.

"I'm sorry," I remember her saying. "I'm not going to lie to you. Kids can be very cruel sometimes."

"Blub," I said, sniffling, nodding.

"*Bu-ut,*" she suddenly singsonged, shifting gears and catching my eye, "it'll be easier for you to make friends, real friends, with nice girls if you'd just try . . ." She paused, but she didn't really need to finish the sentence. I knew what she was thinking: *if you'd just try to lose some weight.* All the wonders of the world—friends, fun, fabulousness—would be mine if only I'd get it together and stop being so damned fat. Which was a point she'd been hammering for a while; she just finally found something to anchor it to.

I nodded glumly, knowing she was right.

It was all my fault.

When she walked me in to school the next morning, I stared accusingly at the sun painted on the front door. I had never noticed how phony the sun's smile looked before. I reread the slogan. THE SUN SHINES ON EVERYONE.

Everyone but you, fatso! the sun seemed to be saying, winking snidely. *Have a great day!*

I hated school from then on. Going to the fleas with my dad was pretty much my only pleasure. That and eating, which, now that I think about it, we did a lot of when we went to the fleas. These great big cinnamon rolls the size of your head, with cups of extra white icing on the side, and giant sweating plastic tumblers of pink lemonade to cut the sweetness. Mmm . . . good times.

I'd probably still be going to the fleas with my dad, except that he's not here anymore. Broadway called, or more specifically, the Marriott Marquis Hotel on Broadway. They wanted him to manage their food services. My dad referred to this as his "big Broadway break," although he said it in kind of a wistful way. It's a little weird to think that my dumb little summer job is closer to working in the antiques biz than my dad's, especially since he got me started.

I never knew jobs like mine existed until I went to The Clothing Bonanza to consign some of my own stuff. I didn't have an appointment or anything. I just brought a bag of stuff to the second-floor registers and asked the girl working there if the store bought stuff.

"You got an appointment?" she asked me.

I shook my head.

"I dunno," she said dubiously. "Lemme see."

I passed the bag across the counter. The girl riffled through it, raised an eyebrow, and picked up the phone.

"Yah, hey, Claire?" she said. "I'm sending one up."

Hanging up, she pointed behind me.

"Follow the yellow brick road," she said.

I turned to look. Sure enough, the wood floor was painted black except for a four-inch-wide path painted gold. I followed it down the middle of the cavernous main retail floor, past the wigs and shoes and racks of vintage dresses grouped by decade or by the predominant color of their fabric. When the path led to a door, I stopped. The pink and black sign on the door said EMPLOYEES ONLY! DO NOT ENTER THROUGH THIS DOOR. But the gold path went right up to the bottom of the door.

Looking down, I noticed what looked like a bite taken out of the bottom of the door. I squatted down carefully and realized it was a homemade cat door cut out of the bottom of the regular person-sized door. Peering through it, I could see that the yellow brick road continued behind the door. My heart pounding, I pushed the big door open and followed the painted path up a rickety staircase.

"Your grandmother die?" asked Claire when she looked through the stuff I brought in to sell. I sat awkwardly on a lumpy rose-beige bouclé couch in her makeshift office, an open area in the corner of the floor partitioned off by several clothing racks. Next to the couch were a desk, a chair, and several mismatched filing cabinets.

"What? No, why?"

"This blouse." Claire pulled it out of the bag and inspected the lace by holding it up to the light. "It's your grandmother's, right?"

"No."

"Huh. I haven't seen one of these in a while." She dug some more and made sort of an appraising grunt. "Mmh . . . This Marimekko's pretty unusual. You sure you want to get rid of this?" She held up a lime-green and white shift with a round metal pull tab on the zipper.

"Yeah," I admitted.

"Why?" she asked.

"I have two others at home."

Claire made a low whistling sound. Then she offered me a job.

"I . . . sorry?"

"Part-time. For the summer. You're in school, right?"

"Uh, yeah." The way she said it, I could tell she meant college. I took the job without bothering to correct her.

She laid out the basics: what I'd get paid ("The pay is for shit . . ."), when I'd get paid, and what I'd be doing ("but there's no floor time"). I kept waiting for her to ask if I was sixteen. My plan was to answer yes, even though, technically, I wouldn't be for another six months.

But she didn't.

While she rattled on about the job, I was kind of freaking out inside. I mean, I'd never really worked before. I'd never even babysat before. I was psyched to have a summer job of any kind, especially one that didn't involve scooping poop.

But this was not going to go over well at home. After my

mom had run into her former dance student at the farmers' market, she had become convinced that my summer plans were all set. So far, I hadn't gotten around to telling her that I'd skipped my interview at the animal shelter to go to an estate sale instead. Of course, I reassured myself, as long as my mom didn't run into this particular ex-student any time soon, my change of plans could probably slide clear on through into August undetected.

Claire turned out to be a one-woman Consignment Corner. My job was to be her assistant. I was expected to shadow her as she made appointments with consigners, picked through their stuff, priced it, and logged it in. I quickly learned that Claire didn't share my reverence for the merchandise. She knew vintage, to be sure—she'd worked it long enough to have the styles and designer names at her fingertips. But to her, the clothes were all "just meat." Meat to be piled up, slopped around, slapped with tags, and shuffled off to The Real Deal or discarded and "depped."

When I get up to Employees Only! today, I breathe a sigh of relief. No Claire. Just Rags, or at least a cat that I think is Rags, sleeping on the well-clawed dirty pink couch with the exposed springs.

Claire's habitual lateness works well for me because I actually prefer the company of vintage clothing to people. I mean, technically, I'm never actually alone on Employees Only! because, like the floor's name says, there are other people working there. But it usually feels like I am, because the other employees completely ignore me.

Which is fine by me.

Today, for some reason I can't quite put my finger on, it feels different on Employees Only! It could be because there are no appointments. So, without Claire, it's pretty quiet. Not quiet-quiet, because it never is up here. The industrial equipment creates a constant din, like if you were on a train with all the windows open. Employees Only! serves as a weigh station of sorts, kind of a vintage clothing purgatory. It is a maze of old garments and the huge, ancient machines that process them—the pressers and the steamers, my favorite of which is the Moist-Rite Finishing Cabinet. It looks like a big set of metal gym lockers but is actually a surprisingly efficient steamer. Plus, there are these giant fans, because it's wicked hot up here.

The other employees on Employees Only! are these women I think of collectively as the Lunch Ladies. They sit all the way on the other side of the floor from the Consignment Corner, sorting piles of the clothes the store buys in bulk from vintage clothing wholesalers. They get up occasionally to operate the pressers or add items to the Moist-Rite Finishing Cabinet, then they resume their seats at sewing machine tables to mend clothes bound for the retail floors. Claire says they're from all over—Haiti, El Salvador, Brazil, you name it. New to this great land of ours, they seem thrilled to work for next to nothing with perks like all the dry-cleaning fumes you can inhale.

I don't deal with them directly, because most of the clothing they process doesn't come from individual consigners. I call them the Lunch Ladies because they all bring their lunches from home in old margarine tubs and eat crowded around a card table next to the main dry-cleaning machine. It probably makes their food taste like dry-cleaning fluid, and it definitely requires the couple of Lunch Ladies who speak the same language to yell their conversations. Yet it doesn't seem to occur to them to leave the third floor, much less the building.

At times I've been tempted to point out to them that the Mooks next door tolerates a regular parade of Pickers using the bathrooms and drinking the little thimbles of half-and-half. Surely this is an establishment that might welcome a bunch of gainfully employed brown-baggers, some of whom might actually purchase a cup of coffee or a baked good from time to time.

But none of the Lunch Ladies speak English. So I haven't bothered trying to clue them in.

From the rack, I choose a light blue sailor dress I've been sketching and get out my sketchbook. One thing I love about it is that the buttons don't just have anchors on them, they're shaped like anchors. Also, it reminds me of a dress I had when I was little. Not just young, but actually little. Like four or five, when the only hint of my future girth was my rosy round cheeks. My dress had the same pleats and the same dorky little square neckline with piping all around it. According to the photo albums, my mom used to make outfits like this for me by hand. Back when she used to sew and didn't cringe at the sight of me.

Most mornings, while I sit there by myself, waiting for

Claire, I make these little sketches of the best stuff I find—whatever is the most unique or unusual, along with some stuff that just catches my eye or speaks to me for some reason or no reason. I need to buy some colored pencils one of these days—my black felt-tip pen is just not doing this dress justice.

I started drawing pictures of vintage stuff when my dad and I used to go to the fleas. He'd always buy all kinds of random stuff—his Broadway tchotchkes, of course, plus old vinyl records of Gilbert and Sullivan operettas, commemorative plates of the fifty states, you name it. Invariably, I'd come up with a couple of trinkets I knew I couldn't live without: a blue glass fish, a hula-girl doll with wobbly hips, a Chinese fan. He'd look at me over the top of his glasses and raise a single chubby finger.

"One thing, Ronnie. You can pick it, but it's gotta be just one thing."

So I'd plant my feet and stand there, scowling, trying to make up my mind between the irresistible treasures. Finally, drawing pictures was a compromise he invented for me. It became a way for me to take home as many treasures as I wanted without breaking his rule.

Usually I can get about an hour of drawing in before Claire appears. But today, ten o'clock rolls around and still no Claire. I finish drawing the dress and begin doodling pictures of myself waiting around with my thumb up my ass. Claire hasn't told me the password for the computerized inventory system yet.

When I get bored of that, I start sketching a pair of opera-length gloves a consigner brought in last week. Just then the phone suddenly rings, startling me.

"Hello," I say, expecting Claire.

"Hey, um, Veronica?" It's Bill.

"Yeah?"

"What's going on?"

"Nothing. You?" I say, even though there's only one reason Bill ever calls up here. The chute is clogged.

"The chute's clogged, man."

"What do you want me to do about it?" I ask, though I already know exactly what he wants me to do about it.

He wants me to buzz The Nail.

And The Nail just happens to be the one thing that I don't like about Employees Only!

CHAPTER THREE

The Nail is this guy named Lenny. He's the only person that I am actually required to interact with, unless you count the consigners. Which I don't.

Lenny is the guy who stocks the store's inventory, picking up racks of consignment items from me and taking them down in the freight elevator to The Real Deal. He's also in charge of unclogging the frequently clogged chute to Dollar-a-Pound. He only comes to Employees Only! when one of the Lunch Ladies or I ring this old-timey buzzer and summon him up to the third floor. There's really nothing for him to do up here except pick up racks of clothing for transport. Or unclog the chute.

I call Lenny "The Nail" behind his back. It's from this

song. See, at school this year there was this girl named Kay who showed up from England midway through the year and was sort of like my friend for a little while. She was fat, too, only she had a British accent so she was able to get a boyfriend anyway. The boyfriend was named Kurt and he played the guitar and did a lot of open mike. Kay dragged me out to hear him play, like, constantly. My mom was delirious with joy that month, even though I could tell she wished I'd snagged a skinny friend instead. Kurt was part of this scene that wasn't really a scene that called itself "anti-folk." Which was confusing because if anyone had ever asked me what the music sounded like, the first word to come into my head would have been "folk."

Anyway, Kurt wrote this song about spending a summer working as a carpenter's assistant. Apparently, his boss was an unemployed philosophy professor (or so he told us during his pre-song monologue). The guy would always say to him, "Don't just hit the nail. BE the nail." So the song was called "I Am the Nail," and the chorus consisted of repeating that line a few times while strumming a lot and brooding purposefully. *I am the nail, I am the nail, I am the nail . . . Gonna be that nail, I am the nail, I am the nail . . .*

I found the song ironic because the fact was, Kurt had something of a nasty temper and used his voice more for yelling at Kay than for singing. Clearly, he was more of the hammer type. I made the mistake of pointing this out to Kay at lunch one day. She responded by snuffling a lot, then telling me I didn't know what the bloody hell I was talking about.

"Oh, yeah?" I said, tempted to tell her that I knew a thing or two about people who say they love each other but spend most of their time yelling at each other. I wasn't quite ready to tell Kay the gory details about my folks splitting up, but I had rationed myself a daydream or two about our friendship surviving long enough to get to the mythical sleep-over-and-spill-your-guts stage. I pictured us whispering late into the night over a giant bag of M&M's, our voices overlapping as we interrupted each other and finished each other's sentences. I had never let anyone get to know me so well she could finish my sentences. With Kay, I was thinking maybe I might.

"Yah," said Kay, with a deep, soulful sniff.

"Look, Kay," I tried.

"I don't want to talk about it."

"Fine, be that way."

I went back to my sandwich. Kay blew her nose, then shuffled off with her tray. A few days later, one of Kay's new friends informed me that Kay had gone to the assistant principal's office and changed her lunch period so it wouldn't be the same as mine anymore.

So much for that sleepover.

Whatever. I'm so over it, but I still have that dumb song stuck in my head: *I am the nail, I am the nail, I am the nail . . .* As soon as I met timid, squirrelly, flinchy ol' Lenny, I immediately thought of it. Lenny is The Nail if ever there was one.

I usually have to ring the buzzer four or five times to get

The Nail to move his sorry ass upstairs. I don't know what it is with him. Maybe he's stoned all the time like Bill, but I don't think so. With The Nail, it seems like it's part of his DNA. He's probably about my age—maybe a little older, like seventeen or eighteen—but he moves really slowly and carefully, like a much older person. Plus he's one of those thin, fragile types. All translucent skin, pale eyes, and ethereal, wispy hair. He walks gingerly, like he's afraid that if he doesn't step each step just so, gravity will lose its hold and he'll just blow off the face of the earth. Which is as likely to happen on Employees Only! as anywhere, because of all the big industrial fans running 24-7 to keep the dry-cleaning machines from baking us all to a crisp.

I hang up on Bill and hit the buzzer. I end up having to ring it six more times before The Nail finally appears.

"Hey," he says.

"Yo," I reply sarcastically. The Nail blushes and smiles at his feet as if I've said something embarrassing.

"What's up, Len?"

"Oh, um, nothing, you know . . ." His voice trails off. Small talk is not his strong suit, though I'd be hard-pressed to tell you what is.

"The chute's clogged again," I inform him.

"Oh, okay. I'll take care of it."

He lurches over to the bin and sticks his head into the chute. He leans further, shifting his weight, and his top half is momentarily out of view. His pants fall slightly, revealing the elasticized waistband of his underwear and the curve of his lower back. I'm totally skeeved by the sight, and yet I can't not look. I guess I must be curious to see if a guy that skinny has a butt crack, and it seems obvious the answer will be revealed any second. But then he sort of rolls over onto his back, bringing his knees up and shimmying deeper into the tunnel. His feet and the cuffs of his jeans dangle as he works. He's not wearing any socks, and I notice a dark maroon line running up his leg, starting just above his ankle and disappearing into his jeans.

THUNK! THUNK! comes from inside the chute. Then a shuffle and kind of a whooshing noise, which tells me the clot has been cleared. Then both his hands emerge, like they always do right before he's going to pull himself out.

But the next thing I know, they disappear again and I hear this kind of muffled *auggh* noise as his feet start to slide backward. Then he's gone.

"Oh my God—Len?"

"I'm okay." His voice is muffled. "I'm just a little—uh, I think I'm stuck."

"You think?" I say, rolling my eyes for the benefit of exactly no one. I peer into the chute and see only darkness. Holy shit, how far has he fallen? There's no freaking way I'm climbing in. If a string bean of a guy like The Nail can get stuck, it's pretty clear what would happen to me.

I consider calling Bill. It's likely he'd come right up and remedy the situation. But then I'd kind of owe him, and that's an unacceptable option. I could stick something down for The Nail to grab, like a broom or something. But he is so fragile, it might just poke him deeper in.

"Um, a little help? I'm really kind of stuck."

There's no way around it. I stick my head into the chute and tentatively reach one hand into the darkness. Almost immediately I encounter resistance: The Nail's shoe, a brown-on-brown suede sneaker.

I move my hand farther and wince at the unexpected sensation of his leg hair and bare skin. I take a deep breath, grab hold, brace myself, and pull. At first there is no movement. Then I feel a little shift, though not enough. My hand slips and I almost pull his shoe off.

"Crap," I say. In goes my other hand. I brace with my tummy and pull, harder this time. I readjust my grip and manage to slide him up a few inches. I wipe off my hands and try again. A little more success.

"Okay. I've got it from here," he says.

I drop his ankle and watch both feet emerge. His hands appear, and this time he is able to brace himself as he backs out. He brushes his bangs out of his eyes, to no avail, and smiles sheepishly.

"Thanks," he says. "I've never fallen into the chute before."

"Yeah, well, there's a first time for everything," I say, my irritation temporarily trumped by my relief. The moment passes when I remember that I touched him. I wipe my hands on my skirt. Yeesh. The Nail skeeves me to no end. The fact that he's so damned friendly makes him even more annoying.

"So, okay. Chute's clear, check. Any racks ready to go downstairs?" he asks.

Oh, good. Right. Give him a rack and he'll leave. Excellent. "Um, yeah. That one."

But he doesn't leave. I don't know why. He's supposed to leave. That's basically the extent of his job: take the racks and leave. *Leave,* I beam at him silently. *Leeeeaaaavvveeee.*

But no, he stays. The next thing I know, The Nail starts to inspect the clothing on my racks, which I'm pretty sure isn't part of his job. I watch him closely, hating him for being there and poking around, touching what I like to think of as my stuff. The Nail has this way of seeming to be on the lookout for something, which makes me start to wonder about him. Maybe The Nail gets over by looking all meek, but has some sort of racket going. Admittedly, I'm suspicious by nature. But then, when I see him sneaking peeks at labels and running fabrics through his fingers, I think that maybe I'm not so off base.

While he pokes around, I pretend to be engrossed in a shoebox full of consignment paperwork. But out of the corner of my eye, I watch The Nail. He seems drawn to a rack where I keep all the really good finds, the stuff I'm not quite ready to see go downstairs. Sort of my Consignment Corner Greatest Hits, if you will. First he fiddles with the bolo tie on a Western shirt I bagged and tagged the day before. Then he drifts absently to the next item, a real one-of-a-kind find: a campy pair of pink flannel pajamas with an unusual print of frolicking foxes and hounds. He pulls the collar forward with one thin finger and squints at the label. Then he rolls one of the cuffs of the pajama top between his thumb and next two fingers and closes his thin eyelids for a moment.

I can't help it; I turn and look right at him. For a second he gets this serene look on his face, almost like he's dead or something. Then he opens his eyes and catches me watching him.

Before I can look away or say anything, he says, "Do you think I could have these?"

"No!" I snap instinctively, though as soon as I say the word I begin to panic, thinking he's going to ask me to tell him why not. Thankfully, he nods sagely, accepting my refusal as if he expected it all along.

I should have known he'd want the pajamas. They're really special and I have lingered over them for a few weeks, not wanting to say goodbye and send them to The Real Deal. They're from the 1930s, soft as butter and in mint condition. I have fingered the same cuff myself no less than a dozen times. There's nothing in this world that's as soft as vintage flannel.

Suddenly I lunge forward and snatch the hanger off the rack. Startled, The Nail lets go of the pajama cuff. The sleeve falls limp.

"Oops, these can't go downstairs yet. Sorry."

The Nail nods again and says nothing. Without looking at any of the other items, he takes the metal clothing rack and pushes it in the direction of the freight elevator. The Z-shaped base of the rack stabilizes it, but also makes it list to the side. So he keeps having to stop and reposition himself as he pushes it along. Occasionally the casters lock up, which slows him down even more.

"Later," I say under my breath like a curse as I watch him slowly navigate across the floor. Alone again, I realize that my heart was pumping. More than anything, I am surprised by his nerve. Did he actually think I would just let him take the pajamas? That I'd be so charitable as to not know how to say no when the timid little dork asked for something so seemingly minor?

I play and replay the incident in my mind. It doesn't make any sense. Why would The Nail want my beloved pink hunting-scene pj's? They're women's pajamas, too small to fit him (*way* too small for me, not that that's really the point) even if he did swing that way, although I can't imagine that he does. There's no way a guy like him has a girlfriend. So what would he want with them? Is it possible he knew I wanted them and for some reason that made him want to take them away from me?

By lunchtime I'm totally worked up over this, but Claire still hasn't shown up, so there's no one on Employees Only! to tell. The Lunch Ladies are gathered around their table, leaning in and shouting, laughing riotously at each other's jokes, shoveling food to their mouths like lunch is some kind of raucous Olympic event.

Where IS Claire, anyway? When the Lunch Ladies start to clear their dishes, I stand up, feeling restless and irritated. Much as I don't want to, there's no other choice but to go downstairs and see if any of the Florons have seen her.

One flight down, the door with the cat door carved into it, where I once paused on the yellow brick road before crossing the threshold and ascending to Employees Only!, is right next to the Real Deal dressing rooms. So when I go downstairs, I practically bump into the Floron manning the dressing rooms. Who happens to be Zoe.

After what happened at the Mooks this morning, I'm more wary of her than ever. But there she is, all six feet of her, sprawled across two barstools at the counter that defines the entry to the dressing room area. She's flipping through a catalog, her legs up and her big fishnetted thighs crossed at the knee. A big pink and black sign above her head warns, ONE PERSON IN DRESSING ROOM ONLY! To her right, three pairs of shoes are shuffling at the bottom of a leopard-print dressing room curtain.

I approach her cautiously, summoning up my nerve. "Do you know where Claire is?" seems like a straightforward, and thus safe, question. Until I ask it, that is.

"Beats me," says Zoe, without looking up. She picks up a flyswatter and pretends to flog herself with it for the benefit of Ginger, who turns out to be slouched down behind the counter, drinking a soda.

Ginger giggles her approval.

"Seriously," I try again. "Has she called in? She was supposed to be here about a decade ago."

Ginger comes around the counter, screwing the cap back on her soda. Zoe and Ginger exchange glances. Zoe puts down the catalog and sighs dramatically.

"Look, New Girl," says Zoe. "I know you just started working here, but there's something you ought to know about Claire."

Ginger makes a mournful face.

"Claire's very sick," Zoe informs me. Ginger nods solemnly.

"She is?" I ask.

"Yes," says Ginger. "Claire has a terminal case of . . ."

"*Cun*-junctivitis!" blurts Zoe.

They both burst out laughing.

"Pinkeye?" I ask, making them laugh even harder.

"Don't worry, it's not *cun*-tagious!" adds Ginger. The way she enunciates the last word suddenly clues me in.

"It's really for the best, all things *cun*-sidered," says Zoe.

"Yeah, yeah, her *cun*-dition is fatal!"

They try to keep going, between fits of laughter.

"Oh, oh, I've got one," says Ginger, flapping her hands and trying to catch her breath. "They're *cun*-sidering . . ."

All of a sudden Zoe straightens up like a prairie dog. "Well, hey, Claire!" she says brightly.

Ginger practically falls over, suddenly busying herself with straightening a rack of gauze peasant blouses. I turn and look around for Claire. In a moment, Ginger looks up hesitantly, then realizes.

"You bitch," she says to Zoe.

"Suck-ahs!" Zoe doubles over, slapping her thigh.

"Forget it," I mutter, heading back toward the stairway.

"Hey, New Girl! Wait. Come back!"

"Yeah, we have something to tell you."

"Seriously, come back."

"We're sorry. Please?"

"I have to get back." I toss the lie over my shoulder.

"No, you don't," announces Zoe. *How does she know that?* I pause, my hand on the Employees Only! door handle.

"Come on," she coaxes. "We won't bite."

I stand there, frozen, dreading what I know is going to come next. *Dumb-ass,* I say to myself. *With all the crap you've put up with all these years, where do you get off thinking that this job, this store, this world will be any different?*

"What's your name again, New Girl? Vera?" asks Zoe.

I look up, surprised. I can't believe she's even close.

"Veronica," I say.

"Veronica, close enough," she says. "Come on, we need a word with you."

I'm still frozen, hand on the door. My heart is pounding.

"Unless you'd rather sit upstairs and wait for your boss with the *cun*-tagious *cun*-dition . . ."

I can tell from her voice she's smiling. I turn and nervously return the smile. *Could I run? Just bolt up the stairs, just like that?*

"Attagirl," says Zoe, wagging her finger at me. She yells across the floor at another Floron, "Hey, Gwen, watch the dressing rooms for five!"

"Yeah, right. Five," says the girl.

"Five, ten, whatever. You owe me."

"For what?"

Zoe answers with a burst of haughty, knowing laughter.

 43

Then she grabs me by the hand and pulls me forward into the stairwell. Ginger follows, smirking. Zoe doesn't let go until we're down on Dollar-a-Pound. Only instead of going to the right, into the back area behind The Pile, she pushes open a door marked DO NOT PROP THIS DOOR OPEN! and then proceeds to prop it open with a brick. The door leads to a loading dock where trucks pull up to load and unload bulk shipments of clothing.

"Ta-da!" says Ginger. "Welcome to our salon." She gestures broadly to the loading dock.

"Someday, all this will be yours," says Zoe, putting an arm around my shoulder and adopting a fake deep voice. Ginger squeaks with appreciative laughter.

Even with Zoe practically (and inexplicably) hugging me and Ginger giggling like a chipmunk, I'm tense, waiting for the inevitable attack.

I wish they'd just get it over with.

There are no trucks around, so Zoe and Ginger plunk themselves down on the concrete shelf, their legs dangling. Ginger pulls over a cardboard box, reaches inside, and pulls out a tablecloth. She covers the box with the cloth, then produces what appears to be the Mookie's bag from this morning.

"Donut?" she says, opening the bag and extending the open end in my direction.

Her smile seems genuine, but instinctively I resist.

"No, thanks."

"Aw, c'mon, take one," Ginger insists, shaking the bag. "We've got, like, a million."

"No. Really."

Zoe gives me the evil eye. "It's because you're fat, isn't it?"

"Oh my God, Zo!" yells Ginger. "I can't believe you said that!"

"What, called her fat?" Zoe says. "Look at her. She IS fat."

"Zo, I swear, you are such a bitch!" To me, Ginger adds, "I'm sorry she's such a bitch."

"That's right, I'm a bitch," says Zoe.

Then Zoe unzips this little white furry purse she always carries and begins digging through it. Which is good, because I can't look at her. I'm actually too shocked and startled to feel the cut of her words. It's a funny thing about being fat. People will say all kinds of mean shit behind your back and even in your presence, but no one will ever look you in the eye and call you fat to your face. Or at least no one has to me, until now.

While she's digging, she's kind of talking to herself. I hear some of the words: *"Fatso, Fatty Patty; Fatty-fatty-two-by-four, can't fit through the lunchroom door; want some fries to go with that shake? Lard-ass; Buffalo butt . . ."* But they're not aimed at me. It's more like she's reciting a grocery list or something.

"Check this out," she says finally, coming up with a small plastic rectangle and holding it up.

I reach for it, but she pulls it back. She pats the concrete next to her, mouthing the word "sit."

I sit, half expecting her to say "Good girl" and pat my

head. She looks me in the eye and hands me the little plastic thing.

"Second grade," she says meaningfully to me, before announcing loudly, "for your information, I am NOT a bitch. What I am is refreshingly honest. Most people just can't handle that."

Ginger gives a rueful snort.

I look at what I'm holding. It is a small laminated school portrait, maybe two inches by three inches, of a little girl. She's wearing a light blue shirt with the top button unbuttoned. She has very short bangs, tight pigtails, and several chins. She's smiling so hard that her eyes are almost closed, like she's Chinese or something.

"You were fat?" I say, trying to comprehend that Zoe ever wore light blue, much less that she was ever a fat little kid. She seems like she was born in black vinyl boots and fishnets.

"Hello?! Not was. IS, baby. It's just that now I'm, like, six feet tall, a'ight? Trust me, it's *aaaall* still there. It just has more places to go." She shakes her shoulders and kind of bobbles her head for emphasis.

"Oh," I say, handing back the picture. Zoe looks at it herself for a moment.

"I always hated it when people offered me food, too," she tells me. "Acting all nicey-nice but totally moving in for the kill."

For a moment, Zoe seems lost in the memory. Then she sort of waves it off and tucks the photo back in her purse. She flashes her signature toothy grin.

"So relax," she says. "One fat bitch to another."

She takes a donut from the bag and hands it to me.

"Seriously," she says.

I hesitate for a moment, but it is no use. With Zoe, you don't get a lot of choices. Besides, it is strawberry-frosted, with rainbow sprinkles. The pink glaze blinks sleepily in the bright sunlight. What can I say: I'm a sucker for sprinkles.

"Attagirl," says Zoe. "So, what do they call you?"

I have no idea what she means, so like an idiot I say, "Who?"

"Your friends. Do they call you Vee or something?"

I don't have any friends. I mean, I had one for a little while, but she cleared out pretty quick. And there's Bill, I guess, but he doesn't really count. Somehow, I don't think the truth is the way to go here.

"Uh, actually, everyone just calls me Veronica." *Except my dad,* I think. He calls me Ronnie. Only he hasn't called me anything in about six months.

"I like Vee," says Zoe. "I'm going to call you Vee."

"O-kay," I say, trying to act nonchalant. I've never been called anything that wasn't basically a slam on my size before. I feel myself slipping it on and liking it. *Vee. My friends call me Vee.*

"Donut, Zo?" asks Ginger.

Zoe makes a face and pushes the bag away.

"Please, I've had like twenty. I'm good."

I take a bite of my donut. The glaze is warm and melts on my tongue. The sprinkles are stale in a good way, crunchy and sweet.

"Soooo, how's life upstairs?" Ginger asks me.

"Um . . . okay." I chew, stalling. I'm not quite sure how much to tell them.

"Oh my God, it must be so much fun," gushes Ginger. "I had to go up there a few times last year, and every time I did I just couldn't believe some of the clothes you get in *cun* . . . I mean, *consignment*."

"Oh, yeah?" asks Zoe, who seems bored by any conversation that does not revolve around her.

"Totally. One time there was this dress that was made entirely out of beads and it was in the pattern of a flag . . ."

"It's still up there," I tell her.

"No way," says Ginger. "Shit, I was sure Claire snagged it."

"Ha-ha. Pay up!" says Zoe.

"Fuck," says Ginger. She digs a wadded-up bill out of her pocket and hands it to Zoe. "It's this dumb bet," she explains. "I STILL say Claire's a klepto."

"It would seem that Claire is a total *cun*-undrum," says Zoe. "Ha-ha-ha." She wiggles the bill, making the president do a little dance.

"This doesn't prove shit," insists Ginger. "I had my aunt drop off a ton of good stuff with her, really valuable shit, just to see if she'd take the bait, and none of it ever made it downstairs."

"So you think she stole it?" I ask.

"Totally." Ginger gives me an impatient look, like I'm the densest person she's ever met. "I mean, think about it. Upstairs, there's nobody watching. A blouse here, a pair of shoes . . . some of that stuff can fetch a pretty penny online, if you know what you've got."

"I guess," I say.

"Totally," repeats Ginger. "Some of that merchandise has huge resale value, if you know where to take it. I'd be tempted to get in on that action myself, but on the floor there's no way."

Zoe nods. "There's cameras all over the store. If anyone on the floor swipes stuff, the management cans them so fast, they skin their asses on the staircase."

"Well, okay, so today Claire hasn't showed up or called or anything. Do you think she got fired?" I ask.

Ginger shrugs. "Wouldn't be the first time."

"Okay, okay," says Zoe, clapping her hands. "New topic. Vee, are you banging Barnacle Bill?"

"What?"

"From Dollar-a-Pound, you know," says Zoe, leaning in excitedly. "Well, are you?"

"No! Oh my God, did he say something?"

Zoe and Ginger laugh.

"Nah," promises Ginger. "He's just, well, sort of . . ." Ginger's voice trails off.

"Hard up?" I ask, my hackles rising.

"Not *that* hard up," snorts Zoe.

"Shut up!" yells Ginger. "That was, like, once and it was a million fucking years ago."

"*On the gooooood ship Loll-i-pop . . . ,*" trills Zoe.

Ginger smacks her with her purse, a gigantic hobo bag. "Shut UP!" she hisses again.

"Ow!" complains Zoe, pouting.

"Why do you call him Barnacle Bill?" I ask, both out of curiosity and to end their squabble. Zoe grins. "Because Sailor Boy gave Ginge here a bad case of the crabs."

"Jesus, will you shut up? It was just a fricking yeast infection. I am so never telling you anything ever again, I swear." She crosses her arms.

"Yuck," says Zoe, making a face. "Nasty."

Just then I notice someone leaving the store and starting to walk in the opposite direction. I can tell immediately that it is The Nail because of that odd walking-on-eggshells way he moves.

"Man, what is with that guy?" I gripe.

"Who?" asks Ginger. Then she looks and elbows Zoe. "Hey, Zo, look. D.B.W. . . ."

"D.B.W.?"

"Dead Boy Walking," explains Zoe. "He calls in sick all the fricking time. One of these days he's going to call in dead."

"Oooh, who would you rather do it with, Vee?" squeals Ginger. "D.B.W. or Bill? Death is not an option!"

"Except for D.B.W.," I say, which cracks them up.

I get a little thrill when I make them laugh, and I'm tempted to tell them about my own nickname for Lenny, even though that would mean telling them the whole story about Kay and Kurt. And on top of that, I get an even bigger thrill realizing that it is not obvious to them that I have never done "it"—even in the loosest sense of that word—

with anyone yet. Unless you count letting my cousin stick his hand up my shirt at a Fourth of July picnic last summer.

Which I don't.

But before I can say anything, I suddenly notice a familiar pink sleeve hanging out of The Nail's backpack.

CHAPTER FOUR

"OH. MY. GOD. He stole them!" I say, pointing at The Nail walking with his pack on one shoulder, a pink flannel sleeve dangling out of the top flap. "That asshole stole my pajamas!"

"Why do you keep your pajamas at work?" asks Ginger.

"I don't. I mean . . . they're not mine exactly, they just . . . arrghh . . ." I flap my hands like I'm trying to dry them, not sure how to explain. "They came in as consignment and they're really good. I told him not to take them, but look!"

"Ohhhhhh!" says Zoe, drawing in her breath sharply. She elbows Ginger. "Oh my God, he's totally working for Claire!"

"No WAY!" says Ginger.

"Of course, he's like her slave! It's perfect."

"Totally!" Ginger's black-rimmed eyes are huge.

"You've got to follow him!" says Zoe.

"Follow him?"

"Of course!" she says. "See where he goes, if he meets up with her or if they have some secret warehouse or whatever. Come on, don't you totally want to know?"

"I guess," I admit.

"So go after him! We'll cover for you."

"Yeah, I dunno." I think about the great job Zoe did covering Dollar-a-Pound for Bill.

"Seriously, we'll take care of it. I promise." Zoe gives me this intense look, like she's reading my mind. "Go on, follow him. Investigate. Find out what he's up to. And then, when you've cracked the case, come back and find us. Okay, Vee?"

"Yeah, yeah, totally. We want to hear *everything*!" Ginger is practically jumping up and down.

Since they clearly aren't going to take no for an answer, I get to my feet.

There's really not a lot of choice with Zoe.

So I start down the street after The Nail.

Given the fact that Lenny moves like a snail, I quickly realize that I will catch up with him in no time. At which point it dawns on me that I don't want to do that. I'm not sure why. As terrifying as it sounds, I sort of like the idea of me running after him in this crazy layer cake of a skirt, yanking the incriminating evidence from his bag, yelling accusations, and then stalking off triumphant.

And yet I can't bring myself to actually do it. I start walking slower and slower until it's like I'm doing an impersonation of him. I don't exactly think that Zoe and Ginger are right about Len and Claire. But it suddenly occurs to me: *What if they are?* What if Claire does have Len doing her dirty work? I mean, why else would he take a pair of old flannel pajamas . . . girls' pajamas, no less? Unless he's a total perv and he needs them for some sort of weird pervy stuff that he does that has nothing to do with Claire.

Or everything to do with Claire.

I suppose this means Zoe and Ginger are right. It definitely seems worthy of an investigation.

But why me? This is so not me, this girl detective thing. I never got into reading that Nancy Drew stuff, or signed up for the Puzzlebusters Club, or whatever überdork activities you do if you give a shit about getting into college. Sure, I can tell Bakelite from plastic from across the room. I can tell you whether a beaded cardigan is authentic or reproduction, and I know all the original colors of Fiestaware by heart. But that kind of knowledge was not really obtained out of a desire to go on some sort of bizarre stakeout of the weirdest boy on the planet.

Besides, let's say Ginger and Zoe are right and The Nail and Claire turn out to be partners in crime, running a big vintage clothing resale business off stolen merchandise and pocketing all the money they pull in. Why exactly am I supposed to care? I mean, yeah, okay, it's wrong. And it's pretty insulting to think that they thought they could get away with it right under my nose. A thought comes to me suddenly—maybe Claire hired me because she thought I'd be too dumb to suspect anything? I imagine her sitting at the desk that is now mine and laughing to herself. *Perfect, I'll hire this one. She'll never catch on.*

A wave of anger takes me out of my dream, and my mind is immediately filled with another thought. What if Ginger and Zoe are the ones who are playing me? What if they think this whole thing is hysterical, filling my head with imaginary crime rings and devious collaborations between unlikely partners? What if sending me out here was simply an elaborate scheme to have a good laugh at my expense?

As The Nail carefully turns a corner and I hang back to avoid overtaking him, this strikes me as the most likely scenario. I picture them back by the dressing rooms, Zoe bending over the counter with her butt in the air, pretending to be me snooping around—The Incredibly Gullible Fat Girl Detective—while Ginger hums the *Mission Impossible* theme song: *"Doodley-doo, doodley-doo, doodley-doo, DA-da."*

Yet for some reason I continue to follow him. I put on my cat's-eye sunglasses, well aware that they conceal nothing. That dumb refrain loops through my head: *I am the nail, I am the nail, I am the nail* . . . It makes me think about Kay again. Me and my big dumb mouth. If only I had just shut up about her asshole of a boyfriend, we'd probably still be friends now. We'd be hanging out and having fun, working some lame-ass summer job together. Instead of me wandering around, acting out some dumb Nancy Drew story: *The Case of the Purloined PJ's.*

Gonna be that nail, I am the nail, I am the nail . . .

My confidence plummets with every step. *What if it's not even the same pajamas?* I mean, that seems impossible, but you never know. *Or maybe there's some perfectly good reason he needs them.* Some reasonable and perfectly innocent reason, like . . . Okay, I can't think of what that might possibly be.

Slowly, slowly, sllllooooooowwwwly I stalk him. I walk behind him for eight long blocks, hanging back to keep out of sight. The Nail walks so slow, it isn't funny. You'd think he was somebody's grandfather, for chrissakes. *Maybe he is actually old.* Or he could have some weird aging kid disease, like a kid I saw on TV once. Walking behind him, I notice that his hair is so pale, it is almost white.

Finally he comes to a three-story house. While I wait behind a minivan parked across the street, he carefully navigates the steps and goes inside. After a minute, I go stand in front of it and squint at the front door. On the right-hand side, there are three buzzers, the middle of which reads L. CASTOR. I have arrived at the lair of The Nail.

O-kay, I say to myself. *Now what?* I step back and survey the building. It's gray, with aluminum siding and some dead petunias in window boxes on the third floor. The second floor, which I'm guessing is Lenny's, seems to have dark curtains drawn, despite the fact that it is July. It looks like a house that your grandmother would have and you'd think of any excuse in the book to avoid visiting. And if you weren't actually able to get out of it, you'd spend every minute inside shifting in your seat, looking forward to being anywhere but there.

I notice that there's a drip, drip, drip, and I realize that there are air conditioners—one on the first floor, one on the second—hanging out of the windows on the side of the house. If I wasn't wearing a gigantic, fluffy tulle skirt—and if I was someone like Catwoman instead of her lumpy sidekick, Fat Girl—I'd be able to climb on the car in the driveway and hoist myself up the side of the drainpipe. I almost laugh out loud at the thought. I have not scaled anything since I shredded my palms attempting to pass the rope-climbing requirement for seventh-grade P.E. My pits stain at the very thought of this. That's so not happening.

So I wait a while longer. There's no other way to say this: The Nail's house looks trashy. Like his family is on welfare or something. *Oh God. Maybe that's it.* Maybe he's stealing to feed his family? Could that be it? How much could reselling vintage stuff—even really top-quality stuff—possibly make? Especially swiping it one item at a time. Maybe there's more to it somehow. Maybe if I stay a little longer, I'll find out.

I am the nail, I am the nail, I am the nail . . .

But on the off chance that Claire has actually shown up at work and is wondering where the hell I am, I abandon the stakeout and head back to the store.

"Hey, Veronica?" Bill calls after me as I tiptoe in and start to make a running dash for the stairs. Bill is adept at foiling my attempts to enter Employees Only! without engaging in conversation with the Florons.

"Yeah?"

"Can you check if there's anyone in the girls' john? I have to go, uh, clean it."

I narrow my eyes and shoot him a look. But I do it anyway, since I have to go myself. No one is in there.

"Yeah, actually," I tell him when I come out.

"Oh," says Bill, disappointed. I don't know why he likes to spend time in the ladies' room, nor do I really want to know why.

"I think one of them is sick, too," I tell him. "It could be a while."

Bill sighs, taking a bag from a Picker and weighing it.

"Seventeen dollars," I hear him say.

"Say what?"

Bill digs through the bag. He pulls out a pair of bowling shoes and shows them to the guy. "Shoes, man—they'll get you every time. It's like a salad bar. Shoes are the cherry tomatoes."

"You got that right." The man tosses the shoes back into The Pile. While Bill is reweighing his bag, I tiptoe up the stairs. Thankfully, I make it all the way up to Employees Only!, where—surprise, surprise—there's still no sign of Claire.

I'm at my desk for two seconds max when the phone rings.

"Claire?" I say.

"Paging Spy Girl!" chirps Ginger. "Come in, Spy Girl! Report to Spy Girl Headquarters for a full interrogation, immediately."

"Yeah, um, I can't leave right now," I tell her.

"Yes, you can."

"If you're not down in five minutes, we're coming to get you," booms Zoe, who has clearly just grabbed the phone from Ginger.

"Over and out!" I hear Ginger yell in the background before Zoe slams the phone down.

Once again, not a lot of choice with Zoe.

I go downstairs and find them at the counter by the dressing rooms. Zoe is behind the bar, tending, perched high on her stool. Ginger stands in front of her like a cocktail waitress or something. Ginger grins and waves when she sees me. Zoe's head is down, eyes closed as she shakes her head from side to side and sings along with a track on the store's sound system.

"Jet Boy, Jet Girl.
I'm gonna take you round the world.
Jet Boy, I'm gonna make you penetrate,
I'm gonna make you be a girl.
Ooo-woo-ooo-ooo. He gives me head."

"Shut up, shut up, Zo, Vee's here."

Zoe glares at her.

"So?" she snarls. To me, she demands, "How'd you do?"

"Uh, not so good. I kind of lost track of him."

Ginger guffaws, like she thinks I'm kidding. I shrug.

"Seriously?"

I know how stupid I sound, but I really don't know what to tell them. "I just . . . I mean, he got to his house and everything, but there wasn't really anything to see."

"Oh, yeah?"

"Yeah. Sorry."

Ginger and Zoe look at each other.

"So . . . what did his house look like?" coaxes Ginger.

"I mean, like a house. It was, um, kind of old."

"Uh-huh, like how?" They're both leaning in, hungry for details.

"I dunno . . . it looked like it hadn't been painted in a while. The paint was all, you know, dirty and flaking off? And there were all these blinds on the windows, so I couldn't see in or anything."

"Totally," breathes Ginger. I've come to notice that it is her favorite word.

"It was kind of gross," I add quickly. "A total dump."

"Did you see Claire?" asks Zoe.

"Nope, didn't see anyone but The N—" I catch myself. "I didn't see anyone but him."

"Oh, this is great!" crows Zoe.

"Totally," chortles Ginger.

"What?"

"You totally have to go back!" urges Ginger.

"I—what?"

"To blow the lid off their whole operation, don't you see?"

"Uh, I don't really . . ."

"It's perfect. He's their eyes and ears at the store, taking the stuff, bringing it back to their hideout, while she's managing everything from behind the scenes."

"Yeah, well, count me out."

"What do you mean?"

"I mean, I'm not going to do it."

"But you have to! You saw him take the pajamas. You have evidence of a crime being perpetrated."

"Yeah, but what am I supposed to do, ring the doorbell? And be all, 'Hello, I'm here to bust you for stealing. Have a nice day.'?"

"Noooo," says Ginger, looking to Zoe for help.

Zoe tilts her head, considering. Suddenly she claps her hands together. "I know!" she says.

"What?"

"You could make a *suggestion*," Zoe says.

"Hey, yeah!" says Ginger.

"I don't . . ." I look from Zoe to Ginger. "A suggestion?"

"Follow me," says Zoe. Leaving the dressing rooms unattended, she walks all the way across The Real Deal. We cross the yellow brick road. We pass the decade racks and the Wig Wall. We duck under the Harley-Davidson hanging from the ceiling.

"Presenting," says Zoe, using her arms to make a frame in the air, "the feedback box."

"Ta-da!" adds Ginger.

I look through Zoe's arms and see a pink birdhouse nailed to the wall. It is marked FEEDBACK BOX! in large black letters that closely resemble those on the EMPLOYEES ONLY! sign and virtually every other sign in the place. I've never noticed the birdhouse before, probably because I spend so little time on The Real Deal. Also probably because it is partially obscured by a much bigger sign that reads DUDE, WHERE'S MY CART?, which I'm guessing is the spot where the Florons relocate carts of merchandise that have been abandoned on the retail floor.

The roof of the Feedback Box! is adorned with a very realistic sparrow or lark or something. Given the obscure location and tiny size of the box—not to mention the even tinier size of the hole for inserting comments—the extent to which management values customer input seems pretty obvious. There isn't even a pad of paper for "feedback" to go on, although a long string hanging off the birdhouse suggests that once upon a time there was a pencil.

"I . . . I don't get it," I say.

Zoe smiles indulgently. "This is where you put suggestions. About, you know, anything. For example, you could *suggest* that all songs by Bob Marley be put on the no-play list, for example."

"We did that," admits Ginger. "Didn't work."

"It was just a *suggestion*," says Zoe, shrugging, like *no big deal.* "Do you see?"

I nod.

"Another *suggestion* might be that a certain extremely deceased boy be investigated for stealing. For example."

I cringe at the thought. "I dunno," I say.

"What?" says Zoe. "It's just a *suggestion.* Nobody has to know that it was your suggestion. It could have come from anyone. That's the beauty of the feedback box."

"Yeah, I just . . ."

"Got a pen?" interrupts Zoe.

"Uh, no." I buy myself a moment. I mean, what's the harm? It's not like he's going to get fired or anything. The

worst that might happen is he'll have to answer some questions, maybe get watched more closely. Right? Besides, the truth is, he IS stealing. Although now that I've seen his house, I'm pretty sure I know why. And I'm not entirely sure I blame him, even though he could have chosen something else to steal. If anyone was going to have those pajamas, it was going to be me.

"How 'bout an eyeliner?" offers Ginger, plucking one off a rack displaying several next to a rainbow of false eyelashes.

"Purrrrrfect," says Zoe, ripping off its packaging. "Now all we need is paper." She digs through her furry purse and finally produces a Mookie's Donuts coupon, which she hands to me. One side reads TASTES BETTER IF YOU CALL IT A S'MOOKIE. 20¢ OFF. The other side is blank. Then she uncaps the eyeliner.

"Look, it's your shade," she says, winking and holding it out to me.

"I don't know," I say.

"Vee, honey," scolds Zoe, her voice dripping with concern. "When are you going to stop being a scared little girl and stand up for yourself?"

"I . . . what?"

"This *boy* . . . this total freaking loser . . . he goes to where you work and he sees your nice stuff and he snags it, just like that. Stuff you care about. Are you seriously going to tell me that's okay?"

"No! I mean, it's not like that. It's just . . ."

"What's not like what? He's not a freak? He didn't steal your stuff?"

"No, no. It's just . . ."

Zoe puts a hand on my shoulder. "Sweetie, come on," she says, her voice soft as a marshmallow. "You *know* we're your friends, right?"

"Um, I guess."

"Well, then wake up. Guys pull this crap all the time. Especially with the girls they know won't call them on it."

"Yeah," adds Ginger, nodding knowingly.

"Come on, kiddo," says Zoe. "It's time you learned how to speak up for yourself."

"By making an anonymous tip?"

Zoe smiles ruefully. "You gotta start somewhere."

I look to Ginger for help, but she only nods.

"Oh, all right," I grumble.

"Attagirl!" crows Zoe.

I take the eyeliner and try to disguise my handwriting by printing in all caps. I keep it short and to the point:

LENNY STEALS.

"Good," says Zoe, reading over my shoulder. "Don't crumple it up or they might think it's trash," she instructs.

While Zoe watches, I carefully fold the coupon twice and thread it into the little hole. As I do, the real-looking fake bird scrutinizes me suspiciously, like it is worried that I might be disturbing its eggs by poking a foreign object inside its nest. I half expect it to fly down and peck my eyes out.

"Well done," pronounces Zoe, once the note is tucked inside. "I told you she had potential."

"Totally," agrees Ginger. "You should see about getting transferred downstairs."

"Uh-uh," I say. "I am strictly an upstairs girl."

"You are SUCH an upstairs girl," agrees Zoe.

"Uh, thanks . . . I think," I say.

"Oh, shut up, that's why we love you."

Zoe is looking me straight in the eye when she says this, and it's like looking directly at the sun—I actually have to turn away. I realize for the first time that she can be just as disarming when she's being kind as she can when she's being cruel.

"We've got to make a pact, though," adds Zoe suddenly.

"What for?" I ask.

"To stay on him. I mean, he's going to keep doing this, right? It's up to us to make sure he doesn't get away with it."

"Right," I say.

"So here's the deal. We keep an eye on him when we see him. We maybe follow him again?" She gives me a look, making it clear that by "we" she means me. Ginger and I nod. "And if we see anything *unusual*, we'll report it immediately."

"To who?" asks Ginger, wide-eyed.

"To each other, duh!" snaps Zoe. "It'll be . . . our Secret Spy Girl Pact." She holds out her hand, palm down. "Okay?"

"Okay," I say. Ginger nods. We pile our hands on top of Zoe's.

Immediately, Zoe yanks hers back. Ginger and I pull back our hands like we've been burned.

Zoe laughs. "Come on, Spy Girls," she says.

Together, the three of us walk back across The Real Deal, kind of struggling to keep from laughing about the Feedback Box! and our secret pact. Which feels really, really unfamiliar, like something you'd only see in a movie. It makes me think of this time I saw these two girls hanging out at the Mooks. With no warning, one of them shot her straw wrapper right in the other one's face. And then they both just laughed. It totally blew me away. Because when I see a straw wrapper fly through the air at me, it's like a declaration of war or something. I knew right then I'd never have a friend like that, a friend you can pull wacky shit on and not get hated for it.

And I never have.

Until, maybe, now.

Life is so weird that way. When I woke up today, I never could have predicted any of this. Zoe and Ginger making a scene at the Mooks. The Nail falling into the chute, then stealing my pajamas. But I *really* never would have thought that today would end up with me getting to be friends with Zoe and Ginger. Hanging out and dishing, making a secret pact, laughing together, any of that stuff.

It's so funny. They've always seemed so, I dunno, tough or something. The way Zoe says whatever the hell she wants, the way they made that scene in the Mooks. But then, out of nowhere, they give me this glimpse of their other side. Looking out for me, getting mad at The Nail on my behalf, and helping me get back at him for stealing my stuff. Inviting me into their club and making me feel like I'm part of something, for once. It feels kind of like it does when I snag a great find at the fleas, something rare and entirely unexpected. *Zoe and Ginger: diamonds in the rough.*

Like my dad always used to say, *Who'd a thunk?*

Who'd a thunk? Definitely not me.

CHAPTER FIVE

To keep up my end of our Secret Spy Girl Pact, I start walking by The Nail's house each day on my way home from work. It always looks the same—flowers dead, window shades down—and I never see The Nail, or anyone else for that matter, going in or coming out of it. I almost begin to wonder if I imagined that this was the house.

It doesn't seem possible that it can be, since I never see anyone who seems to have anything to do with the house. Occasionally, I linger across the street for ten, fifteen minutes. Nothing. There's always a pile of mail and several newspapers on the porch, but I can't be sure if they are the same ones. I mean, I guess I could go up on the porch myself, but what if someone did show up?

It makes me think: Who is The Nail, anyway? Does he live alone? He seems a little young for that, but maybe. Or maybe he lives with someone who's old and can't get out much, like a grandparent or somebody. But then wouldn't I see him with groceries or something? At my house, my mom is constantly going to the grocery store to stock up on her key staple items: diet soda, diet bread, diet yogurt, frozen diet entrees, fruit, and these awful Scandinavian crackers that taste like cardboard. Oh, yeah, and fake butter.

Maybe this isn't his house after all.

At first Zoe and Ginger jump on me whenever I come in, pestering me for stakeout details. But after a few days of no news, they lose interest. I actually begin to worry that if I don't turn up something juicy soon, Zoe's going to write me off entirely. Ginger still waves at me when she sees me crossing through The Real Deal, but often Zoe just gives me a bored smirk. *Come on,* I can tell she's thinking. *Let me know when you dig up some good dirt. Otherwise, don't waste my time.*

But then one afternoon, after more than a week of stalking The Nail, I see him. He's standing on the front porch, but he's mostly in shadow, and at first I'm so eager to make sure it's him that I completely blow it and don't hang back. And as soon as I'm sure that it's him, I kind of freeze like a deer in the headlights. I have this fleeting wish that somehow he won't notice me standing right square in front of his house, wearing, of all things, a bright pink ruffled polka skirt with about a thousand layers. I'm only too aware that it makes me look like a giant strawberry-frosted cupcake or something. Or a sports team mascot, maybe.

Or a very, very inept Spy Girl standing in front of a house she's supposed to be staking out.

"Veronica?" The sound of my name turns my head to the voice, which is, of course, The Nail's. He is holding the door open and clutching several envelopes in one hand. His backpack is still on his shoulder. "Hi. What's up?"

"Nothing," I say by default.

"Do you live near here?"

Do I live near here? Noooo. Then why are you here? Ummm . . . Actually, I do live near here. Oh, really? Where? Uhhhh . . .

I panic. He must be onto me. He knows I have been stalking him. Shit, shit, shit. This is not how I planned it at all. Or rather, I have not planned this at all. All I really know is, I really want to be the one surprising him. So instead of answering his question, I decide to ask my own. In this way, I can refuse to let go of my moment.

"I think you know what I'm doing here, don't you?" I say. I use my most suspicious, haughty voice, very Joan Crawford or some old movie person like that.

The Nail looks confused.

"Do you want to come in?" he says.

I pause, but I don't really have a choice. I drained an extra-large iced mocha smoothie on my way out of work and I am about to wet my pants.

"All right," I say. We go inside and I follow as he carefully climbs the stairs. An eternity later, we arrive on the second floor. He opens his apartment door, puts his keys, backpack, and mail down, and turns on the entryway light.

"Bathroom?" I say.

"Down the hall, on your left."

I stagger there and barely make it. *Ahhhhhh.*

When I come out, I tiptoe around to try to explore before The Nail realizes I have emerged. The apartment has that powder-scent-air-freshener grandma's-house smell and a lot of heavy, dark wood curio cabinets with ugly figurines in them. I don't see any piles of vintage clothes, and the one closet I peek into has a vacuum cleaner, two hockey sticks, and an old set of golf clubs.

Down the hall, I find a bedroom that I'm guessing is The Nail's. It has a twin bed, a bookcase, and very little else. He does, however, have the same vintage sci-fi film festival poster from two summers ago that I keep on my bedroom wall.

What I don't have, however, is what I find in the living room. There are two matching couches, covered in plastic, and almost nothing else except fish tanks. The fish tanks are on every available surface in the room, including the couches, plus two big ones on the floor. I look around and do a rough count. There are maybe fifteen of them.

The curtains in the living room are drawn and the lighting is very poor, except for some fluorescent bulbs in the tanks. He must raise some kind of weird nocturnal fish. Except most of the tanks have mesh tops held on by what looks like duct tape. Weird nocturnal jumping fish? I crouch down next to a mesh-covered tank and peer inside. There is no water, and I come face to face with this big black and orange striped thing . . .

There is a moment when it feels like everything happens

at once. The thing raises its head and looks at me and I try to stay cool and not scream, but instead I end up making this gurgling noise as I run into the next room, which turns out to be the kitchen. Len, who has his head in the fridge when I burst into the room, fumbles and drops a glass bottle. Then there's glass on the floor and a puddle of lemonade running down the sloping linoleum and collecting under the stove.

"Shit! Oh my God, I'm sorry! Are you okay?" I say.

"Yeah, I'm okay," he says. But there's a small spot of blood on his pants leg.

"No, you're not. You're bleeding."

"I am?" He looks down. "Oh. It's okay," he says. He sits down and rolls up his pants leg. Very distinctly, I see that vertical maroon line again, which I now realize is a really intense-looking scar running the length of his calf like a racing stripe. He carefully picks out a glass shard protruding from the front of his shin, then presses a dish towel against the bright red spot where it was lodged.

I'm about to ask about the scar when he says, "I'm guessing you saw my pets, huh?"

"Uh, yeah!" I say. "What the hell?"

"Sorry, I should have said something," says The Nail. "But they're all harmless. The snakes and all but one of the lizards have had the venom removed. And they can't get out unless I take them out. So there's really nothing to worry about."

"Oh, okay. I feel much better," I say in my most ironic voice.

"Good," says The Nail. Irony seems wasted on him.

"Listen, why don't you sit down so I can clean this up?" I don't really want to, but my heart is pounding and there's a chair right there, so I sit. His kitchen table is yellow, and it has the same boomerang pattern as my grandma's. I trace the pattern with my finger, something I do when I'm feeling anxious.

"I'm sorry," I say. "About freaking out and the lemonade and all . . ."

"It's okay," he tells me again. "It's my fault, really." He notices what I'm doing. "Do you like that table? It's my grandma's."

"My grandma has one just like it."

"Really? Wow, that's some coincidence. I've never seen one like it before."

I look at him suspiciously. "Ha-ha," I say.

"What?"

"This is only the most popular fifties Formica pattern ever made. There's like a zillion of these in the world."

"Huh, how 'bout that?" he says as he goes and gets some tweezers. He carefully picks up the pieces of glass and puts them in a paper grocery bag. His precise, methodical manner is well suited to this kind of task. While he works, he is completely silent. I hear the refrigerator hum, and I can even hear some of the fish tanks bubbling in the next room.

I can't help it. I ask him about the tanks.

"My grandma gave me a turtle when I was a little kid," The Nail tells me. He tilts his head to one side, squinting at the floor. Then he finds and extracts another tiny shard. "I was in this really bad car accident."

"Oh, yeah?"

"Yeah. I was in and out of the hospital a lot. I even had to learn to walk again. I guess she thought it would be good for me to have a pet that was slower than me." The Nail smiles shyly. "Anyway, the turtle died at some point, but by then I also had a tokay gecko and a couple of corn snakes. And then I started collecting rarer breeds, like water monitors, stuff like that. My grandma was okay with it, so I began using the living room. But I really need to find homes for some of them. I'm running out of space here."

"Are you, um . . . okay now?"

He shrugs. "I mean, as okay as I'm ever going to be. I wouldn't suggest choosing me for a relay race team, but other than that . . . Okay, I think that's the last of it."

The Nail stands up carefully, steps on the garbage can pedal, and tosses in the bag of glass.

"You like stuff, don't you?" he asks.

"What?"

"You're a collector, right? You collect vintage clothing and stuff."

"Maybe," I say warily. "What's your point?"

"Is that how you started working at the store?"

"Maybe," I say again. I don't want to say anything that might be used against me later.

"You go to the fleas, too," he says softly.

"Okay, are you stalking me?"

"What? No," he says, leaning back against the kitchen sink. "I've just seen you there before. At school, too."

"You go to the fleas?"

"Sometimes," he says. "There's a guy there who sells reptile and amphibian supplies. You know, in the far corner."

"Oh," I say. The far corner is where they sell new stuff, like hand lotion, pet food, soda, and multi-packs of socks. "You go to HHS, too? How come I haven't seen you?"

"I dunno. Probably because most of my classes were in J-Vo," he says. "I'm done, though. As of June."

"Oh," I say, calculating in my head that this means he's seventeen, maybe eighteen. Building J, otherwise known as J-Vo, is where they have all the vocational and technical classes, like Auto Shop. It's out back, behind the terrace where they make the teachers who smoke go. My interest is piqued. I've never seen anyone my age at the fleas. And I've never known anyone who's set foot in J-Vo.

I guess he sees my look, because he says, "It's not such a bad place. There's all this giant kitchen equipment and junked cars and stuff."

"Do you . . . collect stuff?" I ask cautiously, meaning the pajamas.

"Nah," he says. "I'm not really into stuff."

"What about your lizard collection?"

He thinks for a minute. "I mean, I guess you could say that. But I don't really think of them like that. They're not *things*. They're pets, you know? Don't you have any pets?"

"Uh, no," I say. I want to tell him more, but all I venture is, "I had a cat once. It died."

"Maybe you should think about taking care of one of my snakes," he says cheerfully. "I'd help you get set up with the cage and the pinkies and stuff."

"Pinkies?"

"Newborn baby mice. Snakes love them."

"Mice Krispies?" I ask.

"Mice whuh?"

"Krispies? Like Rice Krispies?" Nothing. "Forget it, it's a joke," I say. "No snakes for me. No offense, it's just my mom would kill me. Plus, I'm not big on slimy things."

"They're not slimy," he says.

"Slimy, scaly, whatever," I say. "It just creeps me out, okay?"

"They're not scaly either."

"Yeah, okay. Whatever you say, Lizard Boy." So help me God, it just slips out. For a second I dare to believe that he didn't hear me.

"What did you just call me?"

The Nail's eyes are still the color of dirty water, but now I see them flicker like the water has a current to it.

"Nothing," I mumble. I'm tempted to apologize, something I'm not usually a big fan of but which seems like probably the right thing to do at a time like this. I mean, he's a freaking cripple, right? I should be nice. But just then I see a woven basket sitting there in the hall, with something pink hanging out of the top. It is the pajama sleeve, almost waving at me. It's like a cape in front of a bull.

"What I should call you," I say, my voice wavering a bit, "what I really should call you is Thief. What the hell makes you think you can go taking other people's stuff?!"

"What are you talking about?"

"Oh, I think you know, don't you?" I go to the hall, grab

the pajama top, and storm back into the kitchen, waving it at him for my finale. "*Especially* when you asked 'Can I have this?' and the answer was NO!!"

"I can explain," says The Nail quietly.

"Don't bother," I say. "I don't want to even know what you and Claire have been up to. I just want you to know that your klepto days are over. AND that I'll be taking this with me." I ball up the pajama top and am about to stuff it in my bag when The Nail suddenly grabs hold.

"No," he says quietly, holding on tight.

"What the hell is your problem?" I yell, and begin to pull.

"You don't understand," The Nail begins mumbling, pulling back. Or maybe what he is saying is, *You wouldn't understand.* I can't tell, because I am too busy yelling all kinds of crazy shit at him. It feels very, very important that I win this struggle.

I should know, after all those seventy-five-cent Fridays at the store, what is going to happen next. But I'm so wrapped up in the moment, bracing my Chucks to get the best angle, watching The Nail's face turn red as he tries to twist and wrench the pajamas from me, that the sound the fabric makes when it finally gives comes as a complete and total surprise to me. What's worse, it rips on a seam and I fall backward, holding everything but one sleeve. The fall hurts, and I struggle to retain my outraged demeanor, but somehow the ridiculousness of the situation dawns on me. I mean, here I am, sitting on The Nail's kitchen floor, my butt soaked with lemonade, clutching a torn piece of fabric.

"Oh my God, are you okay?" asks The Nail. He looks

horrified at the sight of me on the floor. I remember the glass and hope that The Nail really did find all of it. I reach behind myself to adjust my layers of polka skirt and I'm relieved to not find blood on my hand.

"I think so," I say. He reaches to try to help me up, but years of being a big girl have taught me not to let people do this. I carefully get myself to my feet.

"I'm sorry," says The Nail. "You're right, I shouldn't have taken them."

"Damned right," I say. "I could lose my job over something like this!" Which probably isn't true, but I'm pretty sure he doesn't know that.

"I'm sorry," he says again.

"Good," I say. "You should be. If I ever catch you taking stuff again, I'll totally bust you. You got it? I mean, I don't care how much money Claire is giving you . . ."

The Nail looks confused, and his chin begins to quiver.

"I was just trying to help Violet," he says.

"Violet?" I ask. The Nail nods and leaves the room. I blot the seat of my skirt with one of his dish towels while he's gone. It occurs to me that I should probably just get the hell out of his apartment before he comes back. Clearly, he's about to produce his dead grandma, or worse.

But unfortunately my curiosity is piqued.

Just then, The Nail returns. He seems quicker and more surefooted here in his own space. He has something curled up in the front of his T-shirt, and at first I mistake it for a kitten. Then I realize that it is the lizard I saw before. The animal seems very comfortable resting in his embrace, and I notice for the first time how beautiful its markings are. Most of its skin is black and it has tiny black nails on its toes, but all over its back and head are dots and dashes in shades of orange ranging from pale peach to deep sunset. It opens its eyes and blinks, and The Nail strokes its head.

"This is Violet," he tells me. "She's a juvenile blue-tongued skink. Of all my pets, she's . . . well, I don't like to say favorite. But she's really, um, special."

"Wow," I say, unable to take my eyes off the lizard. She's a pretty spectacular-looking creature. She almost looks like an elaborately beaded purse. "She's . . . wow."

"Yeah," agrees The Nail. "But she's got a rare bone condition, and I'm beginning to wonder if she's going to make it."

"Jesus," I say.

"You can pet her if you want. Go ahead, she's not slimy or anything."

Against my better judgment, I tentatively touch her tail. It is muscular and cold, but he is right, not slimy. The Nail pets her head some more. I touch her again, on the back this time. The Nail smiles and exhales deeply.

"She likes you," he says.

He totally gets to me when he says this.

"Spud," I say.

"What?"

"The cat I used to have. His name was Spud. He was the same color as a potato, get it?" I haven't thought about Spud in years. Under my bed, there's a shoebox of photos that probably includes several of me grinning like an idiot, with Spud hanging compliantly from my arms.

"Kidney failure," I add.

"That sucks," says The Nail.

"Thanks." I wipe my nose with the back of my wrist and stare at Violet.

"Look," I finally say, "forget about the pajamas. I've got some pretty valuable vintage clothes of my own that you could sell. I'll bring them in on Monday and you can take them to Claire. It ought to cover Violet's medicine or whatever."

He turns his red-rimmed eyes at me and gives me a confused look.

"Claire?" he says.

"Nice try," I say. I give him a look to let him know that I know about Claire.

"I just wanted to make Violet a blanket out of them. She's in a lot of pain, and I thought if I had something nice to wrap her in, she'd be able to rest and stay warm. They seemed really soft."

I look at him and oh my God, he's serious. He was seriously planning to make some kind of lizard sleeping bag out of the top he swiped. As if he's reading my mind, The Nail adds, "She's not that big. That's why I only needed the top."

I realize that I have two choices. I can walk out the door, break out into the light and the heat of the day, and run back to the store, gasping for breath, my feet slapping on the pavement all the way. Get myself yet another smoothie, round up Ginger and Zoe, and say, *Man oh man, Spy Girls. Have I got a story for you.*

Or I can stay right where I am.

The lizard Violet blinks her beady eyes again. Cautiously, I extend my hand and touch her head. She is cool and sleek, not the least bit slimy.

I close my eyes and pet her again. Her skin feels softer than vintage flannel.

CHAPTER SIX

When I come in the next morning, there's a snake on my desk. In a fish tank, that is. With a lid, gravel, a water dish, and a note:

> Yours if you want.
> Not slimy, no venom.
> Len

It's a little snake, maybe two feet long, mostly black with a slight sheen. We didn't make any sort of arrangement about this. But since I ended up hanging out at The Nail's house after my ambush attempt, I can't say I am surprised. He talked a lot, giving me details about most of his pets, which range from a bunch of tree frogs to an anaconda. There was a pretty interesting newt called an ambassador or something, and some kind of gecko with pale yellow skin like a plucked chicken. And he told me more about Violet, of course, who is clearly his favorite.

Plus, he cooked me dinner.

I don't really remember the last time someone cooked anything for me. Unless you count nuking, which I don't. And even that's been a while.

I didn't plan on staying for dinner. It just sort of happened. I hung out and we drifted back into the kitchen, and then he just sort of pulled out pots and pans and stuff while we were talking. He definitely moves quickest in his kitchen. It's a small space, so he doesn't have to cross any wide-open spaces. He seems to relax there, and his limp almost disappears. Before I really realized what he was doing with the pots and pans, there was a plate of pasta in front of me. With cheese sauce.

"Do you want grated Romano on top, or does that seem redundant?"

"Um, wow. No, yeah. Grated cheese sounds good."

And it was good. I ate enthusiastically, for once not feeling self-conscious the way I usually do when there's another person there. I even had seconds.

"Do you cook much?" I asked him between bites.

"Why, does it taste bad?"

"No! I just—"

He smiled secretively. "I taught myself to cook when I was little. Self-defense—no one in my family can cook. Cheese

 83

sauce took a long time to master. I can't tell you how many times I set off the smoke alarm before I read up and found out about making a roux."

"Wow, you're like a real cook."

"Nah, I wish. Maybe someday. That's why I started taking culinary classes through vo-tech."

"My mom would kill me if she knew I ate this," I admitted.

"Why? Are you lactose intolerant?"

"No. But she's fat intolerant."

"Huh?"

"Forget it," I said, getting up and clearing my plate. It felt kind of nice that he just didn't get it. "I should actually get going. Thanks for dinner. It was great."

He smiled, a dish towel over one shoulder.

"Anytime."

I got home after seven, which was good because my mom had a yoga student. When she gives private lessons—yoga, modern dance, Pilates, you name it—the living room is strictly off-limits. Which is good because I get to skip the usual Q and A.

At seven-thirty, my mom appeared in the doorway to my room. Her hair was swept up in a scrunchie and she was wearing the idiotic workout stuff she wears even when she's not teaching. A burgundy tank top, low-slung cotton pants, and a pink oversized T-shirt with the collar cut off, like someone out of a bad eighties music video. I mean, okay, I wear stuff from the past, but my look is cultivated. My mom's like some prehistoric creature that stayed in the swamp too long and missed out on evolution. Only, in her case, it wasn't the swamp, it was the StairMaster.

"Did you get dinner?" she asked suspiciously.

"Yeah, I nuked something." This was an acceptable answer, since there's nothing in our freezer but Weight Watchers frozen meals and the bags of peas she offers clients as ice packs.

"Mmm, okay." Right answer. "Long day?"

"Uh, yeah."

"It must be really rewarding, helping out with all those poor homeless animals."

"Yeah, it . . . uh, it's good." I heard a nagging voice inside my head, reminding me that I'd never gotten around to mentioning that I don't exactly work where my mom thinks I do. *Say something,* the voice said. *She's in a good mood; tell her now. She's bound to find out sooner or later.*

I am such an idiot. I really should have said something when I started at the store. Now she was looking at me, waiting for details. I had to say something.

"There was this snake," I finally said.

"Oh?" she said. "They have snakes?"

Shit, why did I say "snake"? Now, if she ever runs into that dumb shelter lady at the farmers' market again, she's going to say something, and what if they don't have snakes? Of course, snake or no snake, if she runs into her former student again, I'm screwed no matter what because she's bound to thank her for giving me the job. I pictured my mom confronting me, her face all pinched and red with anger . . . anger and embarrassment: *"She said you never even bothered to go to the interview!"*

I winced at the thought.

"Not usually," I stammered. "Just this one. It was no big deal. It just took a while to, uh, deal with it . . ."

I was about to say more, but thankfully the doorbell rang. My mom's face flooded with relief, and it was immediately apparent that talking to me was nothing more than something to check off her list. Like watering a plant. *Done, check.*

"Oh, that must be Ken." She consulted her watch, a tiny thin strap encircling her tiny thin wrist. "He's early tonight." Ken being her eight o'clock yoga student, I presumed. She paused for a second, clearly wanting to say something else to me by way of smoothing over the exit she was about to make.

"You look good, sweetie. I'm really proud of you."

"Oh, yeah?" I ventured. Her compliment took me by surprise. Was it that obvious that working at the store had been lifting my spirits and helping to erase my grim memories of the dreary school year that preceded it? Could she tell that making a couple of friends had been an unexpected benefit of taking this job?

"Yes!" she replied. "Sticking to your points is hard work, but it seems like it's really starting to pay off. Keep up the good work!"

And, with a broad smile, a flip of ponytail, and a flash of thong-clad behind—good Lord, Mom—she was gone.

Namaste, lady.

I flipped through my sketchbook and found the sketches I'd done of Len and Violet that afternoon. Even if I'd splurged on some fancy colored pencils, I probably couldn't have done justice to her sunset shades. I pulled out a regular pencil and began shading Len's hands holding her. But I couldn't get it right, and it ended up looking like he was all tensed up, afraid of dropping her, which was all wrong. He cradled her with a confidence and gentleness that I was only then realizing as I became frustrated by their absence in my sketch. I've never been good at hands or faces.

Yet another reason I've pretty much stuck to drawing clothes, until now.

When I see the snake on my desk, I consider buzzing The Nail and getting him to just take it away. But I don't. I'm not going to take it home, because my mom would ask questions. Instead, I do nothing, so it spends the morning on Employees Only! There's no one there to protest. Claire's been missing for almost two weeks now, a development that seemed bizarre at first but which now seems to support Zoe's theory about her being a klepto. I consider asking the Lunch Ladies if they know anything about what happened to Claire. The fact that they don't speak English makes me rule out this idea.

It's funny—I never would have thought I could do this job by myself. When Claire was here, she was so busy, bustling around depping stuff and barking orders at me. Now I can do things at my own pace and in my own way. True, not everything is easy. I can't log new items in by computer because Claire never revealed the inventory system password. But I started keeping my own written log, which seems like an acceptable substitute. That way, if a consigner calls, I can usually track down an item and rattle off how it was categorized, where it ended up, and what the sale price was.

At noon, Len stops by to say hi. I still think of him as The Nail, but pretty much only when he's not around.

"You don't have to keep it," he says.

"I'm not."

"Oh. Okay. So I'll take it home after work today."

"Nah, that's okay. It can stay."

"So you'll keep it?"

"No, I didn't say that. I said it can stay."

"Oh. Okay."

Len's mouth twitches like he's confused but amused. I pull some grocery bags of intake (consignment clothes I haven't sorted through yet) off the spare chair and offer him a place to sit.

He sits and takes the little snake out of the cage. I go through some of the intake and we don't talk for a while, which is surprisingly comfortable.

"What about Potato Two?" he finally says.

"What?"

"Potato Two," he repeats. "After your cat."

"Spud," I correct him. "Not Potato. And no."

"Okay, then what? You can't just call it 'It.' "

"Spot," I suggest.

"He doesn't have spots."

"Duh. It's an ironic name. Like calling a poodle Spike or something?"

"My grandma used to have a poodle," he recalls.

"Yeah, mine, too. I think when you become a grandma, they issue you a poodle."

"That and a boomerang table," he adds.

"Exactly," I say.

Len smiles, transfers the snake to his left hand, and brushes his bangs out of his eyes. They don't quite reach his ears, so they immediately fall back down in front of his face, like a curtain. His hair is almost the exact color of sand. Holding one hand higher than the other, he pours the snake from hand to hand like he's emptying a pitcher of water in slow motion. When the top hand releases, he raises the other hand and uses the first one to catch the flowing snake again. Then he cups his hands and the snake curls itself up inside. With a free finger, he strokes the snake's head.

"I like it up here," he says. "It's so . . . peaceful."

I look around. The Lunch Ladies are having lunch, yelling at each other over the rumble and grind of the folding and pressing machines and the dull roar of the giant exhaust fans.

"Yeah, peaceful. That's how I'd describe it," I say.

"It is," says Len, allowing the snake to travel slowly through his hands again.

"Actually, I know what you mean," I admit.

"Must be nice," says Len. "Being left alone. The girls who work downstairs can be awful. You have no idea."

"Oh, yeah?" I say.

"There's this one girl, Zoe? Do you know her? She's the really tall one with the black hair?" He holds one hand way over his head to suggest her height.

"Uh . . . no." I don't know why, but I can't bring myself to tell him that not only do I know her, I'm sort of her friend. Maybe.

"You should seriously steer clear of her. She is pure evil. She cannot be trusted."

"Oh, yeah? Like how?"

He doesn't answer. Instead he says, "A lot of the girls that work downstairs boss me around. The customers can be just as bad. 'Hey, you! Get me these shoes in a ten and a half!' "

"Seriously?" I wish he'd get back to Zoe.

"And then there's my favorite part of the job: cleaning up puke."

"You have to clean up puke?"

Len smiles down at the snake. "I'm the store runner, remember? I have to go get lots of things. Including, on occasion, the mop."

"Ugh. I'm so sorry."

"It's okay. I've had to deal with worse things."

"Like what?"

"I'll tell you some other time." Len looks up and extends his hands toward me. "You want to hold him?" he asks.

"Nah, that's okay," I say, stepping back.

"Okay," says Len. He gets up to put the snake back.

"You can stay," I say noncommittally. "You know, if you want."

"You sure?" asks Len. "I don't want to be in the way."

"You're not," I tell him, hoping he'll get back to talking about the Florons. But he doesn't, and somehow it doesn't feel right to ask. Considering I'm trying to stay off that topic myself.

The next day, he comes by at noon again. This time he's carrying a brown paper bag.

"Lunch?" I ask.

"Yup," he says, pulling out a plastic bag from inside the paper one. Inside are light brown crickets, hopping all over each other.

"Um, I'm *so* out of here," I say. "Sorry, I just . . ."

"It's okay. Give me ten minutes."

I make a Mookie's run to avoid having to witness the carnage. Clearly I'm not cut out to be a real snake owner, and I'm grateful that The Nail's willing to do my dirty work. So much so that I decide to bring him back a donut.

I peek out the back door, and once I'm sure Zoe and Ginger aren't out on the loading dock, I slip out this way. "Slip out" being an inaccurate description, since hoisting myself off the loading dock requires hitching up whatever I'm wearing (today, a long black flamenco skirt with three asymmetrical tiers of ruffles—red, orange, and yellow) and vaulting myself over the edge. Still, it beats the alternative: walking across The Real Deal. The more I hang out with Len, the less I want Zoe and Ginger to know.

Unfortunately, I forget to prop the door open when I leave. Which means that on my return, I either have to swim through a sea of Pickers or attempt to navigate The Real Deal without being noticed. I opt for the latter, walking fast and looking down.

"Hey, Spy Girl!" calls Ginger. "Any news?"

"Nada," I say, glancing over but not stopping.

"C'mere, Vee," orders Zoe.

I freeze in my tracks. Reluctantly, I walk over.

"Ooh, goody. You got me a snack," she says, reaching out and snatching the waxed paper Mooks bag out of my hands.

She unwads the top and peers down into it. "What is that, a lemon log?"

"Oh!" I say, surprised. "Actually, I . . . uh . . ."

Zoe rolls her eyes and makes an irritated face at me.

"Relax," she snarls. "I don't want your stinkin' cruller."

"Oh, right."

She rewads the bag and hands it over with mock disdain. Then she smiles big.

"You're not used to being fucked with, are you?"

"I, uh," I stammer.

"Too cute!" she says, reaching out and, I swear to God, pinching my cheek. "Love the skirt. Very cha-cha-cha. Stop by later, a'ight? We'll hang."

"Sure," I say, practically crashing into a display of two mannequins in matching Nehru jackets and love beads in my haste to get to the stairs.

As I leave, I can't help wondering if Zoe is saying anything to Ginger about me behind my back. Or not saying anything. Just giving her a look, and Ginger giggling and nodding back like, *I know.*

It's not like that, I remind myself. *They actually like you, that's just how they act. They're diamonds in the rough, remember?* I know I'm right, but I'm tempted, just the same, to look back over my shoulder and see.

But I don't. Because the thing is: if I'm wrong, I don't want to know.

When I return to Employees Only!, only two pitiful crickets remain in the cage. Len kindly removes them so I don't have to watch the inevitable afternoon snack.

Len gives me a confused look as I hand him the Mookie's bag. He peers inside, then brightens.

"People don't usually bring me stuff," he says.

"It's not for you," I say.

"Oh . . . okay."

"Len? Hello? It's a joke?"

"Oh! I thought you . . . Never mind. Thanks."

Carefully, he takes the donut out of the bag, sets it on my desk, and studies it.

"Wow," he says, and I have to agree. A Mookie's lemon log is a sight to behold: a pale yellow ruffle of icing along the top, and shiny buttons of the darker yellow filling at each end. "I thought donuts had to be round."

"Live and learn," I say.

He picks it up and turns it admiringly. Then he pinches its waist and holds out half.

"Here," he says.

"No, it's okay," I say, instinctively waving him off. "I, uh, I had a big lunch." He takes a bite, then closes his eyes and sort of moans.

"Oh my God," he says.

I grin, pleased. "I know, right?"

"What do you call this?"

"It's a lemon log. You like it?"

"It's sublime."

He proceeds to devour the rest of his half.

My heart is kind of pounding, but I don't know why. It's not like I made the donut, for God's sake. But still, I feel sort of thrilled to have introduced him to lemon logs.

 93

"Come on," he urges. "You gotta have a bite. Please?"

I look at him and he gives me this little-boy look. Truly pathetic.

I roll my eyes for emphasis, even though I've been hungry for it all along.

"Oh, all right," I say. Taking a bite, I think of the cafeteria motto of the Sunshine School: FOOD TASTES BETTER WHEN YOU SHARE IT. *Sure it does,* I used to think.

But damned if it isn't the best lemon log I've ever had.

CHAPTER SEVEN

By the end of the week, I find myself looking forward to Len stopping by at lunchtime. And not just because the alternative is catching crickets for the snake myself. I still think of it as just "the snake," and I still won't touch it. But I like watching Len hold it, and I like to sketch it when he's holding it in his hands.

One day, he asks to look at my sketchbook.

I almost say no, because it's really just my random doodles, most of which suck. But then I hand it over. He takes his time with it, flipping through page after page of drawings—dresses, gloves, skirts—so slow it makes me want to jump out of my skin.

"I like it," he says when he gets to the end.

"Yeah, okay. Thanks. Whatever."

"How come you draw clothes that way?"

"What way?"

"All . . . empty."

"Um, that's how they . . . are up here?" I gesture at the racks, confused.

"Yeah, but how come when you draw them you don't make up people to wear them? Or draw yourself in them?"

"I dunno," I say, surprised by the question. "I just don't." I take a breath, then add, "I like the clothes. I'm not so hot on people."

"Oh, yeah?"

"I mean, not all people," I add quickly, realizing how I probably sound. Len raises an eyebrow.

"Tell the truth," he says. "You never liked me."

"That's not true."

"Come on."

"What's your point?" I argue. "You probably hated me, too."

"Nope."

"Oh, please! I used to be a total bitch to you."

"Yeah, I guess. But I always thought you were, I dunno. Different."

I meet the gaze of his pale eyes. His lip twitches, and out of the blue I wonder what it would be like if he kissed me. My sarcasm steadies me.

"Yeah, I'm different, all right," I scoff.

"You are," he says, missing my tone as always. "Just not quite in the way I thought."

"What way was that?"

"Relax," he says. "I didn't mean anything bad. I just always kind of wanted to talk to you, to maybe get to know you. But whenever I saw you it seemed like you just wanted me to leave, so I never got the chance."

"Sorry," I say. "I just never . . ."

"It's okay," he says in a way that lets me know it actually is. Silently, the snake glides between his intertwined fingers.

I'm relieved that he stopped me before the rest of my words slipped out: *I just never thought of you as an actual person before.*

"It's okay," he says again.

So I nod. I open my sketchbook and find a blank page. My pen finds the paper and my eyes find Len's hands and the snake.

I've got to admit, it's more challenging to draw something that moves. I try not to look at Len's face, and I lean forward to keep him from looking at mine. Those clear eyes of his make me nervous, a little. Sometimes I think he can see inside me, what I'm thinking and feeling. Things I might not even know yet. Things I might not even want to know. Which kind of scares me.

On the positive side, I think I might be getting a tiny bit better at drawing hands.

The thing I like about hanging out with Len is that we talk, but we don't have to talk. I've never known anyone I could just sit with, not talking, and have it be okay. Except maybe my dad, but that was so long ago I'm not sure if I actually remember or I just think I do.

When Zoe and Ginger and I hang out on the loading dock, there are definitely times when I just sit there and don't talk. After all, Zoe takes up a lot of airspace with her rants. And Ginger grabs every spare silence she can to chime in. But it's not really the same thing.

Occasionally I ask Len about Violet, how she's doing. He usually says she's the same. Sometimes "a little better." Sometimes "not so good."

"How can you tell?" I ask him.

He shrugs. "I just can."

Len himself doesn't look so good sometimes, but I'm not sure if that's because I see him more often so I've been noticing more. Some days, he looks extra thin, extra pale. Like a vampire or something. My mom would be thrilled if I looked like him. Once she got sick for a week and she couldn't eat anything but saltines and ginger ale. First thing she did when she felt well enough to get out of bed? Got on the scale.

She'd love Len. Of course, I have no intention of telling her about him, much less bringing him home or anything. She'd get all overly hopeful and giddy at the thought that I have not just a Friend but a *Boy* Friend, even if it's a boy that looks kind of sickly and dead most of the time and limps around carrying bags of crickets.

I keep meaning to ask Len if *he's* okay, but I don't want him to feel weird. It's like when people try to give me a hand getting up—maybe they don't mean anything by it, but maybe they do.

The thing about having Len visit me each day is that I am increasingly aware of the lurking threat of getting busted for violating the Secret Spy Girl Pact. Len's visits to Employees Only! are not so risky, because Zoe and Ginger never come upstairs. And I make sure never to leave with Len, even if I have to make excuses. Each afternoon, as I leave the store, I always fear that I'll run into Zoe and Ginger and they'll grill me about my after-work plans. Or, worse, rope me into an impromptu Secret Spy Girl Stakeout of Len's place.

I keep thinking, *Maybe I should just tell them?* I mean, they're supposed to be my friends, right? Why couldn't I just say to Zoe and Ginger, *Hey, wanna hear something funny? It turns out there's actually a good reason D.B.W. took those pajamas!*

But then what? After they asked questions and dragged the whole story out of me, they might just laugh the whole thing off.

But then again, they might not.

It's just better this way, I finally conclude, even if it means keeping them in the dark. What they don't know won't hurt them.

Or me, for that matter.

Then one day, the minute I get to work, the phone on my desk rings for a consignment appointment. As soon as I hang it up, it rings again—another consigner, a new one this time. And then it rings again. Finally, after about ten calls, I call downstairs to Bill.

"Y-ello?"

"Hey, was there, like, something about the store in the newspaper or something?"

"There was?"

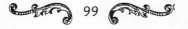

"No. I mean, I don't know if there was, that's why I'm asking you. The phone up here has been ringing all morning. It's like the whole freaking world is suddenly dying to consign."

"Ohhhh . . . ," says Bill knowingly. "That's because it's August."

Bill explains that every August, we get totally trounced at the store. The college kids come back and proceed to sell everything they own and buy new stuff to replace it.

"That's why we're on 'extended back-to-school hours' down here now. It's killing me, man. Any interest in a little overtime?"

"As if. No offense."

"Yeah, I figured. Still, if you change your mind . . . HEY! The Pile is NOT a dressing room . . . put your clothes BACK ON . . . Hey, Veronica, man? Sorry, I gotta go . . ."

Bill hangs up abruptly. Almost immediately, the phone rings again.

"Yeah, hey, is this the place where you can sell your stuff?"

A few calls later, I take the phone off the hook.

Around noon, Len stops by with a paper bag.

"Snake lunchtime?" I ask.

"Nah," says Len. "I didn't get a chance to pick up any. I'm going to have to get some later."

"Sooo, what's in the bag?"

Len shrugs and hands it to me. I open it and find an extra-large smoothie inside.

"I ran an errand for Bill and I just sort of thought you might want one. It's really hot out." He lifts up his T-shirt and mops his face, revealing his absurdly flat stomach and the waistband of his underwear. Low-slung pants are not a fashion statement for him. Just a fact of life for a butt-less boy. "That's the kind you like, right?"

I take a sip. It's coffee-flavored, not mocha.

"I usually get the mocha kind."

Len looks crushed. "I'm sorry," he says. "I tried to call you from Bill's phone before I went out, but your line was busy."

"No, actually, it's really good," I say quickly. "I just never tried this flavor before . . . I mean, thanks."

He looks pleased. "No problem."

"You want some?"

"Uh, okay." He takes the lid off and drains about half the cup. "Not half bad," he says with surprise.

"Okay, explain how you've lived here forever and yet you are not wise to the many splendors of the Mooks?"

Len shrugs. "We didn't have much money when I was growing up?"

"It's hardly haute cuisine."

"Yeah, well, I dunno. We had donuts sometimes, but we always got them at the grocery store. You know, the tiny ones with the powdered sugar?"

"Sure," I tell him, not adding that I used to talk my dad into buying me a roll of them when he'd take me on a grocery run. I'd eat the whole roll in the cart before we'd even make it to the checkout. My mom would bust me every time because of the telltale white smudges on the thighs of my stretch pants where I'd wiped my sticky palms.

"Your phone's off the hook," he says, pointing.

"Yeah, I know. It's the consigners. I'm getting slammed up here," I tell him.

"Oh, yeah?"

I gesture to ten or more trash bags of consignment items, piled in a semicircle wall around my chair. "Yeah," I tell him.

"Do you want help?"

I give him a look. "Nah, that's okay."

"What, you don't think I can do it?"

"Um, actually . . ."

"Do you have any idea how long I've been coming here?"

"No."

"Try ten years."

"Yeah, right."

"Okay, as an actual employee a lot less, but I used to come here with my grandma when I was a kid. She got practically all my clothes from Dollar-a-Pound. Sometimes she'd consign stuff and drag me along for that, too. So before you write me off . . ."

"Okay, okay, you're hired." I'm startled by Len's outpouring of information. I'm also intrigued by his burst of enthusiasm. Plus, the truth is, I do need some help or I'm never going to dig myself out. "But look: up here, I run the show. So you've gotta do what I say."

Len nods. I take a long draw from my smoothie and survey the situation.

"Okay, start with that bag over there." I point. "Dump it out on the floor. Then pick up an item and hold it up. I'll tell you what to do with it."

Len hitches up his jeans, braces one foot against my desk, and hoists the first bag. His upper body is stronger than I would've thought, but his legs shake and look ready to buckle. I make a mental note not to assign him any more heavy lifting. He tips the bag and a cascade of fabric rolls out. A musty cloud of dust fills the air.

"P.U.! Attic," I say, waving the mothball scent away.

Len selects a plaid pair of pants.

"Dep," I order. Obligingly, he tosses them at the chute, missing by a mile.

"No problem, we'll get it later. Keep going," I say.

Next up: a stained tan polo shirt. "Dep." A skirt with a broken zipper. "Dep." A T-shirt with armpit rings and the words KEEP AMERICA GREEN over a big pot leaf on the front. "Bill will love that. Definitely dep."

"Definitely dep," agrees Len. This time, swoosh, down the chute. He grins.

"Two points," I say.

"Huh?"

"Two points? Hello? Jesus, were you never forced to watch basketball?"

"Basketball, no. Hockey. My grandma's a Bruins fanatic."

"Ooh." I cringe. "Brutal."

"Hey," says Len brightly. "Check this out."

He holds up what appears to be a tuxedo jacket.

"Nice," I say, going over to inspect it. "That's a keeper."

The lining is shot, but otherwise it looks fairly decent. I tell Len, "Good eye," and wander off to drag another bag over.

"What do you think?" Len says.

I look up and see that he's slipped the jacket on over his T-shirt and is puffing out his usually sunken chest. The effect is startling. The jacket sits squarely on his shoulders, which makes me realize that he actually has shoulders.

"What?" he says self-consciously, letting out his breath. For a second, he sounds like me.

"Nothing. I—you look good," I say, flustered.

"Shut up," he says. He takes the jacket off and throws it at me. But he's smiling.

I throw it back at him.

"You should keep it," I say. Which I mean, because it did look great on him. But as soon as it comes out, I realize that I'm also fishing for the Secret Spy Girls.

"Nah," he says, throwing it at me again. "I've already got ten of them."

My heart lurches for a second before I get that he's kidding. "Right, and cummerbunds in every color of the rainbow," I say, throwing the jacket back at him again.

"Cummerwhuh?"

"You know. Those fancy wide waistbands that go with tuxedos?"

"Right, right. Yup, I've got a million of those."

We go on sorting for a while, falling into a comfortable rhythm of dumping bags and churning through them piece by piece. It's hot, I'm sweaty, and I'm running on fumes, seeing as I've had too much caffeine and too little food.

And yet it's like the fleas, only better. I look up at one point and realize that it is later than I thought. The fans are still cranking, but the sewing machines are not—at some point, the Lunch Ladies must have gone home.

"Okay, last bag," I tell Len. "The rest can wait." He nods solemnly and dumps it. The item on top of the heap is sort of fuzzy-looking, and butterscotch-colored.

Len picks it up and lets out a low whistle.

"Whoa," I say. It's a pair of men's suede fringed pants.

"Dep?" asks Len hopefully.

"Nooo . . . ," I say, starting to feel a little light-headed. "I think you need to try those on."

"What?!"

"Hey, didn't you agree that whatever I say goes?"

"Yeah, but . . ." Len squints at the pants. "No way."

"Look, this is my job. I need to see if they're fit for The Real Deal," I say, trying to sound like this is official business. I point to a pair of racks of off-season coats. "You can change back there."

"Do you ever try stuff on?"

"Sometimes," I say, turning my back to give him privacy and so he can't see that I'm lying. For extra modesty, I close my eyes while I wait.

"Ahem."

I turn around. Len is standing there wearing the pants, which, surprisingly, fit him great. I guess that's the answer to the question of who should wear fringed suede pants: people who don't have asses.

"Howdy," I say.

"Okay, fine," he says. He rotates clumsily in place for my benefit. "Laugh it up."

"I'm not," I tell him. "Seriously, you look good."

"Oh, yeah?" He looks me right in the eye.

"Yeah," I say.

"So this is fun for you?"

"I guess so . . . yeah."

"Okay, then," he says, returning to where we dumped out the bag and digging through the contents.

"What are you doing?"

He pulls out something long and shiny and holds it up.

"Your turn," he says.

This is ridiculous.

I don't have to do this.

I should just tell him to leave.

There's no way I'm going through with this.

"Veronica?"

I poke my head out from behind the rack. "Look, forget it. It doesn't fit, okay?"

"Let me see."

"I told you, forget it."

"I won't laugh. I promise."

The dress Len selected is a floor-length red satin sheath. In it, I feel—and probably look—like an overstuffed sausage. And that's without even getting it zipped up. I take a deep breath and try the zipper again. It moves a millimeter and bites me.

Fuck.

"Veronica, come on out. There's no one here. Except me, and I'm wearing chaps, I think."

I laugh and the zipper retreats some more, so my whole back hangs out. Then I take one more deep breath and grab a burgundy smoking jacket off the rack I'm crouching behind. I belt it tightly around me, then I emerge.

"Those are not chaps," I explain. "Chaps are worn over pants."

"Let me see," he says.

"No," I tell him, biting my lip, but he's watching my eyes, not my mouth. Slowly, he comes up to me and undoes the silk rope belt.

I know I could stop him with a look. Or a touch.

But I don't. I look down and see his hands spreading the lapels and exposing the tight, shiny, bulging front of the gown. Instinctively, I jump when I feel the slightly clammy touch of his hands as they make it to my lower back, where the gown gapes open like a canyon. I feel my body tense up as his hands travel up my back, exploring the soft, squishy terrain. I brace myself for the laugh that I know is coming any moment.

He lets out a long breath.

I look up at him, narrowing my eyes protectively.

His bangs swing forward as he leans in and closes his eyes and I realize a second before it happens—

Oh my God oh my God oh my God

shit yikes The Nail oh my G—

—that he's going to kiss me.

There's this sudden rush in my chest, which I assume is

because, even with the dress unzipped, it is cutting off my circulation, and also, between my legs, there's a warmth, sort of, and my mind of course is racing, racing. My thoughts are still screaming, *Oh my God oh my God oh my God oh my God!*

This is so weird.

The Nail is kissing me.

Holy shit. The Nail.

And how much weirder is it that I kind of don't want to make him stop?

I kind of maybe even want to kiss him back.

I somehow manage to keep the freaking-out in my head.

And my lips sort of unfreeze and start to move against his in a way that I hope does not seem robotic and weird.

I want to lift my arms because I've seen that in movies and it feels right to do that, and I also really, really want to touch his hair to see if it is as soft as I've always suspected, even though I've never consciously thought about it. But I'm afraid the dress will rip right down the side if I do, so I leave my arms at my sides . . .

. . . and luckily there's the fringe right there . . .

. . . so while we stand there and kiss and kiss, my hands are twiddling, twiddling away at the soft tendrils of leather.

Did I mention he's just the right height?

For kissing, that is.

And his hair is, yes, that soft. Even softer.

I find out about his hair when we take a breath and then move to the old couch, where Rags often sleeps. He takes the tuxedo jacket and spreads it out over the part where you can see the springs.

"How chivalrous," I say, which sounds like something my dad would say, which makes me think of my dad, which makes me decide to try not speaking for a while.

Instead, I lower myself carefully onto the jacket and fold my arms across my chest. My heart is going *boom, boom, boom,* keeping time with the *chung, chung, chung* of the industrial ceiling fans. I cross my legs, wrapping the robe around my knee and tucking it under my top thigh.

"Len, I . . . ," I start to say.

"Shhh . . . ," he says. He closes his eyes and puts one arm around my shoulder. "Listen."

Uneasily, I lean into him, keeping my hands firmly positioned so the robe won't flap open when my weight shifts. My head is against his shoulder and I smell the mustiness of the couch mixing with the smells of his soap, his sweat, his skin.

"To what?" I ask.

"It's so quiet," he whispers. *Chung, chung, chung* go the ceiling fans, like giant propellers revving for flight.

"*Phhh,*" I hear myself exhale awkwardly.

Chung, chung, chung. Like we're taking off.

"Close your eyes," he says.

Reluctantly, I close my eyes.

Chung, chung, chung.

We sit so still, just breathing, listening to the fans. It's almost like I'm dreaming, because I feel myself growing smaller and smaller, nestled there beside him. Lighter and lighter, like a bird under another bird's wing.

Chung, chung, chung.

Keeping my eyes closed, I slowly unclench one hand.

Timidly, I reach out until I find the warmth between his arm and his T-shirt. *Chung, chung, chung.*

I feel him turn and kiss me again. My forehead this time. Then my nose. Then my mouth again.

And just like that, we take flight.

CHAPTER EIGHT

en works his way down some more. The top part of the smoking jacket parts and the straps of the dress shift because the back of the dress is wide open. Before long, the top of my vintage bomber bra peeks out. Len's bangs brush against my neck and he kisses the tiny embroidered rose that sits smack at center stage. He looks up at me and cautiously traces one finger back and forth along the lace edge of the cups.

"You're beautiful," he says.

"Shut up," I tell him.

"Why does that embarrass you?" he asks.

"Because I'm not, okay?" I say quietly, snapping out of the moment for a second. "And I'm actually kind of okay with that. So do me a favor and just don't lie to me."

"I'm not lying," he tells me. "I wouldn't do that. You can trust me."

I want to tell him that I *never* trust people. I just don't, okay, and it has worked out pretty well for me so far.

But then he kisses me again.

"And," he whispers, "I think you're beautiful."

I open my mouth to protest.

And then I shut it again.

And I close my eyes.

And kiss him back.

When I get home, much later, I ease the side door closed behind me and tiptoe through the kitchen.

I glance around the counters for a note. No note. I can't hear the tinkling strains of her yoga music, so I know she's not teaching. She could be asleep, but I doubt it. It's not that late. And she can't be out, because there would be a note. Still, maybe she just ran out for a minute? If I can just get to my room . . .

"Hi, sweetie." No such luck. Her posture immaculate, her ponytail like an actual pony's tail, my mother sprints into the kitchen.

"Hey, Mom."

"Long day, huh?" She consults her sports watch.

"Uh, yeah."

"They're really giving you a workout, huh?" This comment comes with a big grin. She clearly loves the idea of her slothlike daughter getting a workout of any kind.

"Uh, yeah." *You have no idea.* I hide my blushing face in

the fridge, looking for something edible I can pluck and take with me to my room. "You're not teaching tonight?"

She reaches past me, grabbing a bottle of water. "Nope. I had a last-minute cancellation." She sits and removes her scrunchie, shaking out her hair. Then she redoes her perfect ponytail while launching into a monologue. "Actually, it's sort of funny. Paula, you know Paula, has this dog named Kimba. Is it Kimba? Maybe it's Simba. At any rate, she was thinking she might be sick, because she was sleeping so much. The dog, that is. And the next thing she knew, the dog climbed into a basket of clean laundry—clean white laundry— and had puppies! Can you believe that?"

"Yeah," I say, my voice a conversational flyswatter.

"Not just one or two, either!" continues my mom, her voice darting away and buzzing just out of reach. "I think she said there were six of them. Anyway, she cancelled her lesson because someone's coming over to look at them." She sighs like this is a major tragedy. "But even if she finds homes for one or two, the rest may have to go. Dorothy's is a no-kill, right?"

"A . . . what? Who?"

"Dorothy's animal shelter. You know. Dorothy Milner? *Your boss?*"

My boss? Oh, no. *Shit, shit, shit!* I knew I shouldn't have blown that whole thing off. It was so obvious it would come back to bite me eventually.

"I . . . uh . . ." *Deep breath.* "Look, I know you're going to be mad."

"Mad? Why?"

"The thing is . . . um, I don't work there . . . anymore."

"You don't? Since when?" Her voice is as crisp and frosty as a frozen french fry. Which we haven't kept in the house since Dad moved out.

"Okay, it's just that . . . I didn't actually get that job."

"I don't understand. Dorothy said she'd hire you even without . . ."

"Yeah, see, I got this other job instead," I interrupt her, talking fast. "And I've been going to work every day, honest. I kept meaning to tell you, but I just . . ."

"What kind of job?" she asks suspiciously. You can tell she's envisioning me working at the Mooks, or worse. *Well, Mom, I'm an ice cream tester. Yup, they pay me in ice cream, and my job is to sit there on my butt and eat ice cream all day long.*

"It's at a store. The Clothing Bonanza?"

"The *used* clothing store?" she says, incredulous. You'd never know from the way she says it that she used to embroider smiley faces on the worn-out knees of my overalls and take her most worn-out pairs of jeans and sew on corduroy triangles to turn them into skirts. "The one with the dirty clothes all over the floor?"

"Vintage clothing," I correct her. "And that's Dollar-a-Pound. I don't work on the Dollar-a-Pound floor."

"You're working as a . . . *salesgirl?*" She says it like it's a synonym for "prostitute."

"No, I work upstairs. In the Consignment Corner? That's where people bring clothes that they . . ."

"I know what consignment is," she snaps.

"Oh."

"Do you mean to tell me they actually hired you? Off the street, with no experience, no references, nothing? Do they have any idea how old you are?"

"Yes!" *Well, actually, no.* "Jesus, Mom, I'm not a baby. Lots of kids my age have summer jobs." I know because I see them all over—the boys who rip tickets at the movies, the girls who walk the summer camp kids around town on those long wrist-leash ropes.

My mom looks like she's trying real hard not to burst a blood vessel. "Veronica," she says carefully, "I'm sure you're doing a *fine* job. I just don't see why you felt the need to lie to me."

"Well, gee, let's see. Could it be because you're always so busy trying to run my life that I can't get a word in edge-wise?"

"Veronica, that's not fair."

"Come on. You decided on this dumb pooper-scooper job for me and you didn't give a damn what I wanted."

"I was trying to help. You've never had a job before."

"Yeah, well, I have one now. A good job, something that interests me. The work's good, the people are good . . ."

Her radar goes off. "What people?" she says.

"You know, the people I work with."

"Other girls?"

"Yeah, Mom. I know that sounds impossible, but I actually have friends at my job."

"Well, that's great. I know this has been a hard year for you, socially." *Year?* Try "life." "Do you know them from school?"

"No. I mean, this one boy goes to my school. I mean, he did."

"A boy?" Immediately, I wish I hadn't brought him up.

"Yeah."

"Is he one of your friends?"

"Yeah. I mean, kind of."

"And do you and your friends get together after work? Do they invite you over to their houses?"

Get together after work? I picture me and Len on the couch. I feel my cheeks getting hot. Not quite what she has in mind, I'm sure.

"I mean, yeah, uh, I guess," I stammer. "Not a lot. Okay? Jeez, what's the big deal? I thought you wanted me to have friends."

"I do want you to have friends, Veronica. You know that. It's just that . . ."

"What?"

She sighs. "Sweetie, I just worry about you. I've just seen you get hurt before. It's just, well, you know. Girls can be cruel."

"Yeah, well, like I said, one of my friends is a boy."

She gives me a really serious look. "Boys can be worse. A girl like you needs to be careful, Veronica."

"A girl like me?"

She looks impatient. "Veronica, look. I have nothing against boys. Some boys are fine. However, some boys know

that a girl who hasn't had a lot of attention before will do anything to get it. And so they take advantage of that. Do you know what I'm saying?"

"This boy's not like that, Mom," I say, rolling my eyes and trying to sound nonchalant.

"I hope so," she says.

She doesn't sound very convinced.

In my bedroom, I stay awake for hours, playing and replaying every little detail of the evening in my head. The way he leaned in when he kissed me the first time. The way I kissed him back. Did I know, on some level, where things were headed when I told him he could help out? Did I actually want him to kiss me? And if I did, did he know I did? Yikes, did he think I was coming on to him with that whole *"You need to try these pants on"* business? I mean, I wasn't. But if he thought I was, did he kiss me just because he thought it was what I wanted? Or because the way I was acting made him think I'd let him?

Good God, could my mom be right? Did I seem like I was just trying to get his attention? Like I was desperate for his attention?

No way, I tell myself. Jesus, he was as nervous as I was. Maybe more. Plus there was all that stuff he said. About how I looked. And how I could trust him.

But he had his eyes closed. A lot. And it was dark. Was that because he didn't want to look at me? Oh God, why did I let him talk me into putting on that stupid sausage casing of a dress? And why did I wear that ridiculous pointy bra to work today? I mean, I didn't know when I put it on that anyone would actually *see* it. But I must have looked like such a freak to him.

But then I think about how he looked at me. How he kissed me—right on my stupid bomber bra even. How he seemed so genuinely grateful that I let him near me.

I turn onto my side, close my eyes, and start to drift off to sleep. With one finger tracing up and down my bra strap and the other hand tucked between my legs, trying to trick my mind into believing that my hand is his.

The next morning, I wake up early, no alarm. I start to put together one of my usual aggressively idiosyncratic outfits, but I just can't help myself. Instead, I pull out my favorite dress. It is a peach taffeta prom dress, with rhinestone spaghetti straps and a frothy, multi-tiered tulle skirt. It didn't fit when I got it, so I ripped out the side seams and added contrasting accent panels of salmon taffeta. It is the goofiest, sappiest thing I own, and yet my love for it defies reason. I put on a men's T-shirt underneath it to hide my bra and my flabby upper arms, the part my mother refers to as "mermans" (even though her own arms are chiseled) after some fat dead singer who had them. I have this pair of peach Bakelite combs that match the dress and that I always consider wearing with it but generally decide not to because they're a little too matchy. Skipping my usual pigtails, I shove the combs into my hair and stand before the mirror.

I practice smiling at myself, then make a face.

I can't believe I'm doing this.

I'm dressing up for The Nail, for God's sake.

I brush my teeth twice, sniff my pits a thousand times, consider and reject the idea of dipping into my mom's makeup supply. By the time I get out the door, I'm running late. Not hideously late, but late enough that if I actually had a boss, I'd be in some minor amount of trouble.

I stalk down the block at twice my usual pace. My tulle layers whoosh-whoosh against my legs as I march along. In my head, to the beat of my stride, I suddenly hear that old refrain, only with new words:

Kiss-ing The Nail, kiss-ing The Nail, kiss-ing The Nail . . .

Gonna kiss that Nail, kiss-ing The Nail, kiss-ing The Nail . . .

Despite myself, I can't help smiling at the thought.

When I get to the store, I scramble in through the loading dock, successfully gambling that Zoe and Ginger will not be around but will have left the door propped open in flagrant disregard of the sign. This saves me the fifteen minutes I usually spend trying to extricate myself from conversations with Bill, Zoe, and Ginger on the lower two floors. Instead, I can clomp straight up two floors to Employees Only!

My mad dash comes to a grinding halt when I arrive at the Consignment Corner. Because when I get there, I immediately notice that someone is already there, waiting for me. Waiting on the couch, specifically—Len and my couch from last night.

At the sight of me, she rises and extends her hand.

"I'm Shirley," she informs me. "You must be Veronica."

Shirley has an inch of bright blue eye shadow over each eye, an upswept hairdo crowned with a giant clip shaped like a butterfly, and no chin, just a ski slope from her mouth to her neck. She's dressed in a military-looking polyester suit with a constellation of brass buttons. It's lime green, so she looks like a giant pear in it. I'm not exactly one to talk, but she has an extremely wide butt.

Zoe, who likes to be an authority on everything, will later describe Shirley as, and I quote, "batshit crazy." But when I meet Shirley, I don't know this. Due to where she's sitting, I assume that Shirley is the new Claire. After all, Claire is now Long Gone (much of her personal stuff—several plastic trolls, a grass skirt and a flower lei taped strategically to her computer monitor, the bust-of-Elvis lamp—remains in place as a sort of shrine to her memory), though the reasons for her leaving have never been shared. At least not with me. I no longer expect Claire to reappear, but it has crossed my mind that at some point the Powers That Be might send someone upstairs so I don't have to keep doing her job as well as mine.

But Shirley turns out not to be the new Claire. She explains that she is a floor manager (I immediately think: *Floron* manager) and that Claire will be replaced "shortly." She then turns the conversation to another topic: efficiency. She has a way of emphasizing certain words with her index fingers. Sort of like a flight attendant pointing out the exit rows.

"You may not be *aware* of it," she tells me, pointing to both sides, "but the store's *efficiency* is at an all-time low. If *improvements* are not made, there may need to be *oversight* to determine the causes of inefficiency and to address the *exigencies* of the situation."

I nod. I have no idea what she is talking about.

Eventually, I realize that it comes down to this: she's bugging me to move the consignment goods faster.

How? Shirley is full of opinions.

"Dep this!" Shirley says briskly, plucking a windowpane lace blouse I rescued and tagged during the marathon session Len and I had with the backlogged intake. "In fact, dep the whole rack."

"O-kay," I say, startled to hear someone other than Claire and me use the word "dep." I suddenly realize that Shirley's mannerisms seem so familiar because she must be the manager I've seen Zoe impersonating. Having her come to Employees Only! is unsettling. By definition, Florons, and the managers of Florons, never leave the retail floors. Plus, Shirley's clearly oblivious to the fact that I spent the better part of yesterday evening carefully culling the very items she's now telling me to toss down the chute.

She starts digging through some of the trash bags Len and I didn't get to when she quickly stands up.

"What on earth?" she says.

I look, fearful that I've left my sketchbook out.

But no. She's looking right at The Nail's snake.

"That's not . . . really mine," I tell her, which probably sounds about as stupid as any lie I could have made up.

"Really?" she says, dubious. She peers inside. "What kind is it?"

"I have no idea."

"Hmmmm . . ." She smiles. I don't. "Problem is, the health department is supposed to make an unscheduled visit this month, so I'm afraid you'll have to dep the snake."

"What?"

Shirley smiles, her non-chin slipping into the abyss. She has these gray smoker's teeth. "Just get the snake out of here, okay?"

After she leaves, I buzz Len. Repeatedly.

He finally emerges, wearing the tuxedo jacket (I insisted he keep it) over a dark gray hoodie sweatshirt I've never seen him wear before. He looks ridiculous, since it is about a hundred and ten degrees up here. But also bulky and cute, sort of like a kid whose mom has made him wear extra layers to go play in the snow.

"Hey," I say.

"Hey," he echoes. "Wow. Nice dress."

"Yeah?" I say, wrinkling my nose. I want to tell him that it's actually my favorite, but I suddenly feel self-conscious, so I don't. "Nice jacket."

"Thanks."

He pats my fluffy skirt lightly.

We both grin like idiots.

It's bizarre. I can almost convince myself that nothing happened last night. That things are the same as they ever were. But they're so not. And just knowing that gives me a little charge that makes me want him to kiss me again, right now, in front of the Lunch Ladies and everything.

"What's with the hoodie?" I ask.

"Huh? Oh, I got it from Bill."

I cringe. Now's probably not the best time to tell him not to take fashion suggestions from Bill.

"Look, we have a problem." I tell him about Shirley and how she said to "dep the snake."

"Hey, that's it," he says.

"What's what?"

"The name we've been looking for. 'Dep.' Dep the Snake?"

"Len, seriously, you've got to take it home. I could get in trouble."

Len grins.

"Guess I'd better not let her find out about this." He moves the side of the kangaroo pouch over to reveal that inside it he is cradling Violet, her nose and one nubbly black foot protruding from her pink vintage flannel snuggle sack. Her eyes look crusty.

"Len?!" I yell.

Len looks guiltily over his shoulder, though none of the Lunch Ladies are paying any attention to us.

"Are you crazy?" I ask him, lowering my voice to a whisper. "What if someone saw you? Plus, is that even good for her?"

Len covers her up with the pocket again. "I read somewhere that they do this kind of stuff for, like, babies that are born too early? And this zoo in Australia has started doing it for immature bats, too."

"Yeah, okay, but last I checked, Violet's not a bat."

Len sits down at my desk and sighs. "I'm just not sure

what else to do for her. I don't think she has that much longer."

Just then, out of the corner of my eye, I see the door to Employees Only! open. From behind it peek two heads: one high up, with jet-black Cleopatra hair; the other, much lower down, with long white-blond, pink-streaked ponytails.

"Len, listen, you gotta go. I've got work to do. Here, take this rack downstairs." I grab a Z-rack and yank it away from the wall. *"Come back after,"* I whisper.

I practically shove the Z-rack at him, cringing as I do because as soon as it is in motion, I realize that if I knock him off my chair, Violet's health may become even more compromised. Luckily, Len blocks the rack with his arm, then uses it to pull himself off the chair.

"Later," I say, though not in a snotty way. As he lurches across Employees Only!, pushing the rack, Ginger raises her eyebrows at Zoe and they practically run across the floor to my corner.

"Oh my God, D.B.W.! Yikes! What did he want?!" Ginger practically drools at this development.

"Um, it's, like, his job? To get stuff from me? He's the store runner?" I try to sound nonchalant, but my heart is racing. Even though my head insists, *They don't know; they can't know,* I can't help but worry, *Yeah, but what if they do know?*

"Yeah, but did he ask you about anything? Does he know we're onto him?"

"Uh, no. He's, like, the definition of clueless." The snide comment rolls off my tongue, but it leaves a bad aftertaste in my mouth.

"Totally," agrees Ginger. "What a freak."

It would be a good moment to say something in Len's defense. Maybe I could just kind of say something and stick up for him without quite letting on what happened last . . .

"Ooh, nice dress," says Ginger, admiringly, pinching my skirt and holding it out. "Turn around."

I obey, twirling in place. The moment to rush to Len's defense evaporates—poof!—just like that.

"Not bad," says Zoe. "The fleas?"

"Yeah, but it needed a little, you know, fixing up here and there."

"You did that?" asks Ginger. "Get out! You're so creative."

"Mmm-hmm," agrees Zoe, nodding.

Just then, Ginger shrieks. "Zo, oh my God! Check this out! Did I tell you?" She reaches up to admire the flag dress.

Zoe ignores her and looks around carefully, sizing things up.

"So this is The Land of *Cun*—I mean, Consignment."

"Yeah. What are you guys doing up here?"

"What, you've never seen a Floron off the floor before?"

I feel my face get hot. Zoe grins and waves a finger in my face, scolding me.

"Didn't know we knew your bitch of a boss calls us that, eh? Live and learn, honey. Miss Zoe knows all."

Ginger grabs my arm urgently. "Vee, we came up here to warn you. Something's up, and I think you're about to get a visit from The Nutbuster."

"The Nutbuster?"

"You know. Shirley the Squirrelly?" Zoe does her impersonation of Shirley, who, come to think of it, does hold her hands out in front of her like a squirrel begging for an acorn or something. That's where the resemblance stops. Her body is not unlike that of a *Tyrannosaurus rex*: a broad rear tapering up to a tiny torso and spindly arms. Zoe's impression of her is particularly funny now that I've actually met her victim.

"Been and gone," I inform them.

"She has?" gasps Ginger. "Oh my God, what did she say? Did she say anything about D.B.W. and Claire?"

"No," I tell her.

"Wow, that's weird," says Ginger. " 'Cause she totally came sniffing around the floor. Asking us all these questions about the inventory and taking notes. We were totally sure she was onto them."

"I told you, she doesn't know shit," says Zoe.

"That is so not what you said downstairs, Zo. You said . . ."

"Nice snake," says Zoe, changing the subject smoothly. She taps the glass with her long black fingernails.

"Holy shit!" says Ginger. "Is that real?"

"It's not mine," I tell them. As soon as the words come out, I regret them. I see the conversation spinning out in front of me. *"Where'd you get it?" "Uh . . ."*

"Oh, yeah?" says Zoe suspiciously, putting her nose up to the glass. "Somebody consign it?"

"Sort of," I say nervously. Without really thinking, I tell her, "Anyway, I have to get rid of it."

"For real?"

I shrug. "Nutbuster's orders." That makes them laugh, and I have that same jolt of surprise and excitement. I'm still so unaccustomed to having people laugh with me instead of at me.

Zoe puts her nose right up to the glass. "Shit, I'll take it."

"Zo!" exclaims Ginger. "Are you crazy?"

Zoe tosses her hair. "Maybe," she says.

"Seriously, Zo, Maureen is going to totally shit a brick if you bring home a snake."

"Who's Maureen?" I ask.

"Zoe's mom," Ginger tells me.

"Who says she has to know about it?" says Zoe angrily.

This is news to me. I always figured Zoe and Ginger shared an apartment or lived with boyfriends or something. It has never occurred to me that Zoe might have a mom, much less still be living at home.

Zoe turns to me. "You're cool with this, right?"

Jesus, no. Of course I'm not. There's no way I can let her take Len's snake. But then again, I can't tell her that it's Len's snake. And, in a way, it's actually my snake. I mean, he gave it to me. And now that Shirley's told me to get rid of it, I need to find someone to take it. So, in a way, Zoe would be doing me a favor.

Wouldn't she? But what about what Len said? "She's evil"; "She can't be trusted." But how well does he know her? I mean, I thought all kinds of awful stuff about Len before I got to know him, and it turned out I was wrong about him. Maybe he's wrong about her.

That's what goes through my head. But in my heart, I know that it doesn't matter what I think or what I feel. This is Zoe, after all. And with Zoe, there's only one thing to say.

"Totally," I tell her.

CHAPTER NINE

Once they're gone, my hand instinctively flies toward the buzzer. I've got to tell Len about this unexpected development.

But then I pause, pre-buzz.

I know I should probably tell him, but I just can't do it. I mean, maybe I'm being silly to worry? It's sort of mine now, right? So why should he have a problem with me giving it to Zoe?

Well, for starters, because he cares about it. And also, maybe, because he cares about me. Which is probably why he gave it to me.

Fuck.

I think about going downstairs to try to get Dep back from

Zoe. I could tell her something, make up some excuse. Maybe just say, *I changed my mind, all right?* I doodle a bit, thinking. I draw a platform shoe, open-toed; then I ink in a snake sliding through it. I hear the door open and for a second I allow myself to hope that it's Zoe, bringing back Dep.

No such luck—it's just a consigner showing up for her appointment lugging three overflowing Hefty bags. I can tell by what she's wearing that ninety percent of what she's bringing me is going to be unacceptable. There's a long, printed list of what we don't take—wedding dresses, maternity clothes, stuff like that—and the consigners all have to read it and sign it when they start. But the truth is, some days I'm just not in the mood to say no. I figure I can always dep the stuff later and let some lucky Picker think he hit the jackpot.

The consigner is gone and I'm up to my eyeballs in stained maternity clothing when Len comes back. For a second, I try to remember what I buzzed him for. Then I remember what I didn't buzz him for.

"Hey," he says. "You busy?"

"Uh, yeah," I tell him. "Sorry, now's not so good."

"Okay," he says. "We're pretty slow downstairs. Want me to stay and, uh, *help?*" He says the word "help" like it's our private code word, which gives me a momentary thrill. Unfortunately, I'm still a little preoccupied with the whole snake situation.

"Yeah, no. That's okay. Thanks," I say, ignoring his tone and scrutinizing a purple nightgown with bleach spots. I can't look at him. It's only a matter of time. And not much time, I'm guessing.

"Where's Dep?" he asks. *Bingo*.

"Dep?"

"The snake. Dep the Snake?"

"Oh," I say. "Well, remember how I told you The Nut—I mean, Shirley—said I had to get rid of him?"

"You sent him down the chute??"

"No!" I almost laugh at the thought. A snake in The Pile. Now, that would liven things up in boring old Dollar-a-Pound. I imagine Bill holding his seltzer bottle out in front of him like a fire extinguisher. "Back it up, snake, man!" he'd yell, defending his precious Pile by soaking the snake and everything in sight.

Len is not laughing. He looks pained.

"Well, then, what did you do with him?"

"I, um, I found someone who was willing to take him."

"Who?" demands Len.

Dreading his reaction, I say quietly, "Um, well, you know that girl Zoe?"

"You're kidding," he says, a look of alarm crossing his face. "Please tell me you're kidding."

"I told you I'm not good with slimy things," is all I can bring myself to say.

He stares at me in disbelief, then shakes his head and turns to leave without saying anything else. Of course, he moves like a wounded turtle, so I'm actually able to walk over and cut him off. I touch his arm and try to catch his eye.

"Len, hey? Look, it was a bad idea," I say.

"What the hell were you thinking?"

"I just—I dunno. I just thought . . ."

"I thought I could trust you."

"You can!"

Len makes an angry snorting noise.

"Look, I screwed up, okay? But I can fix it. Let me fix it."

"Don't," he says sharply. "You've already done enough." And then, more quietly, "I really thought you were different."

His bangs shield his eyes. Angrily, he shakes me off and pushes past me. Though I could catch him again (twice, probably) before he gets to the freight elevator, I let him go. He presses the button, then waits, his back to me.

"Len!" I yell across the floor, causing the Lunch Ladies to look up in unison like a flock of startled sheep.

Len doesn't even flinch. *Goddammit.* I know it wasn't probably such a great idea, but the intensity of his reaction surprises me.

He says nothing, doesn't turn my way, and just boards the elevator when it comes. I have this funny lurching feeling as I watch it go down. It's almost like part of me is riding with him. I feel my stomach jumping up into my head on the way down.

Look, something happened and I need the snake back. That's what I'm going to say to Zoe.

When I find her.

I want to fix things with Len badly enough that I've decided to venture down to The Real Deal for what I hope will be a quick snake repossession, no questions asked. However, Zoe seems to have vanished. I check the dressing rooms and the cash registers. She's not in the wig section or over by the thigh-high vinyl boots or by the rainbow curtain of feather boas. She's not under the motorcycle that hangs from the ceiling or next to the rearing unicorn statue. The decade racks—Fifties, Sixties, Seventies, Eighties, and "Contemporary"—turn up nothing but a bunch of Florons I don't recognize. A few of them look like Zoe—dark blunt-cut hairstyles, fishnet stockings, Glam eyeliner. But none of them are six feet tall.

I listen intently for Ginger's nervous laugh. I probably wouldn't hear it over the sound system blasting The Cure, but I strain for it anyway.

Goddammit. Why the hell did he give me his dumb snake in the first place?

Maybe this is for the best, I realize. I mean, let's face it. Zoe and Ginger aren't dumb. They're going to put two and two together sooner or later and figure out that something's up between me and Len. And when they do, they're going to have a field day. I'm not going to be their cute, funny Spy Girl anymore. I'm going to be one of the store's many freaks to them, like Bill and Len and Shirley. You know her, that freaky fat girl who's hot for the Dead Boy.

But that doesn't have to happen, because now, without even meaning to, I have clearly offended The Nail to the point where he won't ever talk to me again. Which is good, right? Problem solved, trouble averted.

Then why am I headed down the stairs instead of up?

Oh, right. Because, without actually meaning to, I kind of fell for Len with the inexplicable swoon that I usually reserve for particularly quirky pieces of Bakelite jewelry. The boy just *got* to me. So now, even though I've somehow flubbed things to the point of providing myself a convenient out, I don't want to take it.

"Hey, Bill."

"Veronica, hey! What's shaking, baby?" Bill's T-shirt du jour reads REALITY IS FOR PEOPLE WHO CAN'T HANDLE DRUGS!

"Not a lot." My voice is flat, no-nonsense. "You seen Zoe?"

Bill looks crestfallen. He shakes his head.

"All right. Thanks," I say, heading back toward the stairs. Bill calls after me.

"Hey! She might've just gone out to the Mooks. I think I saw her, but that could've been a while ago. It's been like a revolving door down here, man. Lenny punched out, this one's on break, that one's on break. All play and no work around here today." Bill scratches his chin thoughtfully. "Actually, I could use a smoke myself. If you want, you could go with me and, like, check for her?"

"Yeah, okay." Like I have a choice. Bill nods to this guy Earl, who also works on Dollar-a-Pound.

"Going out for a while, man," Bill tells him proudly. Jesus, you'd think we were off to the freaking prom.

Earl scowls back to show this is fine by him. He looks like he's been to prison. He's bald, with a thick neck and a mustache like an upside-down version of the handlebars on one of those banana-seat bikes. Once I noticed there were letters tattooed on several of his fingers, but I've never gotten close enough to read the words. Earl calls out as Bill holds the door open for me.

"Yo, Bill! Get me an apple fritter."

"Ten-four, good buddy," says Bill, sounding pleased to serve as Earl's foot soldier. As if this makes him tough by extension.

We walk down the block, Bill smoking and chatting away. He tells me about how Earl's parole officer came by the other day, but she came while Shirley was on Dollar-a-Pound, so Earl freaked out and hid in The Pile. On account of how it was okay for parole to know he had a job at the store, but it was NOT okay for the store to know he was on parole.

"Aw, man, I just about lost it, you know? It was so funny! But meanwhile he was seriously losing his shit. You know?"

"Seriously," I agree, even though I'm not really listening. I'm looking at the crowd out in front of Mookie's, lots of people clustered like there's some kind of fire drill going on. Just then there's a siren, and from around the corner a cop car comes flying.

"Shit, man," says Bill, stopping suddenly. I know Bill's feelings about the police well enough to know he's not going any farther. I stand there with him and watch in total disbelief while the cops go in and come out a few minutes later.

"Oh my God," I say. Because the cops are escorting two girls to the squad car. Two girls named Zoe and Ginger.

"Shit," repeats Bill. "Those two pull some serious shit, but this is some crazy shit."

"Yeah, crazy," I agree. Reason number eight hundred and twelve why not to hang out with Bill: Risk of catching a bad case of his stupid stoner way of talking.

My heart is pounding, though. What the hell could Zoe and Ginger have done this time? I feel like I should do something, say something, but I'm just kind of rooted there with Bill. This has to be a misunderstanding, right? I mean, Zoe and Ginger act pretty insane sometimes, but I can't believe they'd actually get themselves arrested. Would they?

When the cops drive off with Zoe and Ginger, we shuffle closer to the Mooks. People remain out front, holding their coffees and looking nervous. Bill sidles up to a fellow traveler: a guy with a long, messy ponytail like his, plus a stubbly chin and round wire glasses.

"What went down, man?" Bill asks, bumming a cigarette even though he's got a pack of his own.

"I don't know, man," the guy replies. "Somebody said they saw a cobra or something. Then everybody just went nuts and they called in the goon squad and shut the place down."

"Whoa," says Bill.

I feel like I can't breathe. I sit down right there on the sidewalk, the tulle layers of my prom dress poufing out with a loud *shhhuushh*. I feel cold concrete on my flanks.

Girls can be cruel.

Bill squats down, trying to balance while holding his cigarette away from my face.

"He's going to kill me," I say to myself.

"Aww, man, he's not," says Bill consolingly. "If anyone's going to take the heat for not getting him his apple fritter, it'll be me."

I shake my head, but I don't even try to explain. Bill extends his hand to help me up, but I shake him off. Why do people seem to think I need help getting up? I'm fat, okay? I'm not crippled.

I walk over to the front door of the Mooks and try it.

"Veronica, no!" yells Bill, clearly envisioning me meeting my death at the hands of a vicious monster serpent. Apparently, this is not a scary enough vision to make him drop his cigarette and run after me.

The door is not locked. I pull it open and stride into the Mooks.

CHAPTER TEN

As I enter the Mooks, the smell of donuts and coffee is comforting enough to almost make me forget why I'm there. The sight of the place brings me back. It looks like a bomb went off. There are chairs tipped over, tables askew. For reasons that are not immediately clear to me, there's flour all over the floor and some of the tables and chairs.

Most of the Mookie's employees are sitting around one of the larger tables. A few of them are behind the counter, and one of them is actually sitting on the counter. The one on the counter is the first to notice me come in.

"We're closed," she informs me. Her voice carries none of the false cheer of retail.

"Yeah, uh, I . . ." I almost turn and leave. But instead I tell her, "I'm, um . . . it's . . . about the snake?"

"Yeah?" she says.

"I, uh . . . I know something about the snake."

She stares at me for a moment.

Then she yells, "Mr. Singh!"

A man appears at the counter and I instantly recognize him as the man who gave Zoe the free donuts. He looks tired, and there is flour all over his striped polo shirt.

"Yes?" he says.

"This girl says she knows something about the snake."

"I . . ." I suddenly worry that this is going to lead to me sharing a jail cell with Zoe and Ginger. "It's not my snake!" I blurt out. "I just . . . I know the guy who owns the snake, and I just thought maybe I could help get it back to him? It's not poisonous . . . I mean, venomous . . . or anything."

Mr. Singh looks even more tired.

"Your friends," he says finally. "Tell them not to come into my donut shop anymore."

"They're not my friends," I tell him sadly.

Mr. Singh doesn't look convinced. He motions for me to follow him and takes me behind the counter.

The display wall of trays of donuts under fluorescent lights momentarily distracts me. I've never been so close to so many donuts before, and I am struck by how lovely they are, all lined up in rows. They look almost like jewelry, some of them; edible bracelets painted with glistening frosting and adorned with jewels—colored sprinkles, toasted coconut, cinnamon sugar. I am tempted to take one, even though I know Mr. Singh will see me and besides, I am not even hungry.

"There," says Mr. Singh, and I turn and look.

On the floor lies what I almost mistake for a long piece of dough lying in a pile of flour. Then one end twitches and I realize it is Dep the Snake and he is either dead or about to die. There's flour all around him, too, although the floor shows through here and there like he thrashed around for a while. But the sickening part is there's a shoe print in the flour right across his middle, and he's wider there, where he was clearly flattened. Oddly, there is no blood.

"Oh my God," I say, wincing.

Mr. Singh takes a pair of tongs and pokes Dep tentatively with them. There is a reflexive recoiling, which makes me recoil, too. He pokes again, harder this time. Just to be sure, I'm guessing, but still it is awful to watch. The sharpness of the poke sends Dep onto his back, exposing a creamy yellow underside. I always thought he was black all over, but I guess I was wrong.

"Stop it," I say.

"Dead," he announces. I want to say *You think?* but I don't. I stare hard at Dep, and for a second I almost believe he's still breathing. But then he looks blurry all over, and before I realize what's happening, I close my eyes and feel myself start to crumple.

From very far away, I hear a voice saying, "Mees? Mees?! Mees!"

When I open my eyes, the first thing I see is the girl who was sitting on the counter. She's leaning over me.

"Mr. Singh!" she yells in my face. "She's awake."

Mr. Singh, whose polo shirt is a little tight across his belly, runs over. He reaches out to help me to a chair, and I actually let him.

"Are you okay?" he asks me.

"I guess," I say, even though my head is killing me. I fainted once before, at a blood drive at school, so the feeling was awful but familiar. At school, I fainted before they could even take my blood. I lost it when I walked in and saw a bag of blood, which I guess I should have realized would be part of the scenery at a blood drive. Luckily, like ten other kids fainted, too, including this senior named Tyler Turk who was pretty much universally worshipped, so everyone was too busy talking about him to use the information against me.

"I'm sorry," he says. "I should not have let you see your snake."

"It's not my snake," I tell him again. He nods.

"Can I get you anything?" he asks. "Some water? Donut?"

"Nah, that's okay," I say quickly. I just want to leave. But as I stand up, an employee pushes a big flat broom by us and I remember.

"Um, actually," I say, "can I have the snake? It sort of belongs to someone . . . I mean, not the people who brought it here, but, I mean, it's . . ."

Mr. Singh tilts his head to one side. He looks confused, but also maybe a little concerned.

"Look," I tell him. "The person who owns the snake? He really cares about it. And since I'm sort of the reason things got so messed up, I feel like if I bring his snake back, maybe I can sort of make it up to him? A little."

Mr. Singh sighs and shakes his head. "It has been cleaned up. I'm sorry."

"Cleaned up where?" I ask.

Which is how I end up standing behind the Mooks, digging through the Dumpster with a pair of tongs that may or may not be the ones used to check Dep for signs of life. In addition to the tongs, Mr. Singh has provided me with a donut box (the correct size and shape for transporting twelve donuts or one dead snake). Thankfully, it seems that Dep was the last thing tossed, so I find him quickly.

See, Len, I think to myself, *I do care about you. Okay, I might be partially to blame for this mess, but it should count for something that I'm willing to go Dumpster-diving to retrieve your dead snake.*

I gently lift Dep, so gently that I end up dropping him again. The sight of him slipping back into the garbage heap and landing with the ungraceful thump of deadweight almost causes me to vomit.

I steel myself and try again. This time, I get a firmer hold on him and manage to land him in the box. I close the lid and feel intense gratitude for the lack of a cellophane window. I walk around to the front of the store and I'm surprised to find that Bill, his hippie friend, and a couple of other people are still standing there.

"Veronica! Hey!" says Bill. "We were just getting ready to send out a search party."

"Clearly," I say, looking at the proliferation of butts littering the ground.

"What's with the donuts, man?" he asks. "I thought they were closed."

"They are," I say, but that's all I say. Bill nods and takes another drag.

"You wouldn't by any chance have an apple fritter in there?" he asks hopefully.

"Um, no."

Bill nods again, looking worried.

"Listen," I say to Bill, "do you think you could punch me out? There's something I gotta go do."

I walk quickly to Len's house, box in hand. I'm not sure what I'm going to do if he's not there. Worse, I'm not sure what I'm going to do if he *is* there.

As I walk, I try to figure out something to say to him. "I brought back your snake, but it's dead." *No.* "There's no way to explain this, so . . . here." *Uh-uh.*

I remember this scene in the movie *A Clockwork Orange,* which Bill made me watch once and which actually turned out to be better than I would've thought. The main guy in it has this big pet python or something, and he comes home to find out that his parents have gotten rid of it. "He met with like an accident," is what they tell him.

Regardless of whether Len has seen the movie, I don't think this explanation is going to fly.

As I turn the corner and start up his block, I notice movement on Len's front porch. There's this huge guy with knee-high boots like a jockey or something, and he's backing out Len's front door, lugging something heavy and looking backward over his shoulder. Almost immediately another big guy emerges (this one is not wearing boots), holding up the other end of what they are carrying, which I realize suddenly is one of Len's fish tanks. Boots takes a few more steps and almost wipes out on the stairs, apparently due to his buddy's overeager assistance.

Boots says something sharp that I can't quite hear. He shifts the tank to where his leg connects to his body and uses the back of his free hand to wipe his brow. As I get closer, I hear Boots mutter, "Let's go, let's go. We don't have all day."

The other guy says something back. He is shorter and has sort of a mashed nose, making him look like a flounder or something.

I hang back, watching from behind a parked station wagon. *What the hell is going on? And where the hell is Len?* It looks like these guys are stealing his pets, which makes no sense. I mean, they couldn't be that valuable. Could they? And even if they are, which I doubt, what am I supposed to do? They're not *my* pets.

I mean, I guess I could call the cops anonymously, or something. But to do that, I'd have to run back to the store, and the burglars would probably be long gone before help arrived. Besides, the cops would probably trace the call to the store, and to me. And then they might put two and two together and ask me about Zoe and Ginger and what happened at the Mooks. How would I explain that? Not very well, considering I am currently carrying a dead snake (THE snake from the Mooks, no less) in a donut box coffin.

Zoe and Ginger. It suddenly occurs to me: *What if they were right after all?* What if Len has been stealing stuff from the store . . . not just half a pair of pajamas, but lots of stuff, expensive stuff? What if he *is* involved in some big crime ring and this is some sort of, you know, payback or something? You see that in movies all the time. Thugs come and they take the guy's car or whatever to settle a score.

This all goes through my head too fast to process. The point is: These guys might be stealing Len's pets. Len is nowhere to be seen. Someone has to do something.

STOP! I imagine myself yelling as I run up and grab hold of the tank. *You won't get away with this!*

What thuh . . . ? says Flounder Face, looking terrified.

Yikes, let's get out of here! says Boots, abandoning his end of the tank. I picture myself standing there laughing, holding the tank while they bolt down the street.

Yeah, right. As if. I stand frozen behind parked cars, imagining the scene. But I can't just do nothing, so eventually I tiptoe out from behind a car and cross the street slowly, staring at them. Maybe my suspicious glare will scare them off, or something.

I haven't really planned on saying anything, so I just stand there nervously. Scowling, holding my donut box and praying they aren't armed or anything. Maybe a neighbor will see what's going on and call the cops. Or maybe Len's grandmother will come home. I get a queasy feeling then because it occurs to me that maybe Len's grandma *is* home.

Maybe the thugs already took care of her.

"Veronica?" I look up, and there's Len standing in the

doorway. He's still wearing the hoodie with the tuxedo jacket over it. He's holding a piece of paper, and there's a man standing next to him and holding a clipboard. "What are you doing here?"

"I, uh, hey," I say lamely.

Boots grunts and adjusts his hold on the tank. Flounder Face does, too, and they continue down the front steps. I walk up and join Len.

"I came by to, um, talk to you. And then I saw those guys and I got worried they were, um, stealing your pets?"

Len shows me what's on the clipboard. It says *Court Order* at the top.

"Yeah, well. They're not," says Len angrily. "So thanks. You can go now."

He carefully shuffles over to the porch swing and sits. He looks really, really bitter and defeated.

Meanwhile, two more big guys come out of the house carrying a tank. As they go down the steps, I notice the design on the back of the T-shirt worn by the guy bringing up the rear. It is a picture of a raccoon under a butterfly net with the words HAMPDEN COUNTY ANIMAL CONTROL below it. They load the tank into a van parked across the street. It has the same drawing painted on the driver's-side door.

"What happened?" I ask.

Len runs both hands through his hair. "They took everything," he says. "That's what happened."

"Everything?"

He glares at me like I'm stupid. "Everything!" he repeats emphatically. "The tanks, the filters, the pinkies—everything."

"But . . . why?"

"Well, someone from the store—and I'm guessing you have an idea who I mean—told the police some story about me stealing from work. So they got a search warrant to look for all this cash or stolen stuff I'm supposed to have."

"But why did they take your pets? Are they illegal?"

"No. I mean, not to own. But there are pretty strict rules about selling them. I guess they thought that was what I was doing. Now I have to go to court and explain that actually, I'm not a criminal. I'm just a guy with a bunch of exotic pets. If I'm lucky, they'll give them back. Eventually."

"But did they find any, like, evidence?"

Len looks irritated. "Like what?"

"I dunno. Stuff they were looking for? Or just the lizards?"

"*Just* the lizards?"

"I didn't mean it like that."

"What did you mean it like?"

"I mean . . . I don't know. Nothing."

"Look, you should go, okay?"

"Len, there's actually something I've got to, um, tell you. I mean, I feel like this is all my fault and I'm really, really sorry. I know there's no excuse, I just . . . really want you to know how awful I feel. I—"

I look at Len and see that he's not looking at me. His head is hanging down and his hands are in the pocket of his hoodie. I see his mouth moving, whispering.

"Len? Oh my God, do you have Violet?"

Len nods slowly and grants me a peek. "They took her cage, though," he says.

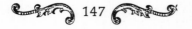

I feel an incredible sense of relief at the sight of her orange-flecked skin. I reach in and give her a little pat with one finger. My fingers accidentally brush against Len's inside the pocket, and I feel a tiny jolt before he pulls away. Carefully, I sit down next to Len. The swing creaks a warning under my weight, so I hold on to the chain just to be sure.

We sit there together in silence and sway a little.

"I'm still mad at you," he says.

"I guess I deserve that," I say. We're so close I can smell his skin, which makes me think of last night on the couch.

Just then, Len points to the box I'm still holding. *Oh, shit, I almost forgot about Dep. How the hell am I going to tell him now?*

"Lemon logs?" he asks.

"Not exactly," I say, taking a deep breath.

CHAPTER ELEVEN

"First off," I say. "Like I said, I'm sorry for giving Dep to Zoe. I know this is going to sound dumb, but I didn't think she'd do anything bad with him."

Len kind of snorts. "I thought I warned you about Zoe."

"Yeah, I know," I admit. "It's just that, I dunno, I just thought . . . Ugh, I don't know what I thought. I really fucked up."

"What were you thinking?"

"I dunno. I wasn't thinking. I mean, I should have known better. I just really thought it would be okay. Which sounds ridiculous now, I know."

Len sighs. "Veronica, you can't trust Zoe. If you do, you'll regret it very soon. The only person Zoe cares about is Zoe."

"And Ginger."

"No," says Len, very serious. "The only person Zoe cares about. Is. Zoe."

"Great, great! I got it, okay?" I start to feel a little indignant about the whole situation. "Look, if there was some way to go back in time and undo this whole mess, I would. If I had a magic wand or something, wham, Dep would still be alive, you'd still have all your pets . . ."

"What did you say?" Oh, *shit.*

"You'd still have all your pets?"

"No, about Dep. Where's Dep?"

I so don't want to do it, but I hand him the donut box. His eyes get big and he looks at me like, *no.* I nod.

"I'm so, so sorry, Len. I just . . ." And then I lose it. I start to cry, really cry. Like Spud dying and then some: loud blurbles, snot running, awful blubbery tears. Len does not cry or put his arm around me. On the positive side, he doesn't tell me to leave, or even to shut up. He just sits there silently next to me.

After a while, I quiet down.

"Sorry," I say again, this time meaning about the tears. I rub my nose with the back of my wrist.

"It's okay," he says.

"No, it's not. I'm such a freaking idiot."

"Veronica, look. I forgive you, all right? You didn't mean for this to happen. You're a good person."

"How can you say that?" I ask him. "I mean, after Dep and all . . . this."

Len shrugs. "Because it's true," he says simply, which almost makes me start to cry again. He reaches for the chain on his side of the swing and pulls himself carefully to his feet.

"Why are you so nice to me?" I ask him.

He frowns. "I have no idea."

So I tell him the whole story. About going downstairs to try and get Dep back, going to the Mooks to try and find Zoe, seeing Zoe and Ginger getting arrested, and going in to find Dep.

"Thanks," he says when I finish.

"For what?"

"For trying to get him back."

Before I can respond, he asks, "Wanna help?"

"*Help?*" I venture, wondering if he means it our code way.

"With Dep."

"Help what with Dep?" I have this weird feeling that maybe he hasn't heard a word I've said. Maybe he's in shock over losing his other pets or something.

"Come on," he says, and slowly starts down the front steps. I walk behind him, carrying the donut box.

I follow him down the stairs and up the driveway that runs along the side of the house. It leads to a small backyard that looks like it was once someone's garden. There's a small shed and a low fence made of white-coated wire roping off about three-quarters of the yard. Behind the fence is one of those wooden signs painted to look like a lady bending over and showing her polka-dotted behind to the world. It looks as though her underwear has weathered many a rainstorm.

"Hang on, okay? I've got to put Violet inside."

I nod. Len goes up the back stairs, leaving me standing there, holding the box.

I look around. In addition to the lady with the spotted panties, there are also a lot of bricks, scattered randomly throughout the dirt in the garden. I see writing on one, so I pick it up. ROY, it says in black paint. REST IN PEACE.

"Oops. Sorry," I say, although no one is there. Carefully, I replace it on the ground. I guess Len does get it. Clearly he's no stranger to pet death.

"How many have you, um, lost?" I ask Len when he returns from inside the house. He doesn't answer. Instead, he goes to the shed and emerges dragging a shovel and wearing a pair of beige canvas gardening gloves.

Len leans on the handle and thinks for a moment. "Twenty-three," he says finally, "not counting fish." He picks up the ROY brick, frowns, and moves it back to the proper spot. "The goldfish, I don't really keep track of. They're all over there by that rosebush, all together."

Len falls silent. Then he points out a spot.

"I think there's room here."

"Oh. Okay," I say. Len picks up the shovel again and takes a stab at the ground. He barely makes a mark. He tries again, but the ground is unyielding. Eventually he unearths about a tablespoon of soil. He lurches over to the rosebush, depositing the dirt on top of the goldfish grave. Then he returns and tries to dig some more.

"Len?"

"Hmm?"

152

"Can I ask you something?"

"Sure."

"Do your folks . . . I mean, your grandma, or whoever . . . are they okay with you turning the backyard into a pet cemetery?"

"My parents aren't around anymore."

"They're—dead?"

There's a long pause. Then Len, his back to me, says, "Uh-huh."

"Oh my God. I'm so sorry."

"It's okay."

"They're not . . . ?" I look around nervously.

"No, they're not buried here."

"Okay, good," I say. Which I realize sounds funny, so I quickly add, "I mean, I'm really sorry."

"Thanks."

"I used to wish my parents were dead," I tell him.

"You did?"

"Big-time. I think it started with *Annie*? You know, the musical? Plus, I was really into orphan books." I'm rambling nervously, but I can't seem to stop. "The parents are gone and the kids have these great adventures. You know, like *Pippi Longstocking*? *James and the Giant Peach*? Plus, my folks totally suck."

"Oh, yeah?"

"Yeah. My mom is, like, anorexic? So she's always trying to put me on some insane diet or another. And since my dad and I aren't, like, total skeletons, she hates us both. My dad's okay, but he got this job in New York? So he just took off and

I haven't seen him in a couple of months. Which is probably for the best," I conclude.

"If you say so," says Len. "Still sounds better than not having them around at all."

"Yeah, I guess . . . ," I say dubiously. "Did they die in the car accident? Your parents, I mean."

"Yeah. I mean, yes and no. My mom did. My dad died a couple years before that."

"Wow. What did he die of?"

"Cancer. At least that's what my grandma always said. Of course, she smoked, too."

"Wait, is she dead, too?"

"No," says Len. "She's in New Jersey. Which is sort of the same thing, I think."

"Sorry?"

"Hello? It's a joke?" says Len, imitating me.

"Okay, I'm an asshole," I say.

"No, you're not," says Len. "But it's going to be a while before I trust you with another snake."

Len scratches the ground with his shovel again. It is starting to rain lightly, which seems to slow him down all the more. It occurs to me that I could probably move more soil with a pair of tweezers than he does with his shovel.

"Hey, can I do some?" I ask. We could be here for hours at this rate.

"No, that's okay." Three more tiny clumps of wet dirt come up in the shovel.

"No, really, Len. Let me help. I mean, he was kind of my snake, too." Reluctantly, Len hands me the shovel and the

gardening gloves and practically collapses on a lawn chair. He blocks the rain with one hand and watches me.

The shovel is heavier than I expected, but I kind of get into the rhythm of it. I must look like a clown, digging a grave in my peach and salmon taffeta ball gown. I yank on the sleeve of my T-shirt and mop the rain and sweat from my face with it.

"You don't have to do that," Len says, though he doesn't get up.

"It's okay," I tell him, trying to sound like I dig ditches all the time. I take another stab at the ground.

"But what about your dress?" says Len. And I look down and let out a little cry of dismay at the sight. My dress, my favorite dress, is totally destroyed. I mean, there's dirt and mud all over it. I try to brush some off, but it only makes it worse.

"It's okay," I repeat. I dig the shovel in again to prove it.

It gets harder to keep my footing as the hole gets deeper. Thankfully, Len says, "That's good," at just about the point when I'm ready to give up.

Slowly, Len approaches the hole, carrying the donut box. I realize almost too late that he's about to open it, so I reach over and grab his hands.

"Closed casket," I say, giving him a meaningful look.

"Ohhh," he says, but he does not argue. He lets me take the box while he uses the shovel as a cane and carefully lowers himself to his knees. I hand Len the box, then kind of squat beside him. He wedges the box into the hole and I am relieved to find that it fits. I stand back up, but Len stays where he is.

I hear him say quietly, "Do you think it hurt?"

 155

"What?"

"When Dep . . . died. Do you think he was in any pain?"

"I actually don't know," I say, which is true but is also a way of sparing him.

After that, Len is quiet for some time. His head is bowed and he is mumbling something that I guess must be a prayer. I didn't know Len was a religious guy, and I hope I haven't offended him by getting to my feet. Instinctively, I look around to make sure no one can see us, but the yard is walled in by the neighbors' fences. Since there's no one there, I try harder to get into it. I close my eyes and try to look respectful.

When I open my eyes to peek at Len, I see he is looking up at me.

"Do you want to say anything?" he asks.

"Nah, that's okay."

"It's all right," he says, his expectation obvious. "Just say what you feel."

"Um, okay." The last funeral I was at was for my great-aunt, who I barely knew. Apparently, neither did the clergy guy, who referred to her as "Rose" instead of "Rae" and started off by saying, "Although I did not know the deceased . . ." Unfortunately, this phrase kind of stuck in my head.

"Although I did not know the deceased . . . I mean, although I did not know him very well . . ." I take a breath and try to start over. "Dep was really a very special snake. He died before he should have, and that was sad."

I look at Len, who seems eager for more.

"When someone—or, I mean, something—dies before it

should, we can't help but ask, Why?" Okay, now I'm on a roll and this probably isn't going anywhere good, but I can't stop now. "And I wish I knew, but I don't. It kind of sucks, and I wish you didn't die. I would have liked to know you a while longer. So I'm really sorry. You were a really good snake. Very pretty and . . . um, nice and all that. I thought you would be slimy, but I was wrong. You weren't slimy at all."

For a moment, I think I'm done. But then I take a deep breath and suddenly blurt out, "I've been wrong about a lot of things lately. About snakes, you know, and, um, about people, too. I'm not trying to make excuses. It's just . . . I've been hurt, okay? A lot. But then, I ended up hurting the one person who didn't deserve it at all. So now I just wish there was some way I could take it back somehow."

My voice starts to trail off and I end up whispering that last part, but I'm pretty sure Len hears me. He reaches for my hand and I help him up.

"Thanks," he says.

"Shut up," I say.

"No, really," he says. "Thanks."

"No, really," I tell him. "Shut up."

And we just kind of stand there close together for a while, looking down at Dep's grave. It's sort of like I'm holding him up.

Or maybe he's holding me up.

Or both.

The rain starts to fall harder.

I turn my face upward, letting my mouth fall open like when I was little and I used to try to eat snowflakes right out of the sky. The cold rain pummels my face. It hurts, but it feels good. I start to shiver, but I don't even care. There's so much that I want to wash away.

I feel something around my shoulders and I realize that it's Len, putting the tuxedo jacket around me.

"Your dress," he says.

"What?" I joke, holding out the muddy, ripped fabric. "It's fine. Everyone's wearing them like this."

"Come inside," he says. "I'll make you an omelet or something."

"That's okay," I say, even though I'm starving. I've already screwed things up so badly today, I figure I should quit while I'm ahead.

"You're soaking wet," he says. "At least come inside and dry off. You can borrow something to wear." He turns and limps toward the back steps.

"Len, come on. There's no way I can fit into any of your clothes."

Len turns back and looks me up and down.

His mouth twitches. He raises one eyebrow.

"That's okay," he says finally.

And so I follow him up the back steps.

Take that, Mom.

Slowly, we wind our way up the creaky back staircase. He fishes out his keys and lets us in. The apartment is dark, but he doesn't reach for a light.

Instead, he reaches for me.

My heart pounds as I kiss him back, like it did the night before but even more so. Since this is my second time kissing him, I feel worldly and brave, yet still jumpy as a rabbit. I like

that it is dark. I want to feel his touch, but I still don't want him to see me.

I break from his embrace and feel my way down the hall to where I remember the bathroom is. I take off my mucky dress and drape it and the tuxedo jacket over the edge of the tub. I consider trying to rinse them out, but I want to get back to Len before I lose my nerve.

There's a bathrobe on the back of the door, a worn plaid flannel one that I hope is Len's. It occurs to me that I'm assuming we're the only ones here. He said his mom and dad are dead and his grandma's in New Jersey, and he's never mentioned a brother or a grandfather or anything.

I hope I'm right.

I put the bathrobe on, then tiptoe out of the bathroom and down the hall to his room. I can sort of make him out sitting on the bed. His eyes are wide and his bangs are pushed behind his ears, where they might stay for a matter of seconds if he doesn't move his head. He's still wearing his perpetually low-slung muddy jeans, but he's taken his hoodie off. In fact, he's completely naked from the waist up. The sharp jut of his collarbone and his strong, ropy arms frame his pale, lean torso. A thin trace line of hair winds its way from between his ribs to the band of his briefs. His shoes are off, the yellow tips of his brown socks fidgeting nervously.

He leans over to switch on the bedside lamp.

"Don't," I say, but it is too late.

I catch a glimpse of my reflection in the mirror on his closet door. The sight crushes me. My hair is wet and matted at the top and frizzy at the bottom. One comb is still in my hair, barely. The other, I presume, is in Len's backyard, or perhaps in the Dumpster behind the Mooks. My face looks puffy. My body is hidden behind the robe, and yet I've never felt more exposed. I catch sight of my thick ankles and I'm paralyzed with fear.

What am I doing here? This is a huge mistake.

But then I look at Len. I can tell he doesn't see any of this. The way he's looking at me makes me suddenly feel that ugly, unlovable feeling melting away like the rain. I start to feel the tiniest sensation of what it might be like to step outside my body entirely.

"Hey," he says shyly.

And I realize right then that my mother is right. I mean, she's wrong, but she's also right. I know that I can trust Len, that he's not that kind of boy.

But I also know that if he were, it wouldn't matter.

Because right now, I would do anything for him.

CHAPTER TWELVE

The next afternoon, I'm at my desk when the phone rings.

"Hello?" I say, expecting Bill but hoping it will be Len, even though he never uses the phone. He didn't swing by at lunchtime, so now I feel all jumpy, like one of those crickets Len feeds his pets. *He always comes by around now. Where could he be? Did something about last night make him change his mind about me? About us?*

"We need a moment of your valuable time," says Zoe.

"Um, right now?"

"*Um*, yes," she says, imitating my tone. "Right now."

I hang up and briefly consider ducking out the back. I don't know what they want, but it can't be good. I haven't seen them since they were taken out of the Mooks by the police the day before. Do they know I saw them? Do they blame me for the whole snake business and for getting arrested?

Oh God. Do they know about me and Len?

I go downstairs and find them by the dressing rooms. There are a bunch of blond girls trying on clothes by the couches and the big mirror. I freeze when I see them, but on closer examination I realize they are probably just clones of the girls at my school. Zoe and Ginger are sitting on the barstools, pretending to read an ancient copy of *Tiger Beat*.

"Véronique!" cries Ginger, catching sight of me.

"What's shaking, Vee?" yells Zoe.

The two of them bestow multiple air kisses on me for the benefit of the audience of dressing room girls.

"Hey," I say, still nervous even though their friendliness seems genuine. "What's up?"

"Oooh, nothing, just sitting here watching the hair on my legs grow. Hey, six items max, Barbie-rella!" One of the blond girls glares at Zoe, but obeys her command.

"Are you guys okay?"

"Okay?" Ginger looks confused. "Uh, yeah. Why?"

"Oh, nothing, it's just . . . um, I just heard something about something happening at the Mooks yesterday."

"Who'd you hear that from?" asks Zoe, raising one exaggeratedly painted eyebrow.

"Oh, I dunno. Nobody."

"Hmmm, maybe she is banging Barnacle Bill after all, dontcha think, Ginge?"

"Totally," says Ginger, grinning.

"A complete travesty of justice," says Zoe, holding the back of her right hand to her forehead and closing her eyes. Opening them again, she adds, "All will be revealed in my fabulous tell-all biography and accompanying made-for-TV movie. BUT that's not why we summoned you."

Zoe pauses. I wait.

"We have *news*," she finally announces.

"Oh, yeah?"

Ginger nods enthusiastically. "You're never going to believe this. Guess who got called into The Nutbuster's office today?"

"Who?"

"Oh, you're no fun. Guess!"

"Um, Zoe?"

"She wishes!"

"Bite me, Ginge."

"You?" I ask, trying to move the game along.

"You are not even trying!" scolds Ginger. "No, think about somebody who is already acting totally suspicious. Somebody who we already have our eye on."

"Somebody who is a DEAD ringer . . . ," hints Zoe.

"Leh—I mean, D.B.W.?" My heart starts to race. *Oh my God, Shirley. Shirley knows about us. Jesus, how could she? Did someone see us that night on Employees Only!? Did she see us? Although if she did, wouldn't she have said something when she came by the next day? Oh Jesus. Don't panic, don't panic.*

"Bingo," says Zoe.

"But what for? What happened?" I don't want them to see how concerned I am, so I try to sound scandalized.

Zoe looks around, like she's afraid someone is going to hear her. Which is ridiculous, because the blondes are too busy swapping sequined halter tops and bending over to see how much their cracks show in various pairs of vintage Jordaches. I think maybe I do actually recognize one of them. She might have sat in front of me in Biology. Shit, the last thing I need right now is some annoying girl from my school pointing me out and cracking up with her friends.

"Damn, Mandy," I hear one say.

"Right?" answers her friend, sticking her butt out a little more and wrinkling her nose, obviously pleased.

Zoe leans in. "Apparently, he came to work with . . ."

Ginger can't restrain herself. "With a lizard in his pocket!" she blurts out.

"Oh, no," I say. *Violet.*

"Oooh, yes," says Zoe, victorious.

"Zoe heard the whole thing through the cat door!" gushes Ginger.

"Who knew you could stoop so low?" I say.

"I took gymnastics once," says Zoe proudly.

"Is that the grossest, freakiest thing you've ever heard?" crows Ginger, one hand over her mouth.

"It . . . uh, wow," I say, my stomach lurching. "So what happened?"

"Uh, hello?" scoffs Zoe. "The Nutbuster does not fuck around. She totally fired his ass."

"Big-time," says Ginger.

"That is so unbelievably . . ." I want to say "sad," but I'm keenly aware that Zoe and Ginger are awaiting my comment.

"... *nasty*," is what I finally say.

"Totally," agrees Ginger.

"I mean, what if he's been carrying it around for, like, weeks?" I add, trying to keep up my cover, but feeling like the biggest traitor of all time.

"Ewwww!" shrieks Ginger.

"What if it's dead or something?" adds Zoe.

"Ewwww!!!" Ginger hits a higher note.

"Yeah," says Zoe, leering. "Think about all those times he's stopped by to get a rack from you, and meanwhile, while he's looking at you, he's got his hand in his pocket and he's stroking his dead lizard . . ." She pantomimes the scene, doing Len as a drooling zombie with one hand going a mile a minute against his thigh.

"Ewwwwww!!!!" shrieks Ginger again. And I just can't help it—when the two of them bust up laughing at Zoe's ridiculous impersonation, I smile. One of the blond girls looks over at us, and I feel a jolt as I recognize the look on her face. For a moment I feel shaky and scared, but then it dawns on me that *she's* experiencing the afraid-someone's-laughing-at-me feeling, not me. I'm over here with Ginger and Zoe, safely sitting pretty on the other side, for the very first time.

"Oh, lizard, lizard!" cries Zoe, plucking a platform shoe from a display and batting her eyelashes at it. She tosses it to me. I catch it, realizing all of a sudden that she is cueing me to perform.

Okay, it is clearly time to put a stop to this. I should just fess up to the fact that not only is Len not the insidious thief they want him to be, he's actually kind of becoming my boyfriend. Which is not such a big deal, right? I mean, they're supposed to be my friends. They could maybe even put aside their disdain for Len and be happy for me?

So I stand up tall, ready to give my speech.

But Zoe and Ginger are staring at me expectantly. Ready to laugh at my antics, ready to sing my praises, ready to weave me tighter into their cozy little web.

Their web indeed, I realize with a rising sense of dread. Like a spider binds a fly that it is about to devour. Everything's fine as long as I do what is expected of me. Play their games, laugh at their jokes, echo their opinions. But one false move and I'm lunch.

"I, uh . . . I mean . . ." I hesitate. I pet the shoe nervously, which makes both of them start to laugh. I guess they figure this is part of my act. I freeze, unwilling to keep doing their bidding but unable to find the words to make them stop.

Impatiently, Zoe grabs the shoe back. She strokes it furtively. "Oh, my darling, darling lizard," she cries out. "They'll never understand about us." Ginger hoots with laughter, clapping her hands, and Zoe grins from ear to ear. She plants a big fat kiss on the shoe.

It is then that I see Len, whose ass does not appear to have been fired after all. He is standing behind a Z-rack that he has been slowly, quietly pushing in the direction of the dressing rooms. When he turns abruptly and lurches off in the opposite direction, he moves faster than I ever knew he could.

Len, wait! I think.

"Fucking freak," says Zoe, picking at a hole in her fishnets.

"Totally," says Ginger.

When I get back upstairs to the Consignment Corner, I press the buzzer and, for the first time ever, I hope Len will come. All those times I rang and rang, dreading the sight of his woebegone self, and now here I am, wishing I could snap my fingers and make him magically appear.

Bzzzzzzzzzzzzt. Bzzzzzzzzzzzt.

Nothing.

Bzzzt. Bzzzt. Bzzzt. Bzzzzzzzzzzzzzzzzzzzzzzzzzzttt.

Still nothing.

Reluctantly, I call down to Dollar-a-Pound.

"Y-ello?" says Bill.

"Hey, it's me."

"Veronica! What's new, pussycat?"

"Uh, not a lot. Listen, I've got a lot of stock for pickup. Have you seen Len?"

"Lenny? Ooh, you know what? You just missed him. He punched out maybe—oh, I dunno, five, ten minutes ago?"

"Oh . . . okay, thanks," I say.

"You know, it's pretty dead down here. If you want, I could come up and get the racks?" There's a hopeful note in his voice.

"No, that's okay." It's just about the last thing I need. "Thanks anyway."

"Hey, that's cool," fronts Bill. "Later, baby."

"Later," I say.

I consider my options. Len's probably left the store, and I'm sure I could find him if I ran out after him, seeing as he probably hasn't gotten far at his usual pace.

But what would I say?

That it was all a big misunderstanding?

That, despite how it looked, I don't go along with Zoe and Ginger . . . anymore?

That one of these days I'm actually going to work up the nerve to tell them about us, I swear. Really!

Yeah, that ought to go over great.

Finally I arrive at a plan that I like: I will leave early and go to Len's, but I'll just leave him a note or something and give him time to cool off. I convince myself that this is for the best.

So I open up my sketchbook to a blank page.

> Dear Len,
> How are you? I am writing to say

No.

> Hey, Len.
> It's me, Veronica. I just wanted to say

No.

> Len,
> I know you might think I'm lying when I say that I am really REALLY

Goddammit! No!

I rip out the page and toss it at the trash can, missing by

a mile. It is hideously hot in Employees Only! today, which makes everything that much more awful. I am sweating so bad that I actually consider taking off the dress I'm wearing. It's just me and the Lunch Ladies up here, after all, and the Ladies won't care if they see my stack of fat rolls upholstered by the tight cotton of the T-shirt I'm wearing underneath. Several of them appear to have tucked their own blouses into their bras and shoved wadded-up handkerchiefs between their boobs to keep themselves marginally cooler.

The current heat wave has taken its toll on Employees Only! One of the Lunch Ladies actually passed out from the heat earlier this week, causing the ever-frugal Shirley to grudgingly address the situation by providing the Ladies with a case of tiny battery-equipped plastic fans. Each Lady now has one at her station and periodically raises it and waves it around her head. When they do this, it looks like they are crossing themselves, which is quite possible since some of them do that a lot, too.

"Hot enough for ya?" my dad always used to say to the vendors at the outdoor fleas. I'd watch them guffaw appreciatively at his lame joke. Even then, I could sense their naked desire to trade their attention and flattery for his money. The thought of my dad makes me wonder how hot it is in New York right now. If my dad's going to the fleas there. If he's happy.

I kick my shoes under my desk, adding them to a pile I keep down there. I hitch my dress higher and reposition the fan under my desk so it blows air up my skirt like Marilyn

Monroe's in that old movie. I'm not going to last much longer in this heat without a smoothie, that's for sure. But the rush of cool air on my thighs gives me the strength to flip through my sketchbook in search of more blank pages. Without really meaning to, I stop on a page of sketches I made of Violet.

She really is a beautiful creature. I've almost forgotten. Her skin is so smooth and silky, and the markings on her back are as intricate as a tapestry if you look close enough. Her eyes meet your gaze with the keen flicker of intelligence, something I keep thinking I'm imagining and then I look into them again and see it anew.

In some of the drawings, she's alone, in her sleeping bag or sunning herself on Len's windowsill. She looks up at me with those smart, knowing eyes of hers and it feels almost like she's looking right through me.

Hmmph, she says, *I thought I knew you. Guess I was wrong.*

It's not like that, I protest, but I can tell she's not buying it. I flip the page to avoid her disappointed stare.

In a couple of sketches, I drew Violet framed in the fabric of Len's hoodie pocket. Len's hand was captured in these drawings as well, his soft, long fingers extending like a shelf for Violet to rest on, his fingertips curving slightly upward to cradle her. I'm surprised to see that one of the drawings of his hands doesn't entirely suck. It actually looks like Len's hands.

Len's hands.

I almost feel sick, is how it feels. What is my problem? How come for once in my life, something good happens and then I have to go ahead and fuck it up?

I start to cry, but I wipe my eyes violently to keep the tears

from dripping on the page. With a sharp, decisive tug, I rip this sketch from the book. Then I take my pen and carefully print the simplest of messages at the bottom of the page:

Len, I can explain.
Please let me explain.
Veronica

I study my note, then crumple it up and toss it at the trash can. Another miss.

"Fuck!!!" I scream in frustration.

I steal a guilty look at the Lunch Ladies. Some of them have turned and are looking my way. I wouldn't have thought they could hear me over the noise of the pressing machines.

"Sorry," I say, though none of them reply. I turn back to flipping through my sketchbook.

"Hey."

I jump at the sound of the voice and slam my sketchbook shut. I turn and see that Len is standing behind me, his backpack slung over one shoulder.

"Oh my God, you scared me," I say back, feeling nervous, yet relieved. We're clearly off to a good start—he's speaking to me.

"Sorry," Len says lightly. "I just wanted to say goodbye."

"Oh my God, seriously? You're fired?"

"Yeah, uh . . . it's actually a long story. Bottom line is, I'm not going to be working here anymore. At least not for a while."

"But why?! Not because of us, right?"

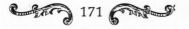

"No." *Whew.*

"Is it because of Violet?"

Len's mouth contorts into a reluctant, bitter grimace like he wants to tell me, but instead he just says, "Not exactly. It's kind of complicated."

"Well, that totally sucks! What are you going to do?"

"I dunno. It's just . . . I mean, the thing is, I'm okay with this."

"Yeah? Well . . . okay." I'm not convinced, but what am I supposed to say? Oh, yeah. I suppose I should say what I was going to say in my note.

"Len? Listen, um, about what happened downstairs?" I can't bring myself to actually say it: *About when Zoe and Ginger were laughing their asses off at you and I just kind of stood there?*

"I don't want to talk about that right now," he says curtly. "I need to ask you a favor."

"Um . . . okay."

"My grandma's coming back next week and I kind of need to have Violet stay someplace else. Is there any chance you could take care of Violet while I'm . . . I mean, while she's here?"

"For how long?"

"Well, a month . . . maybe two."

"A month? Wow, I don't know," I stammer, caught off guard by his request. "I mean, there's no way I could take her home. And if I kept her here . . . Well, it didn't work out so well last time." Understatement of the year. "If Shirley found out, I'd probably get fired, too."

Len waves his hand at me. "Yeah, bad idea. That's okay. Forget it."

"I thought your grandma was okay with your pets."

"Yeah, well. It's just . . . it's complicated."

"Plus, aren't you, like, mad at me?" I ask.

"Yes, I am," he says quietly. "But this isn't about you, okay? It's about Violet."

"Oh."

"I guess I feel like even though you act like you don't give a shit about anyone, maybe, deep down, you might actually care about Violet."

"I do," I tell him, finding one of his eyes through his bangs to make sure he knows I'm serious. *Say the rest,* I tell myself.

"Also, I don't have any other options."

Say it! I scream at myself. *"I care about you, too." Say it!*

But I can't, because I can't bear to hear him say what I know he'll say.

That he doesn't care about me and he never will again.

So instead of saying anything, I hold out my hands and I carefully accept the flannel-wrapped bundle from him. It is surprisingly compact. And warm, from his pocket. I find a large boot-sized shoebox under my desk—which reminds me uncomfortably of Dep—and gently place the swaddled Violet on some folded newspapers inside it. I combine several piles of paperwork to make room on top of my desk for Violet's makeshift habitat.

I bend and focus my desk lamp to shine on her, and I bring Elvis over, too, since Len says she needs a strong external heat source. I cut down three extra-large smoothie cups to make water dishes for her (skinks need a lot of water, apparently) and poke some airholes in the box lid. I promise to feed her dog food morsels with a pair of chopsticks, and I make a mental note to buy some cans on my way in the next day.

"She might move around in there a bit," he tells me. "If you hear her crash into the side of the box, don't freak out. She's just used to having more space."

As if to emphasize his point, the boot box kind of jumps. Len lifts the lid and gives Violet a gentle stroke with one finger, not unlike the way he caressed the edge of my bra. The memory makes my throat feel raw. I turn away and perform unnecessary adjustments to the desk lamp.

By the time Len leaves, he seems satisfied with Violet's temporary setup.

"Thanks," he says, all business.

"Len . . . ," I start to say.

Kiss me, kiss me, kiss me, I plead silently. *Or maybe just touch me on the arm. Just a little tap to tell me everything's going to be all right. I know I don't deserve one more chance, but please give me one anyway, okay?*

"What?" His tone is guarded, accusing.

"Nothing."

CHAPTER THIRTEEN

You know when something bad happens and you think things couldn't get any worse? For me, that's always a sign that things are about to get even worse.

It's like when I went to the dentist and found out I had four—four!—cavities. And then the hygienist, who was kind of hefty herself, did this whole "tsk, tsk" number and gave me this big speech like it was my fault. And THEN, when my dad took me out for ice cream after (I guess he figured, what the hell, the damage was already done), he dropped the bomb that he and Mom were splitting up and he was moving out.

My downward spiral of bad luck starts, of course, with Len witnessing the unpleasantness by the dressing rooms and deciding to hate me forever. But the next day, things take a turn for the even worse. I leave for work in a decent enough mood, all things considered, because it has occurred to me that by keeping Violet I have ensured that I will have at least one opportunity to see Len again. I dress nice just in case today's the day: an old baby-blue prom dress with an elasticized sequined tube top and a full tulle skirt (plus an extra crinoline to get that giant layer-cake skirt look I love so much), with a V-neck men's undershirt, boxers, and my two-toned creepers on underneath. I pick up two cans of Mighty Dog and an iced mocha smoothie on my way in, expecting to spend the morning pouring out my troubles to Violet and strategizing how to get Len to give me a chance to explain.

But when I get to Employees Only!, I find that I have company. Zoe and Ginger are sitting there, waiting for me, in the Consignment Corner.

I have the uneasy feeling that this isn't their first trip upstairs. Maybe because they seem too comfortable up here. Maybe because I found one of Ginger's Hello Kitty baby barrettes next to my chair when I came in one day the week before. My nervousness ramps up when I realize that Zoe is sitting at my desk, less than two feet from where the spotlights are shining on Violet's boot box. It appears to be untouched and the lid is on, as I left it. But still, too close for my comfort.

Zoe is staring at the computer monitor, pecking at my keyboard and trying unsuccessfully to log on to the store's consignment inventory database. Meanwhile, Ginger is trying on the flag dress over her clothes. She cringes guiltily when she sees me, but doesn't take the dress off.

"Hey, Vee," she says loudly, glancing at Zoe.

"Vee, do you have access to this?" asks Zoe without looking up.

"To what?"

"The store inventory database."

"Oh, yeah, no. No one ever gave me the access code. Claire had it, but since she's been gone I haven't been able to use it. I log stuff in by hand." I babble nervously, my mind racing. *Why are they here? How can I get them to leave?*

"Mmm . . . I see," says Zoe, narrowing her eyes.

"Nice dress," I say to Ginger pointedly. Her hair, which now has a couple of blue tendrils mixed in with the pink, looks like an ironic patriotic statement.

"Right?" she says, pleased. "Sorry, I've just been dying to try it on."

"Sure," I say.

Neither of them says anything, which is unusual, so I say, "What's up?"

"Oh, we just thought we'd come up here to chat with you," purrs Zoe innocently. "Why? Is anything 'up' with *you*?"

"Uh, no?" I look to Ginger, but her back is to me.

Zoe stretches in my chair, sticking out her chest and raising her hands to the sky. She's holding a closed ballpoint pen in one hand, and when her arms come down she begins to move it in circles around the cover of my sketchbook, which I suddenly realize is sitting right there in front of her on the desk.

Did I leave it closed?

Or open?

"Reeeeally?" says Zoe. "Because Ginger and I were wondering about something, but we didn't want to *draw* any conclusions . . ." She pats my sketchbook for emphasis.

Open.

"Zoe, I don't know what you . . ."

"Ah, but I DO know what YOU," says Zoe, wagging the pen at me. "And let me be the first to say, Mazel tov!"

"But I . . ."

"*Vee and Dead Boy, sitting in a tree, K-I-S-S-I-N-G,*" sings Ginger. She grins and elbows me. "Sooo, how is he?"

"Yeah, Vee. Tell us," says Zoe. "Is the Dead One a live one?"

"It's not like that," I say cautiously.

"Oh, you're no fun!" says Zoe. "C'mon, you can tell us. That's what being a Secret Spy Girl is all about. Sharing!"

"I thought it was about snooping."

"Yeah, okay, snooping and sharing." Zoe is all smiles. "Seriously, Vee, are you and D.B.W. . . ."

"We're not, uh . . . I mean, it's not . . . ," I say, unsure of what to tell them. *We weren't, and then we were, but now I'm pretty sure we're not, but I wish we still were . . .*

"She's being coy," says Zoe to Ginger.

"Don't be coy!" says Ginger.

"It's sweet," says Zoe. "But so unnecessary. Plus, it's great for us! We'll get in on the action and have some fun, clearly."

"What action?"

Zoe stands up and sighs dramatically. "Vee, darling. Please. We both know you're smarter than that."

"Look, Zoe . . ."

"There's nothing to worry about, Vee," coaxes Zoe. "Nobody has to find out! You said it yourself—the password left with Claire. You're the gatekeeper now: all the consignment clothes have to come through you. So you're the key to making it all look legit. You send stuff out with your lover boy, Claire sells it, we all split the money. Everybody's happy."

What can I say to convince them they've got it all wrong? As if they'd listen to me.

I glance at the shoebox sitting innocently on my desk. Maybe they'd believe me if I showed them Violet? Poor, sick Violet, wrapped up in the torn-off piece of pajama sleeve. I try to imagine Zoe melting at the sight of Violet. I picture Ginger tenderly stroking Violet's head while Zoe coos words of regret and apology to me.

Yeah, right.

More likely, they *still* wouldn't believe me.

Plus, what if they took it out on Violet? To them, Violet's probably no different from Dep.

"Besides," adds Zoe, "I don't know if your boyfriend clued you in on this, but there's some serious money to be made."

"He's not my boyfriend," I say. *Anymore,* I think to

myself. "Really," I add, sounding particularly pathetic. I wish there was some way I could explain or get them to help me. *Let's say he was my boyfriend, but then he changed his mind about me. And let's just say, I dunno, I wanted to figure out a way to get him to maybe start liking me again.* I look from Zoe to Ginger helplessly, searching their faces for some tiny little glimmer of compassion.

Nothing. They both look determined to break me and get me to confess to my crimes. I'm surprised they don't pick up the desk lamp and shine it right in my eyes.

Desk lamp. Violet. *Oh God. Please don't let them find out about her.*

Just then, the phone rings. I hesitate.

"Go on," dares Zoe. "Take it."

"Hello?" I say.

"Hey . . . Veronica, man, it's Bill? Listen, do you think you could come downstairs for a minute?"

"Now?" I ask.

"Uh, yeah, I guess. Unless you're, like, *in the middle of something?*"

He leans really hard on that last part, and it suddenly hits me that he knows Zoe and Ginger are up here and are up to no good. But how? And why is he doing something about it?

"Um, okay, if it's, like, *urgent,*" I say, echoing his tone.

"Yeah, urgent, that's right." He seems pleased to have communicated so effectively. "So you'll be right down?"

"I'll be right down." I hang up and turn to Zoe and Ginger.

"Shit," I say, trying to look despondent.

"Nutbuster?" asks Ginger. I nod.

"That old dyke doesn't know shit," scoffs Zoe. "Play dumb with her and you'll be in the clear."

I nod some more. Zoe seems satisfied.

"Go on," she commands, grabbing me in a kind of big impromptu bear hug, then kind of shoving me toward the stairwell.

"But," I say, realizing that as much as I don't want to stay, if I go and they snoop around more, sooner or later they're going to lift the boot box lid and discover Violet. Probably sooner.

My mind races to find a way out of this mess. But Zoe clearly isn't going anywhere. And if I try to nonchalantly pick up the boot box, they will sense that its contents are worth investigating. I weigh my options, all of which seem useless. Maybe I should just . . .

"Can't keep The Nutbuster waiting," Zoe says briskly. "Don't worry. We'll continue this conversation"—she pauses and raises her artfully painted eyebrows twice for emphasis—"later."

Why should I be surprised? There's never a lot of choice with Zoe. Slowly, I clomp down the stairs, praying they will not discover Violet while I'm gone.

I find Bill sitting on his stool behind the register next to the big scale, clutching a seltzer bottle. For once, he is not wearing a T-shirt. Instead, he has on a button-down shirt, a skinny tie, and suspenders. Same holey jeans, as usual, but from the waist up he looks like an algebra teacher or something.

He hops to his feet when he sees me.

"Veronica!" he says. "Hey, what's shaking?"

"Not a lot," I say.

"Yeah?" he says. "Oh . . . okay. Listen, there's something I've been wanting to talk to you about."

"Yeah, listen, thanks," I tell him. "You really kind of rescued me."

"Oh, yeah?" he says.

"Yeah, I mean, I don't know what they think is going on, but they're really getting kind of psycho about it."

"They?" he says.

"Zoe and Ginger," I say. "That's what this is about, right?"

"Um, well, uh, not exactly," he stammers, setting the bottle down on the counter and fiddling with his tie. I think it might have come from The Pile. Up close, I can see that although it looks like a solid color, it is actually a black-on-black print of piano keys.

"Then . . ."

"It's just that I've been talking a lot with Earl? You know, because he's in the program?"

"The program?"

"Twelve steps? You know, like AA?"

"Oh . . . sure."

"Anyways, he's been telling me how one of the steps has to do with making peace, speaking the truth, and some other kind of shit. And I was in the bathroom the other day . . ."

"Okay, too much information," I say. Lord only knows what Bill does when he hides out in the bathroom at work.

"No, not like that. I was at home taking a shower, and it just, like, hit me, man. I realized that I've never really told you how sorry I am about the way I used to act with you."

"Bill? Um, I think you have."

"No, not really. I know that when you came over to my place to watch movies, well, I wasn't always such a gentleman. You know?"

Unfortunately, I do. The truth is, Bill did a lot of less-than-"gentlemanly" things during our movie-watching days. Basically, after a few bong hits, he pretty much forgot I was there and did what I can only imagine he did when nobody *was* there. Farting, burping, picking his teeth, rolling empty seltzer bottles under the couch, and—my personal favorite—popping open his top jeans button and falling asleep with both hands tucked snugly in the waistband of his briefs. I often finished the nachos myself, then left mid-movie while he dozed.

Meanwhile, I so totally cannot deal with this right now. I actually thought that having Zoe and Ginger ambush me with my sketchbook was the "things get worse" part of today, but clearly that was just the appetizer course.

"Bill, look? That's, um, sweet, but I gotta go."

"Oh. Uh, okay. Maybe we can talk later or something?"

"Yeah, later," I say. *Much later.*

I head for the stairs, and I have my foot on the first one when Bill stamps his foot loudly, then calls out, "Hey, Veronica, can you send down some roach spray if you see it kicking around upstairs? And keep an eye out for Zoe and Ginger. I think they're kind of on the warpath for you."

"Wait . . . what?"

"Roach spray," he repeats, peeking under his shoe.

"No, about Zoe and Ginger."

"Oh, it's just something I heard them talking about in the bathroom . . ." He stops.

"Bill! Why didn't you say anything?"

"I just did."

"No, I mean, before."

"Oh, I dunno. I had important things to tell you. I guess it just slipped my mind."

I sit down on the stairs and put my hands over my face, spreading my fingers into V's over my eyes. I really really don't want to start crying. Because then Bill will definitely hug me, or worse.

But I can't help it. I am just so totally screwed. Why did I ever let myself get drawn into hanging out with Zoe and Ginger in the first place? It's like a zebra saying, *Hey, screw the law of the jungle . . . I can hang out with the lions if I want. They like me!*

Why am I so stupid?

"Aw, Veronica, man," I hear Bill say as his hand awkwardly pats my head. "It's gonna be okay. Seriously."

I look up at him. His head is cocked to one side, and his ponytail hangs down over his left shoulder.

"Follow me," he says. Since what I'm doing—sitting and sniveling on the stairs—is not exactly working for me, I do as he says. We walk past The Pile and the Pickers and step through these huge curtains that hang at the back of Dollar-a-Pound, separating the retail part from the warehouse itself.

I follow Bill past giant towers of clothing items so stained, damaged, and butt-ugly that they have been rejected by even the Pickers. There are these huge, scary-looking industrial machines that take batches of the reject clothing and smush it into gigantic rectangular bricks of fabric, six feet long by four feet square on both ends. The machines then bind the clothing bricks like hay bales, only with metal wire, and then the bricks get stacked by forklift onto wooden pallets, forming these dark, looming towers.

I don't actually know where they go from here. I've heard they get shipped to Africa or wherever people are so desperate for clothing that they'll take whatever gets sent. I have no idea how much it costs to send them or how the store makes any money off them. But judging by the sheer amount of space they take up, they are a pretty big part of the store's business.

After we get past a few rows of them, Bill disappears around a corner. I turn, too, and discover a card table next to a broken window. Through the window, I can see that right outside where we've ended up is Zoe and Ginger's beloved loading dock. Their salon.

The card table has two folding chairs next to it. On the table there's an overflowing ashtray and a rectangular wooden cigar box. "Dominoes," explains Bill. "Some of the guys in Shipping and Receiving play."

He gestures for me to sit.

"This is where I go to clear my head," he tells me. "Especially when the girls' john is *ocupado*."

"Why don't you go to the men's room?"

Bill frowns, considering the question.

"No ambience," he finally says.

O-kay.

I sit down and Bill takes the other chair. He then pulls a purple bandanna out of his pocket and gives it a shake. A couple of tiny twigs and crumbs fall to the floor. He picks up a little clump of something and offers me the bandanna.

I take it and wipe my eyes, even though they're already dry. The bandanna smells musty. When I hand it back, I see that Bill has dug a little drawstring pouch out of his pocket. From it, he pulls a small metal pipe.

"Do you still not smoke?" he asks me. Another reference to our movie-watching days.

Instinctively, I shake my head, but already I'm thinking, *Why the hell not? What exactly do I have to lose at this point?* I watch him light up and inhale deeply. He pulls off and nods, holding in the smoke. When he exhales, he says, real soft, "Look, I know it seems like the end of the world to have your friends turn on you. But actually, I think it's kind of a blessing in disguise."

"Oh?" I say, surprised to hear him characterize Zoe and Ginger as my friends.

"Yeah, I mean, I was seventeen once, too." *Fifteen and a half,* I mentally correct him. *But who's counting?* "Seems like only yesterday." Bill gazes off wistfully, presumably dreaming about bygone years spent doing, well, probably the exact same thing he's doing right now.

"Bill, no offense, but it's kind of complicated," I start to say. He waves a hand at me, dismissively.

"It always is, man. Like the Great One once said, people are strange."

"The Great One?"

"The Great One, you know. The Lizard King?"

"Are you talking about Len?"

"Who?"

"You know, Lenny."

"Lenny?" Bill laughs. "Nah, man. Jim Morrison. Jim Morrison? One of the greatest prophets of our time? *People are strange when you're a stranger . . . ,*" he croons. I shrug. Bill shakes his head. "Man, you make me feel old sometimes."

"You *are* old," I tease him.

Bill winces, then takes another drag and holds it in. "Harsh, dude," he says when he exhales.

"Kidding," I say. "Grandpa."

"Yeah, ha-ha-ha. Now, wait, I was saying something profound. Oh, yeah. When I was your age, I was running all over the place doing whatever the older kids told me to do, having the time of my life and not giving a damn if they were laughing at me or using me or what. But there came a point where I just said, Fuck it. You can live like this, or you can live by your own rules. Dig?"

"Your own rules?"

"That's right. I've told you about my rules, right? The Sacred Rules of The Pile?"

"Uh, I don't think so."

His brow furrows. "How is that possible?"

"I dunno. I mean, maybe you have and I just don't remember."

"Oh, no. You'd remember the Sacred Rules of The Pile."

"Are they the rules listed by the cash registers?"

Bill laughs.

"No, man. Those are just the store rules. This is something else entirely. Sacred Rules. You know. *Life* Rules." He gives me a meaningful look.

"Oh."

"Are you ready? Okay, listen up. Sacred Rule Number One is: Shit is shit."

"Shit is shit?"

"Yeah," says Bill, grinning proudly. "I made it up the first year I started running Dollar-a-Pound. I was in the john one day—"

"I think I've got it."

"Yeah, but dig this. It's a Sacred Rule of The Pile because it's about clothes, but . . ." He pauses dramatically. Jeez, you'd think he was talking about reading tea leaves or tarot cards or something. His eyes are the most un-drooped I've ever seen them. "It's not *just* about clothes. *Capeesh?*"

"Uh, yeah, I guess so."

"Rule Number Two," he continues, "is related. It goes like this: Sometimes shit looks like shit, but if you scratch some of the shit away, you'll see it's really gold. Covered in shit."

Bill nods sagely and I nod, too, but just to be polite. I'm tempted to make a joke about "number two" but he seems really serious, so I don't.

"That's, um . . . cool," I say.

"Wait, that's not all. Rule Number Three."

"Rule Number Three?"

"Rule Number Three is: Be very, very quiet."

"*Why?*" I whisper.

"Oh, not now. 'Be very, very quiet' is Rule Number Three. You've got to spend some time being very, very quiet because, if you do"—he drops his voice to a whisper—"*you will hear the shit talking.*"

I almost start laughing. "Is that the real reason you hang out in the girls' bathroom?"

Bill gives me a hurt look. "I'm trying to impart some wisdom here, okay? The Sacred Rules of The Pile are all you really need to find your way in this mixed-up world."

"Okay, sorry," I say.

Then, without really thinking about what I'm doing, I extend my hand. Bill gives me a questioning look, but allows me to take the pipe.

"It's still lit," he says.

I put it to my mouth and suck on it. A tiny ember glows red and I get a faint, sweet, smoky taste.

"Sorry, man. I guess it's beat after all." He digs a big crumb out of his pouch and pushes it into the bowl of the pipe. Then he hands it back to me.

"Put it in your mouth," he instructs. I do. Bill leans in and positions his lighter. "Watch your bangs," he cautions, so with my free hand I hold them out of the way. Then he flicks the lighter and the flame shoots up.

"Go ahead," he tells me. This time, however, there is tons

of smoke, far more than I expect. Immediately, I'm coughing and banging on my chest, forgetting about my bangs. The back of my throat feels like it's on fire.

"Are you okay?" he asks.

"Yeah," I say between coughs. "Fine." Bill takes a turn, then hands it again to me.

"Try not to cough this time," he says.

"You think?" I say. But I focus on this, and somehow I'm able to hold the smoke for a few seconds. This time, I manage to exhale before having a coughing fit. Which for some reason doesn't hurt as much.

"Hey, Bill?"

"Yeah?"

"Well, what if," I start out softly, not sure quite how to say what I mean. "What if you spend a lot of time by yourself but you never actually hear, you know, it talking?"

"You will," he says. "You just gotta trust."

"Yeah. No, thanks," I say. "Been there, done that."

"Huh?"

"Trusting people hasn't worked out so great for me."

"I hear that, man," he says with sort of a bemused smile. "But I'm talking about trusting yourself." He breaks into song again: *"Don't trust me to show you beauty/When beauty may only turn to rust/If you need somebody you can trust, trust yourself."*

"Dylan," he informs me.

"Right," I say to avoid another music lecture.

"Now, listen. About this thing with Ginger and Zoe. Maybe I could help out?"

"Like how?"

"Well, I could maybe talk to Ginger for you." He chuckles softly. "She sort of owes me a favor."

"Oh, yeah?"

Bill keeps his eyes down, adding more to the pipe. "Kind of. I mean, actually, we're sort of, um, an item."

I can't help but laugh out loud. Is Bill actually several times more deluded than I ever thought?

"What? Is that so hard to believe?"

Yes. "No," I say. "It's just that . . ."

"Yeah, okay, I know. I'm just some old geezer to you, right? Couldn't possibly make it with the ladies?"

I cringe. *Make it?* Somebody has got to set him straight about the way he talks. Bill takes another turn, but when he goes to pass the pipe to me, I wave him off.

"It's not that," I tell him. "It's just . . ."

"What?"

"I mean . . ." *Ugh.* "Ginger is kind of a bitch."

Bill furrows his brow. "Yeah, I used to think so, too," he finally says. "She comes off as very Rule Number One. But deep down, she's not. A prime example of Rule Number Two. And a very excellent surprise, I might add."

As he stares off dreamily, I decide not to share with him the fact that Ginger and Zoe refer to him as "Barnacle Bill" and that his one-night stand with Ginger has firmly established him as the perennial butt of their jokes. No harm in letting him think he parted the curtains—or scratched off the shit—and caught a glimpse of her kinder, gentler self.

"What about Zoe?" I ask.

"Zoe is one hundred percent Rule Number One. To the core."

"Yeah, well, that's the problem."

"Rule Number Three," he insists, waving off my concern. "Trust yourself, remember? You can do it."

"Yeah, okay."

"Seriously, you can."

"Um, Bill?" I almost can't bring myself to ask, but I've got to know.

"Yeah?"

"What about Len? Lenny," I clarify.

"What *about* Lenny?" Bill raises one eyebrow at me, like *hmmm?*

I shrug, feeling myself blush and beginning to feel a little goofy.

"Lenny," he says reverently, "is above The Rules. There is no shit to Lenny. He is the real deal. Solid gold, through and through. As I believe you know."

My heart lurches. "Bill, I'm such an asshole," I confess to him. "I'm the one who's Rule Number One."

"No, you're not."

"Yes, I am. You just don't know. I did all this awful shit to him. I made fun of him and I called him names and talked shit about him. I mean, that was before I knew him, but still. And then I killed his snake. I mean, I didn't, you know, *kill* it. But it got killed, and it was basically my fault. And then I was with Zoe while she had this shoe and she was doing this whole 'Oh, lizard, lizard' thing, and . . ."

"Whoa, whoa, whoa. Veronica, hey, hold up," says Bill,

interrupting my rant. He gives me this amused look and shakes his head.

"What?"

"You don't honestly think you're like Zoe, do you?"

"No. But almost."

"Veronica, listen to me. You may have done some dumb things. I don't doubt that. Who hasn't? But this I know: *you're not like that.* And once you take the Sacred Rules to heart, you'll know, too."

He stands up and hikes up his jeans. "Seriously, kiddo. I may not know shit about a *lot* of shit, but after running The Pile all these years, I know this shit." Bill tucks a wisp of hair behind his ear, frowns, and raises his eyebrows conspiratorially, as if to show that he's not bragging or anything. Then he gives my knee two pats.

"Listen, stay out here as long as you want. If you want to duck Zoe and Ginger, just sit tight. They punch out right at five."

"Thanks," I tell him, my eyelids starting to feel heavy.

He does this dorky little half salute and leaves.

So I sit there, surrounded on all sides by the giant-clothing-brick walls. I wonder if I'm stoned and whether I'm going to start philosophizing about *talking shit, man,* like Bill. I can't really tell, although I do feel kind of relaxed. My mouth feels dry and I really, really need an iced mocha smoothie. And some donuts.

Yeah, donuts.

Just then I notice Rags peeking out at me from behind a pile of clothes.

193

"Hey, Rags," I say. "Here, boy." It occurs to me that I don't even know if Rags is a boy. Is Rags a boy name or a girl name? If Rags is a girl, she doesn't seem bothered by my calling her a boy. Rags saunters over and bounds onto my lap.

"Watch the claws," I say. As if Rags understands me, he sits down carefully and doesn't knead my legs like Spud used to do.

"Good kitty," I concede grudgingly. I pet Rags and notice how incredibly soft his fur is. Like velvet or something. Only softer, sort of. I can't stop petting him. He feels that good.

Oh, Rags, I think, rubbing his ears, *how did I get myself into this mess? Do you know what I'm talking about? Were you just sitting there in a pile of clothes the whole time, watching this whole mess unfold? Why didn't you warn me, Rags? Why didn't you tell me I was screwing up the one thing that ever came along for me that was worth not screwing up?*

Of course, Rags doesn't answer. But he also doesn't leave. He purrs like an engine, on and on and on. Like a train chugging on through the night.

I guess I doze off. Because the next thing I know, Bill is crouched down next to me, shaking my shoulder.

"Veronica, hey, wake up, man," he says. "I told Shirley you were on break, but you might want to go find her before she finds you."

"Whuh?" I say, disoriented. Rags is gone. My neck is stiff, my tongue feels thick, and my throat aches.

 194

"Shirley," he repeats. "She came by looking for you. Said it was important."

Oh, okay, I say in my head as I slowly surface to consciousness. *I get it.*

This is the part where my day really goes from bad to worse.

CHAPTER FOURTEEN

Four Pep-O-Mint Life Savers later (thank you, Bill), I stand outside of The Nutbuster's door. I've already been through a round of thinking I really should just leave right now. Go home and never come back to the store ever again. And then realizing that whatever The Nutbuster does to me, it can't be worse than the crap my mom will dole out. Plus, my address and phone number are totally on file in the store's main office. If I suddenly disappeared and The Nutbuster wanted to find me, it would be absurdly easy.

Before I can work up the courage to knock, the door opens and I come face to face with The Nutbuster herself.

"Veronica!" she barks. "Thanks for coming by."

"No problem," I say. She kind of pulls me in and shuts the door behind me, confirming my worst suspicions. The closed door suggests I am about to get fired, or worse. Just then I notice Rags on one of the chairs facing her desk. I think I see him smile and—is it possible?—wink at me, but then I remember that I am probably still kind of wasted.

The Nutbuster reaches over and kind of shoves him off the chair, saying, "Go on, scat." Rags dashes out the cat door, making me remember what Zoe said about eavesdropping. Next to the door are several neon-pink and black floor signs. PLEASE ASK FOR HELP WITH HATS! says one. WIGS ARE NOT TOYS! admonishes another. BRRR! KNIT TIGHTS! says a third. On this one, the letters are drawn extra wiggly. To suggest they are cold, I assume.

"Have a seat," Shirley orders, so I do.

"I'm sure you're wondering why I called you in today."

"Um," I say. "Uh . . ."

"I don't know if you've heard, but we've been having some problems here at the store."

"Problems?" I echo.

"Fact is, we've had a very difficult time retaining *quality* help here at the store. You have no idea. Theft has always been a problem, especially for employees working the floor . . . but now management feels it would be a good time to deal with the situation *proactively* . . ."

As she continues, I sit there, watching her poke the air and wishing she would just come out and say it. *You're fired.* There, how hard was that? Or: *We think you were helping Len steal from the store, so clean out your desk and get out.* I am practically shaking in anticipation of her wrath. It is almost as bad as—no, actually, it's worse than—the time my mom discovered I had found and eaten all the Halloween candy (one bag of candy corn, two of assorted miniature chocolate bars) she had planned to give out to trick-or-treaters.

". . . so, what do you think?"

Oh, shit. Can I say "About what?" without looking like a total idiot? There doesn't seem to be another option, seeing as she's staring right at me with her little squirrel arms folded, waiting. But of course, she's clearly just fired me, so I don't really need to ask her to repeat it.

"Um, okay," I say.

She smiles crookedly. "I'll need to work out the salary *details,* of course, but I think you'll find the benefits package highly *competitive.*"

"Benefits?" I say.

"Health, dental, you know." She sort of waves her little hands. "I'll send up the paperwork. There's no 401(k) or anything, but we do pay holidays, plus two *personal* days a year."

It starts to dawn on me. "You're not firing me?"

Shirley laughs and looks amused. "Heavens, no," she says. "I wish we could clone you. You've had some *challenges* here, what with Claire gone and you having to do two people's jobs at once. But you've handled it *admirably* well. You even created an accounting system of your own. That kind of initiative is needed here. So I hope you'll take our offer seriously." She sits down, puts on her glasses, and begins going through a file on her desk. Clearly, for her, this meeting is over.

But it isn't over for me.

"That doesn't make sense," I hear myself saying.

"Sorry?" says Shirley, looking confused.

The pot must be making me bold or something, because suddenly I blurt out, "There's tons of stuff upstairs that I should send down, but I don't because I like it too much to let go of it. And some days I don't get through half as much stuff as I should because I'm too busy drawing pictures of the clothes. And I take a lot of coffee breaks. And sometimes . . . sometimes I take stuff."

The Nutbuster looks up at me over her glasses. She almost looks amused. "Stuff? Like what?" she says.

"Um, I dunno." I'm not sure why I added the part about stealing; it's just that she looked so unimpressed by my confession that at that point I kind of felt the need to up the ante. "I, uh, took a pair of pajamas once." Well, half a pair, actually, and truth be told, I didn't actually swipe them, because Len beat me to it, but that's not really the point. "And a tuxedo jacket."

"*Pfft*," she says dismissively. "Swag. You saved the store having to process those things. Do you have any idea how much junk this store processes?"

"What about the snake? I brought a snake to work."

"Yes," she admits. "But when I told you to get rid of it, you did. Following orders gets *noticed* around here."

Where does she think we are, Nazi Germany?

Just then I get an inspired idea. Maybe I can use my new-found status with Shirley to help Len get his job back?

"I asked Len to hold my lizard for me," I announce.

This gets her attention. "I beg your pardon?" she says, one eyebrow raised.

"The lizard, the one you caught Len—Lenny—with. It's actually mine. He was just holding it for me. If anyone should be fired for that, it's me."

The Nutbuster closes her file and takes off her glasses, giving me a confused look. "Leonard was not fired, Veronica."

"He doesn't steal, you know," I continue. "He . . . what?"

"What makes you think Leonard has lost his job?"

"You didn't fire him?"

"No." Shirley looks uncomfortable. "Leonard has some *personal* problems. He decided it would be best to take some *time off*."

"He decided?"

"Yes. What made you think . . ."

Before she finishes her question, I interrupt with my own question. "What about Claire? Why did she get fired?"

"Claire wasn't fired either. She quit."

"Quit?" I repeat.

"Yes. Didn't give us two weeks' notice, either, which would have been nice. But at least she went ahead and hired her replacement first. Would have left us high and dry, frankly, if it hadn't been for you."

"I'm not her replacement."

"Why not? You're perfect."

"But I'm . . . still in school," I say stupidly.

"Yes, that's all right. We can probably find some way to work around your class schedule this coming semester."

 200

"I'm in high school," I tell her.

"Excuse me?"

"High school." Now I'm the one emphasizing. "I'm going to be a sophomore this year."

"Really?" she says slowly. "I had no idea. You don't look like you're in high school. You're so . . ." She pauses, looking me up and down. "Tall," is the word she finally comes up with. "Did Claire know about this?"

"I think so. I mean, actually, I don't know."

"Oh," Shirley says. "Well, I really had no idea. Although perhaps . . ."

"Yeah, thanks anyway," I say, cutting her off. And then, because there's nothing else to say and I'm feeling just sober enough to not start another round of saying stupid things, I get up and walk out of Shirley's office.

My head is spinning with questions and confusion. *Did Len actually lie to me? Why did he say he was fired when he wasn't? What are his "personal problems"? Do they have to do with me? Did he quit so he never has to see me again?*

Is it because of something about the other night? How could that be? The other night it seemed like everything was good, really good in fact, between us. Was that all just an act or something?

Maybe his feelings about me changed after he had a chance to think about everything that happened with Dep. Or maybe he never really had any feelings for me at all. Maybe the whole thing was some weird joke to him. Maybe that's his "personal problem."

Out on The Real Deal, I follow the yellow brick road and head straight for the stairwell. My plan is to go straight up to Employees Only!, grab my stuff, and go over to Len's to find out what the hell is going on.

But when I pull open the door to the stairs, I hear someone talking and I kind of freeze. Because the voice I hear is Ginger's. I pause there for a second, at which point I hear her giggle. And then another voice.

Not Zoe's voice.

Bill's.

I can't hear what they are saying, but my first reaction is to kind of freak out inside. I can't believe Bill would actually go try to talk to her. I guess it's sort of sweet that he wants to run to my defense. But it's so stupid, too. Because now they're going to persecute both of us. And it will all be my fault for telling him about it and letting him see how much it upset me, knowing that he would be unable to stand silent in the face of such injustice . . . *"man."*

But speaking of silence, all of a sudden it is silent down below. I squeeze into the stairwell and ease the door open a little more. Slowly, I lean forward to see if they are still talking on the landing below.

At which point I see Ginger standing on the bottom stair, her head turned to one side and her eyes closed . . .

Totally sucking face with Bill.

Oh. My. God.

I'm so completely blown away by the sight of them that I do just about the dumbest thing ever. I let go of the door and

it slams shut—BAM—like it always does, at which point Ginger and Bill both look up, and I don't know if Bill sees me but I do know that Ginger does because her eyes kind of bug out and her mouth opens, at which point I bolt up the stairs to Employees Only! as fast as my two-toned creepers will take me.

CHAPTER FIFTEEN

Without even catching my breath, I go straight to my desk to check on Violet. The boot box seems to be in the same spot, and my heart races as I lift the lid. I am greeted by the sight of one black pebbly paw with five long black claws extending from the pajama sleeve. It's almost like she's waving hello.

I feel hugely relieved to see that Violet's still there, though I want to make sure she's breathing. Gently, I inch the fabric back and her elongated head appears. Her shiny eyes meet mine and her pale indigo tongue darts out. I extend one finger and touch her lightly on the back of her head, between her eyes. I think she likes that, though it's hard to say for sure. She doesn't exactly purr or anything.

For about half a minute I'm so focused on Violet that I don't think about what I just saw. But then it all comes rushing back. *What the hell is going on?* Was Bill actually telling the truth about him and Ginger? Are they really "an item," as he so proudly put it? How could that possibly be? She's so cool and stylish and everything, and Bill's, well, Bill.

Plus, if they are together, how could Zoe not know?

Jesus. First finding out that Len has been lying to me, and now this.

How can the world be so fucking upside down?

About five, maybe ten minutes later, Ginger appears on Employees Only! Not counting the stairwell incident, this is the first time I've ever seen her without Zoe. She looks a bit like a baby giraffe. Or like Bambi when he first learns to walk. All gawky and splay-legged.

But beautiful. Surprisingly so. There's something about Zoe that just erases everything around her. So much so that I never quite noticed that Ginger is kind of a Pretty Girl. With incredibly fried blue-and-pink-streaked hair the texture of straw, of course, but pretty nonetheless.

"Hey," she says guiltily when she sees me.

"Hey," I reply, waiting.

"Look, what do you want?" she asks.

"I . . . what?"

"Don't be an asshole," she says. "You can't tell Zoe. Got it?"

"Yeah. Okay."

"So, what."

"What?"

Ginger rolls her eyes. "What do you want?"

"I don't know what you mean. Want for what?"

"Jesus, dumb-ass. For keeping your mouth shut, okay? Name it."

"It's okay."

"What's okay?"

"I don't want anything. I won't tell."

"Sure."

"Seriously, I won't."

"Yeah? How do I know?"

"I don't know. You don't, I guess. But I won't, really." I think about what Bill said. "I just . . . I'm not like that," I tell her.

She makes a sort of rueful noise. "Everyone's like that," she says.

I shrug. "Not me."

She fiddles with the dangling bugle beads on the flag dress, her favorite. I gather up my things, hoping she'll take the hint and leave first. I'm not planning on taking Violet home any time soon, yet I'm afraid to walk out and leave her until Ginger is gone.

But Ginger doesn't seem to want to leave either.

"Hey, how'd it go with The Nutbuster?" she finally asks.

"Um, okay."

"Did you get fired?"

"Not exactly."

"Oh, yeah?"

"Yeah." I can't resist telling her. "Actually, she kind of tried to promote me. I think."

"Get the fuck out of here."

I kind of shrug.

"For real?" she says.

"Um, yeah, I think so," I say.

"That's totally great," she says, without enthusiasm. "Really great."

"I said no."

"What? Why?"

I really, really don't want to tell her why, because I know that once she knows, things will change between us. But things have already changed between us. I have a nasty throbbing on one side of my head and I almost feel like what I saw in the stairwell was a dream or something.

Today has been beyond surreal—and getting stoned with Bill was the least of it. All of a sudden, the curtain is pulled back and nothing is what it seems: Len is a liar, Bill and Ginger are having a secret affair. And there I am, too, I guess: the employee Shirley sees as a regular grown-up professional-type person is actually a dumb little kid who screws up everything she touches.

So, basically, it's not so much that I decide to tell Ginger as it is that I pass out from the exhaustion of not telling her.

"Because . . . I'm in high school," I say.

"Get out."

"Seriously."

"No way, really? I thought they didn't hire high school kids."

"They do if they don't know it."

"Holy shit. Vee!" Ginger looks impressed. "How old *are* you?"

"Sixteen. Well, almost sixteen." Close enough.

"No way! Shit, you look, wow, older. I figured you were maybe younger than me, but I was thinking you were at least seventeen. Zoe was sure you were nineteen, like us." She laughs and shakes her head.

"Yeah, whatever. The thing is . . . ," I start to say.

"You should fucking do it."

"What?"

"You should totally take the job. Shit, you can come here after school, right?"

"Yeah, but I dunno . . ."

"What don't you know? You're good at this stuff. I mean, look at the amazing outfits you put together. Plus, you're a great drawer. I mean, you're totally artistic."

I shake my head. "Yeah, whatever."

Ginger looks pissed. "It's NOT 'whatever.' My whole life, people have told me all the things I can't do, all the things I suck at, what a loser I am. Even now, if Zoe found out about me and Bill? She'd laugh her ass off."

"No, she wouldn't," I say, even though I know she's right.

"Tell the truth," she suddenly demands. "You're his friend, but he totally skeeves you, right?"

For a second, I think she's talking about Len. I hold my breath, wondering if I should tell her the truth: *Yes, he did used to skeeve me, totally, but then I got to know him better, and now, well . . .*

But then I realize she's asking about Bill.

"No," I tell her. "Bill's a good guy. I mean, he's kind of a stoner, but I guess you already know that."

"Yeah," she says coyly, smiling to herself. "He didn't really give me crabs, you know. Zoe made all that shit up."

"What's her problem?" I ask.

"I dunno. She used to just ignore him. But then, when she found out I liked him, she decided he was the King of the Freaks. She's like that with every guy I hook up with." She gives me a pointed look. "Wait and see. She's totally gonna do it to you, too."

"Okay, but see, there's nothing going on with me and Lenny. I mean, not anymore. Seriously."

"Sure, whatever you say," says Ginger, smirking.

"Honestly. I swear."

"Wanna know a secret?" asks Ginger.

"Okay."

"Promise you won't say anything?"

"Yeah, sure."

Ginger hesitates. "I actually know Lenny pretty well. He used to hang out at my house a lot when we were kids."

"You . . . what?"

Ginger glares and points her finger at me. "You promised!"

"Yeah, but . . ."

"We went to the same elementary school. He was in my little brother Matt's class. They were friends."

"Really?"

"Yeah."

"Have you ever been to his house?"

"Yeah, once. A long time ago, back when he lived with his grandma over on Dorset Avenue. Before his mom . . . do you know about his mom?"

"What, that she's dead?"

Ginger's eyes widen. "Get out. Really?"

"Yeah. I mean, I think so. In the car accident?"

"What car accident?"

"The one where he hurt his leg . . . you know, the reason he walks like that?"

Ginger looks at me suspiciously. "Who told you that?"

"Why?"

"Because that's bullshit. Lenny fell off the monkey bars and broke his leg in second grade. When they did the X-ray, they found this big-ass tumor on the bone. He was in the hospital, like, a million times. I know because my mom's a nurse. She used to sneak Matt in to go see him. That's why he walks that way."

"Oh." I feel more confused than ever. "I thought he was in a car accident. With his mom."

"Nope. Did he say that?" She shakes her head in disbelief. "His mom was never really around much. When he was in the hospital, she showed up drunk a couple of times, so they called social services. And then she just took off. I don't know what the story was, but he changed schools. We never saw him after that. Until he started working at the store."

"So you knew about his pets? And . . . the snake?"

"I knew he was into reptiles, but I didn't realize that your snake was his snake until later. Honest." She looks genuinely apologetic.

"What about Zoe? Does she know about any of this?"

Ginger laughs and shakes her head. "Please! I can't even

believe I'm telling you. You have enough dirt on me as it is. If you tell Zoe any of this, I will seriously have to kill you."

"I told you, I'm not going to."

"Okay, okay. Just checking." Ginger boosts herself up to sit on my desk and starts rummaging through her giant purse. She pulls out a mirrored compact and reapplies her lipstick. Next, she digs out a handful of tiny baby barrettes and clips them randomly into sections of hair around her temples. Then, finding a nail file, she drops the bag to the floor, crosses her legs, and starts filing.

All of a sudden I have an idea.

"Look, Ginger? There is, actually, something you could do. Do you think you can maybe talk to Zoe about calling off this whole Secret Spy Girl thing? I mean, this whole theory she has about Lenny stealing clothes is completely insane. There's nothing going on like that at all, really."

Ginger nibbles on a fingernail, scrutinizes it, and then drops the file back in her bag. She hops off my desk.

"Yeah, I have no doubt, Vee," she says, sighing and zipping her purse. "I mean, I totally believe you, okay? Really. But the thing is, there's nothing I can do. Once Zoe thinks she knows something, it's pretty much impossible to get her off it."

"Yeah, but all you'd have to do is tell her you think there's nothing to it."

"Yeah, no. Sorry," says Ginger, looking extremely unsorry.

"Great," I say.

Ginger looks at me and laughs. "Oh, come on. It'll be okay. She'll lose interest. Eventually. She always does."

211

"Eventually is not good enough," I tell her. "I've got to get her to lay off this. I mean, what if I say something? You'll back me up, right?"

"Yeah, bad idea," says Ginger, talking slow like I'm five years old. "I'm telling you this for your own good. If you want to be dumb, be dumb. Tell Zoe whatever the fuck you want. But remember this: Zoe likes you, okay? You're lucky. If you want to fuck that up, be my guest. But don't go dragging me into it."

"Fuck *what* up?" I say, rolling my eyes.

"Excuse me?" Ginger's voice is testy.

I know I should stop, but I don't. "How can you stand it? I mean, she's supposed to be your best friend and you can't even tell her you have a boyfriend?"

"It's not like that," says Ginger angrily. "What you don't seem to get is that sometimes I *choose* to keep some things to myself so I don't have to listen to Zoe's shit."

"Yeah, but—" I start to say.

"But what, Vee?" says Ginger. "Admit it: whatever you and Lenny have been up to, you've been keeping it from Zoe for the same damned reasons. You want to have it both ways, too."

"Bullshit," I tell her, but she knows she's got me.

"The good thing about Zoe is, you always know what's what. Sure, she can be a pain in the ass, but at least she doesn't feed you some line of bullshit to get you to feel sorry for her or something. Like some people."

Meaning Len, I realize. Jesus, maybe she's right.

"Look," says Ginger softly. "It's simple. I'd rather be the

one having fun and laughing it up than be the one being laughed at. I've already been that girl, okay? I'll be damned if I'm going back."

Her eyes are wide, eyebrows arched. She looks angry. Or maybe, possibly . . . Yeah, she looks scared.

"I've been that girl, too," I admit.

"So you know how it is," says Ginger pointedly.

And I nod, because I do.

Or at least, up until now I thought I did.

Now I'm not so sure.

Just then, the boot box jumps.

"Holy shit," says Ginger, startled. "What the . . . ?"

"It's okay," I tell her. "It's just Violet."

"Who's Violet?" she asks nervously.

I slide the box over and pause with my hands on top. "If I show you, you've got to promise not to tell Zoe."

Ginger nods, eyes wide.

Slowly, I lift the lid.

CHAPTER SIXTEEN

he stink of Violet's dog food almost makes me barf. After Ginger leaves, I pop open a can for Violet's dinner. Violet's beady little eyes follow the chopsticks I use to extract chunks, and when I hold out a morsel she snaps at it. Dipping further into the mucky stew and trying not to gag, I start to feel more and more angry at Len.

"I was in this really bad car accident."

"Both my parents are dead."

"You're beautiful."

"You can trust me."

Liar.

Violet goes *snap!* again. She's got quite a set of jaws on her, though she's smart enough not to bite the hand that

feeds her. At least not on purpose. I've seen Len get nipped once or twice, nothing major. Violet's actually looking pretty good. Maybe she's feeling better.

Or maybe she was never even sick. Was that another lie? Another ploy to get my sympathy? I remember what Len said when he showed me Violet the first time. *"She has a rare bone condition." Sure she does,* I think, offering her another beef chunk. *Snap!* She grabs it and gulps it down, then opens up for more.

"Jesus, slow down," I tell her. "Stop eating like such a lizard."

I fish out another chunk. *Snap!* This time, she bites a little higher up on one of the chopsticks and holds on tight.

"Violet? Hey, uh, let go."

Instead, she makes these chewing motions with her jaw, like she's gnawing on the chopstick. But she does not release it. Gently, I take the other chopstick and poke it into the side of her mouth. A trick Len taught me. Violet moves her head away but does not relax her grip.

"Come on, let go." I try to pull the chopstick out, but it doesn't budge. Len also showed me what to do in this particular situation, but I haven't had to try it yet.

"All right. Hold still," I tell her. Carefully, I slide my hand around the back of her head.

I use my thumb and pointer finger to slightly pinch the sides of her jaw. Her mouth opens a tiny bit wider and the chopstick falls to the floor.

"Okay, that's it for dinner. Time for bed," I tell her. "Sweet dreams," I add. I put the box top back on and weigh it down

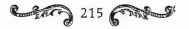

with the desk lamp. Now that she's regained her strength—if she ever lost it to begin with—it seems pretty necessary to keep her from getting loose. I have a feeling that a free-range blue-tongued skink wouldn't go over very well on Employees Only! With Rags, maybe, but not with the Lunch Ladies.

I turn on the Elvis lamp and point the desk lamp's beam downward. In this configuration, the boot box sits in its own private spotlight, like some cabaret act. It makes me think of my dad and his Big Broadway Break. Maybe, one of these days, I'll take the bus and go visit him. Go see his new place, meet the people at the hotel where he works. Hear him say, "This is my daughter, Ronnie," so many times I'd want to kill him. Or hug him. Or both.

Maybe we'll just take a walk, talk about nothing special, hang out. Maybe we'll even get cinnamon rolls and go to the fleas. Like old times.

When I go outside, it is just starting to get dark, though the day hasn't cooled down one iota. I stop by the Mooks for a smoothie. There's a new sign hanging by the registers. It says, MEET MARTIN JIMENEZ, OUR NEW ASSISTANT MANAGER. I look around. Mr. Singh is nowhere in sight.

"Welcome-to-Mookie's-I'm-Carla-can-I-take-your-order?" Through her thick glasses, Carla fixes her bovine gaze on me, showing no acknowledgment that she's ever seen me before.

I guess some things never change.

I get my iced mocha smoothie and linger in front of the Mooks with it for a minute, watching the moths dive-bomb a streetlamp. I stand there thinking, my straw in my mouth.

I want to confront Len.

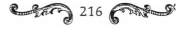

I need to confront Len.

I'm going to confront Len.

I'm terrified to confront Len.

It takes me a long time, longer than it probably takes him, to get myself over to his house and up his front steps. I ring his buzzer, but get no answer. Assuming this is because he's coming downstairs slowly, I stand there, drink some smoothie, then ring again. Finally I sit down on the weathered porch swing, prepared to wait.

"Can I help you?"

I look up and a woman is standing in the doorway, holding the door with one hand and a lit cigarette with the other. She's probably about forty, and she's wearing a tank top, frayed denim cutoffs, and flip-flops. She has light hair with dark roots and her face looks weathered, like she gets too much sun.

"Oh, I'm sorry. I must have pressed the wrong buzzer." I get off the swing. As I'm walking down the steps, I hear her gravelly voice again.

"Who ya looking for?" She cocks her head to one side and looks me up and down, kind of amused. I get this a lot. It's the prom dresses.

"Um, no one. Sorry."

"Go on back."

"Excuse me?"

"Leonard. He's out back."

"Oh. Thanks."

I walk around the front of the house and up the driveway. I practically can't see, it's so dark, but I know I've reached the yard when I step off the gravel and onto the dirt.

 217

Entering the backyard, I see Len on his knees, near the goldfish graveyard. He's wearing the gardening gloves he wore when we buried Dep and he's digging with a trowel. There's a plastic tray of small orange plants next to him—marigolds, maybe. In the light cast by a bare bulb on the back porch, he looks even paler than usual, almost like he's glowing. His neck sort of shines and I realize he is covered in sweat. His bangs shield his eyes, as always.

When he sees me, he wipes the sweat off his brow and awkwardly gets to his feet.

"Veronica," he says. "What are you doing here?"

"I just came by to . . . Look, we need to talk."

"Did something happen to Violet?" asks Len.

I give him a look.

"No," I say.

"Oh. Good. You scared me there for a second."

"For your information, I am capable of taking care of animals."

"I know. I'm sorry."

"This isn't about Violet," I tell him.

"Okay," he says.

"I mean, it is and it isn't. The thing is, I've been hearing a lot of . . . shit." Oh, great, now I sound like Bill. I try again. "I think you need to clear some things up."

"What things?"

"Well, like, I dunno. Why did you tell me you got fired when the truth is, you quit?"

Len pauses. Then he says, "Who told you that?"

"It doesn't matter who told me. It's true, isn't it? You didn't get fired. So why did you lie to me?"

"I didn't."

"Yes, you did."

"No," says Len carefully, taking off the gardening gloves. "I said I wouldn't be working at the store anymore. I didn't say I got fired."

"Yes, you did. Plus, you lied about other stuff. Like being in a car accident? And your mom, who you told me was dead, but I think I just met? And about Violet being sick."

"Violet *is* sick," says Len.

"Yeah, well, great, but what about the other stuff? Huh?" I can't stop thinking about that night on Employees Only! And the other night, upstairs in his room. "You said you wouldn't lie to me, remember? But you did, didn't you?"

"Veronica, look," says Len, shaking his bangs out of his eyes for a microsecond. "I'm sorry. Some stuff is hard for me to talk about. I wasn't sure what you'd say."

"So you just *made stuff up*?!"

"I didn't do it to hurt you."

"Yeah, well, you did! Congratulations!" I spit the words at him. "Are you happy?"

"No."

"You sure? Come on. You totally had me going. I mean, the other night, I almost—" *I can't even say it.* I am such an idiot. I'm such a dumb, pathetic fat girl, so desperate for attention she'll just throw herself at the first guy who lies to her

 219

with a straight face, even a freaking loser like The Nail. "You must be very proud."

"Is that what you think?!" he says angrily.

"What am I supposed to think?" I yell back, shaking.

"Oh, I dunno. Is it so impossible for you to believe that someone actually likes you for you? And maybe even likes you despite the way you act sometimes?"

"What's that supposed to mean?" I shoot back, responding to the second part before the first part has time to sink in.

"Just that you haven't exactly shown yourself to be the most trustworthy person."

"I never lied to you."

"Oh, really? You told me you didn't even know Zoe and then I come to find out she's your best buddy. And that everything that's been going on between you and me, which I thought meant something, turns out to be just some big joke for you and your friends."

"That's not true."

"Oh, yeah? Last I checked, you and your buddies Zoe and Ginger tried to get me fired, killed one of my pets, and got the rest of my pets confiscated by the police." He ticks these off on his fingers—one, two, three—then waggles his fourth finger at me. "Plus, now I have to go to court next week so they can fine me and keep my pets."

"Wait a second . . . what? You think I tried to get you fired?"

" 'Len steals,' remember that? Who do you think is in charge of emptying the suggestion box, brainiac? I know your handwriting."

"Jesus, Len, I can explain . . ."

"And you know what the worst thing is? When I found out, I didn't even care! That's how much I wanted to keep believing that maybe we had something real. I had myself so convinced that maybe you actually had feelings for me that I was willing to overlook all the bullshit you pulled. That's what a fucking moron I am!"

"I do have feelings for you. I mean, I did," I say.

I can't help feeling confused at how this whole situation has sort of flip-flopped somehow and my righteous indignation has kind of evaporated at the same time. I'm still mad at him. I mean, I still want to be mad at him. He's still very, very wrong for lying to me. I know that, or at least I think I do. "You still shouldn't have lied to me," is the best I can spit at him.

Len stares back at me with a look of pure hatred. "You're a fine one to talk," he says finally.

"You've got it all wrong . . . ," I start to say.

"Look, forget it," he snaps. "It's over. It doesn't matter anymore. I'm sorry, okay? Now please. Just go."

And he crosses his arms and just stands there.

He doesn't argue. Or get mad. Or anything. He just looks really, really sad. And I stand there feeling a rising sense of dread and nausea.

It's so quiet. Too quiet.

It's something I learned from my mom and dad when they split up: when all the drama is over and two people really and truly finish with each other, it gets very quiet. They don't care about each other enough to yell anymore.

It's over.

It is very quiet in the yard.

Then Len says again, "Just go. I'll come get Violet tomorrow."

And he turns and limps slowly to the back porch and up the stairs, leaving me alone in the garden.

"I don't know what I was fucking thinking!" I suddenly yell at his back door. "I never should have trusted you, never! After all the shit I've been through, you'd think I'd know better. Jesus! But you know what? Fuck you! Fuck you and fuck your fucking lies and fuck your stupid fucking pets! I don't need you! I never needed you. So ha-ha-ha."

My voice breaks pitifully on that last "ha." I turn to leave, but as I stalk toward the driveway, I trip over one of the bricks.

"Fuck!" I say, fighting not to cry.

I look down at the brick.

DEP, it says. REST IN PEACE.

CHAPTER SEVENTEEN

As I stagger out of Len's yard, the tears can't be held back anymore. I stumble down the block, find my way to the curb, and just lose it. I cry as hard as I ever have for a long, long time. It hurts so bad I want to claw my skin off. I want to throw myself in front of a bus. I want to go home and get into my bed and never get out ever again.

Home. Ugh.

There's no place to go but home.

No place to go but home. Isn't that what Dorothy says at the end of *The Wizard of Oz*? No, wait, that's "There's no place like home." Not exactly the same thing.

Dragging my feet, I can't help thinking about how good it would be if I could go to Dorothy's home instead of mine.

It sounds like the kind of place you'd want to go if you were feeling tired, demoralized, embarrassed, rejected, and just plain sad. A place of comfort, an oasis, where everyone's glad to see you and welcome you just the way that you are. *Oh, Auntie Em—there's no place like home!*

My house is nothing like that. Seriously, my house can be found in the dictionary under "unhomey." We used to have a living room, but the place where the living room used to be is now my mom's dance studio. It looks like someone came through with a giant vacuum cleaner and sucked up all the furniture. No joke: there's a barre where the television used to be. The kitchen has that sucked-up look, too. The countertop is like a desert landscape interrupted only by two objects on the horizon: a microwave and a toaster. There is no visible evidence of food whatsoever: no cookie jar, no glass canister of pretzel rods. Nothing.

I tiptoe in through the side door.

"Veronica?"

"Oh! Jesus, you scared me." My mom is sitting at the kitchen table, reading a book. She neatly puts a tasseled bookmark in her place before looking up at me.

"How was work?" she asks.

"I, uh, fine." I'm suddenly exhausted. It feels like I left the store about a decade earlier.

"Did you go out with your friends after work?" she asks hopefully.

"Uh, yeah, kinda."

"I was thinking. Maybe you'd like to invite some of your friends over one of these evenings? To hang out, or watch a movie or something?"

"Look, Mom, I . . ."

"Veronica, have you been crying?"

I look down and see that she's looking at me, actually looking at me. Her eyes have concern in them, concern that seems like maybe it is actually for me and not just about me. It's very tempting.

"No," I say.

She opens her mouth to say something. Then she shuts it and sort of frowns at me. I know she hates it when I won't let her in, but somehow the more she tries, the more I want to pull back.

"This came for you today," she says. And she hands me an envelope.

The postmark says NEW YORK.

Dad.

I flip it over and go to open the flap. Surprisingly, it gives way with no resistance. I'm pulling out the folded sheet inside when it dawns on me.

"Did you open this?"

"I—let me explain."

"You opened my mail?!"

"Veronica, your father owes us, that is, he owes me some money. I wanted to see if he had enclosed a check. I didn't read your letter, if that's what you're thinking."

"I can't believe you!"

 225

"Veronica, I told you. I looked for his check, nothing more."

"That's not the point. I can't trust you! I can't trust anyone!"

"Veronica—"

"Forget it! Just forget it!" I rip the letter in half, throw it and the envelope on the floor, and storm off to my room.

"Veronica?"

"Veronica, open the door."

"Veronica, I need to talk to you. Please."

"Veronica, if I have to stand here and talk to you through this door, I will. But I'd rather do this face to face. Please, open this door."

"Fine, if you want to be stubborn, be stubborn. You come by it honestly." She laughs ruefully.

"Sure, blame Dad!"

"Veronica, please. Open the door."

I unlock it but retreat to my bed, where I resume my position: sprawled in a facedown flop. I can see in my closet door mirror that my face is red all over.

"Veronica, I'm sorry."

"Yeah, right."

"It's true."

"You just don't get it."

"What don't I get?"

"Forget it."

"Veronica . . ."

"What?"

"I know things have been difficult for you lately." She speaks slowly, deliberately. "You have no idea how hard it is to see you like this."

"What, *fat*?"

"NO. Angry. Sad. Lonely."

"Yeah, well, for your information, I'm not lonely. I have friends," I insist.

"I know, you told me."

"Yeah, well, I do. Good friends. Lots of them."

"That's great. Good friends are hard to come by."

At which point I start to cry all over again.

"What's wrong with me?" I finally say.

"Oh, sweetie," she says, putting an arm around me. I shake her off.

"No, seriously," I say, my voice getting shrill. "What is wrong with me? Nobody has wanted to be my friend since, like, forever. And now I finally meet people who seem sort of like they might actually like me. And then it turns out they don't give a damn about me. Except maybe this one boy, but now I'm pretty sure he hates me, too."

"Oh, honey. It's going to be okay." She tries to touch me again, but I turn on her.

"No, it's *not*!" I snap. "It's not going to be okay. Everything is so royally screwed up that it is never going to be okay ever again. And it is *all* my fault."

"I'm sure that's not true."

"Don't lie to me. I'm sick and tired of being lied to by

everyone. I'm sick of trusting people and having them trick me or laugh at me or lie to me or just plain leave."

"I'm not going anywhere," she says quietly.

"Great," I snarl, turning my back on her.

"Veronica," she tries again. "I am sorry that these people that you thought were your friends treated you so badly. But that does not mean you deserved it."

I sit quietly for a while.

"I kind of deserved some of it," I finally mutter. "I mean . . ." I groan. "I dunno. It's just a big mess, okay?"

"I know."

I shoot her a look.

"Okay, I can imagine," she corrects herself.

"I've got news for you," she continues. "Friendships—all relationships, really—can be messy. The people that are worth knowing are the ones that are willing to roll up their pants and wade through the mess with you." This from the queen of sparkling countertops.

"What about Dad?"

"Sorry?"

"I mean, did things get too messy with him? Or did you just stop loving him, or what?"

"Veronica, no. Your father is just . . . that is, your father and I are just . . ." She looks like she's struggling to figure out a less nasty way to say it. "We're very different people. We always have been. And there just came a time when we realized we didn't want the same things. I will always love your father, in a way."

Right, I think, rolling my eyes as she goes on. "But we just

weren't really on the same page anymore, and it seemed best for both of us to go our separate ways."

"Do I remind you of him?"

"Actually," she says softly, "you remind me of me."

"Yeah, sure."

"It's true."

"Oh, please. I don't look anything like you."

"I didn't say you look like me. I said you *are* like me. In so many ways."

"In *what* ways?"

My mom sighs and stares off past my ear. "When I first met your father, one of the things about him that completely impressed me was how passionate he was about the theater world. I'd never met anyone who knew so much and who spent so much time thinking and talking about any one thing before. It was really extraordinary."

"Yeah. So?" It comes out harsher than I mean.

"I wasn't like that at all. When I was your age, I was incredibly shy. I didn't have any idea what I wanted to do with my life, and even if I had known, I would have been terrified to stand up and say it out loud. So I let your father's passion be my passion. We went to the flea markets together, collected together. For years."

"You . . . you went to the fleas?"

"I did." She smiles bashfully. "This was before you were born. I helped your father track down items, and I collected fabric for my sewing projects. Not seriously, like Ben." Ben is my dad.

"So . . . what happened?"

"It's like I said . . . your father and I are very different. He has always been satisfied by pursuing his interest in theater in that way. Owning little pieces of that world."

She takes a deep breath. "Your father's a good man. But he can be like an island sometimes, and he likes it that way. Me, I need people."

"So Dad doesn't need anyone?"

"No, I didn't say that. He just prefers to keep people at a distance, you know what I mean? An emotional distance."

"Yeah, well, maybe I'm more like Dad," I say defiantly. "Maybe I don't need people."

My mom shakes her head. "I don't think so, Veronica. I know you've had some rough times over the years. And I know you've gotten accustomed to spending time alone and pushing people away. But I don't believe you're actually happy like that. And I wish I could convince you that you deserve more than that."

"I just . . . it's not worth it . . . ," I stammer angrily. "I mean, there's this boy . . ."

And I start to cry all over again. And then, without really planning to, I tell her about Len. And Zoe. And Ginger. And everything.

Well, almost everything.

Obviously, I leave out the juicy parts about me and Len. And the part about seeing Ginger and Bill making out in the stairwell. And about smoking pot with Bill. Also about going over to Bill's house to watch movies earlier in the summer. I actually leave out quite a bit about Bill. Which is funny,

because he's pretty much the only one left who I'm pretty sure I can actually trust. But I tell her most of the rest.

When I'm done, my mom kind of nods and looks like she's thinking.

"It sounds to me like these girls have some self-esteem issues," she finally says.

"Well, Ginger does," I say.

"Sounds like both of them."

"Not Zoe. If anything, she's got too much self-esteem."

"You'd be surprised," she says lightly. "It also sounds like maybe you should give your friend Len a chance to explain," she adds.

I wince, remembering my final rant in his backyard. Please tell me I didn't say "and fuck your stupid fucking pets." I mean, he was inside, but still. I have the uneasy feeling his whole freaking block heard me.

"Not likely," I say.

"Give him time."

I make a face.

After she leaves, I flop down on my bed, exhausted. There's something about my mom—everything has to be a workout with her. Even conversation.

It's so annoying how she thinks she knows everything. About Ginger and Zoe. And Len, for that matter. *Give him a chance to explain.* Explain what, exactly? He lied to me, he didn't care about me, he dumped me. Story of my freaking life. Take my dad. When he moved to New York, he promised he'd call once a week. Turns out, in New York a week is actually about six months long. I wonder if Mom thinks I should give him a chance to explain that, too?

Doubtful. If anyone's more irritated at him than me, it's her.

I flop from my stomach to my side, then my back. I stare at a crack in my ceiling that I've always wanted to pick at. I flop back onto my stomach and I grab my sketchbook. I flip through, looking for a blank page.

But on the way, I pass them. Sketches of Violet and Len. Violet in her sleeping bag. Len holding Violet.

Len's hands.

Violet.

Len.

"Is it so impossible for you to believe that someone actually likes you for you? And maybe even likes you despite the way you act sometimes?"

Goddammit. I rip out the page. And another. And another. *Fucking Nail, you freak. Who needs you?*

Finally I come to a blank page. I pull one of my favorite dresses out of my closet—a seaweed-green bark cloth cocktail dress that looks like one of those outfits Maria von Trapp whipped up from her drapes—and hang it on the hinges of my door. I grab my pencil and try to sketch it, but I mess up. I keep trying again and again, but I just can't seem to make it come out right.

"I don't think you're actually happy like that. I wish I could convince you that you deserve more than that."

Fuck! Meaning what, exactly? Like she's so happy with her perfect little life? Although I guess maybe she is, now that I

think about it. She loves her students and loves performing, even if it is just for them. I mess up the drawing, then scribble all over it, then rip it out. I hate how I draw. I hate everything I do. *Why can't I do anything right?*

I rip and rip and rip. Page after page out of my sketchbook, crumpling and tossing and ripping and ripping. Until all that's left are my sketches of Len and Violet. Pages and pages of Len and Violet.

I look down at a drawing of Len. I think about how he looked when he said that thing about liking me. About liking me *anyway*, even when I screw up or act like an asshole. There was something different when he said it, something I could feel. Was he scared?

Or could that have been me?

Len.

Violet.

And one blank page. Which I start in on, trying to draw the dress again, when—snap!—the point breaks off my pencil. In frustration, I throw it down.

But as I do, I notice something out of the corner of my eye. An envelope and two halves of a letter are sitting on the bed next to me. Where, I guess, my mom left them.

I piece them back together and read:

> *Dear Ronnie,*
> *I know you are probably mad at me. I said I*
> *would write and call. All I can say is I have*
> *been very busy. I know there is no excuse but I*
> *hope you will at least try to understand. Your*

mother always said I was a lousy correspondent and she is probably right.

New York City is fabulous! The Theater District is like a dream come true for a small town boy like me. The lights, the stars, Broadway, it is too much!!! Of course, I haven't caught any shows yet because I am working so much, but my boss, Mr. Manheim, says sometimes the hotel gets twofers for the entire staff. If we do and I get the night off, maybe you can come down? Would you like that?

There are some fleas here like you would not believe. I got a crate of vaudeville 78s last weekend at this spot in Chelsea and I swear the guy almost paid me to take them off his hands! There's one guy who has a stall that's nothing but hundreds of vintage toasters! And there is a coffee shop near there with those cinnamon rolls like at Schneiders's, only better.

I will call soon, I promise.
Love,
Your Father,
Dad

Dear Dad, I write back in my head.
Fuck the fleas,
And the 78s,
And the cinnamon rolls.

 234

Just come back and stay.
     No questions asked.
Love,
Your Daughter,
Veronica

CHAPTER EIGHTEEN

That night, I dream about Claire.

She's standing at a bus stop, holding these giant, over-flowing bags of consignment stuff. She has this scarf on her head, a plastic one like my grandma used to wear when it rained, and these big Jackie O sunglasses, so I can't see her eyes. But I know it's her.

I walk toward her, and when I get close, she smiles.

"Hiya, Ronnie," she says. Usually my dad's the only one that actually gets to call me that, but in my dream I let it slide. "You're just in time. I almost thought you were going to miss the bus."

"Why didn't you tell me?" I ask her. "Why did you go and leave without telling me?"

Claire looks confused, then starts to laugh. A great big barrelly laugh. Then, like Alice in Wonderland, she suddenly starts to grow taller. And taller, and taller. And bigger and rounder, too, until she's like those big inflated balloons you see on TV at Thanksgiving. The bus stop comes up to her ankle, practically, and I have to shield my eyes with my hand to keep her face in view.

"They can't fire me!" she calls from way, way up high. "They can't fire me, I quit!"

Just then I turn and Bill's there, tapping my shoulder nervously. "It's the chute. The chute is clogged," he says. "You have to come with me." So I follow him into the store, but inside he starts walking faster and faster, and then he sort of ducks around The Pile so I can't see him anymore. But when I come around The Pile, I see Len up to his knees, digging through clothes.

"It's gone," he says. And without saying more, I know he needs me to help him look. So I wade in and we dig, side by side, even though I don't really know what I'm looking for. And then I see this loop, like one of those hand-straps on the ropes they use to walk the day camp kids around town with, and I know somehow that this is connected to what we're trying to find. So I squat down and reach in and grab it. "I've got it!" I yell, pulling.

But as I do, I hear a ripping sound. The hand-strap gives way and comes off in my hand and I feel myself losing my balance. And then, from very far away, I hear Bill yelling, "Hey! I fixed the chute. All by myseeeeelf!"

And the next thing I know there's a loud noise, like a

vacuum cleaner or something, and me and Len and the whole Pile are falling through space, falling down the chute, sliding through time and space and surrounded by flying blouses and jackets and hats . . . I can't see Len or anything all of a sudden, and I'm seized with the panicked realization that the fabric is wrapping itself around me, like a tornado or something. I'm suffocating, clawing through the fabric, trying to gasp for breath, trying to rip the musty cloth off my face and unwind it from around my neck as I fall and fall . . .

And then I wake up. I'm drenched in sweat, and for a moment I'm not even sure where I am. I see the sci-fi film festival poster, and for a hazy moment I actually think, *Did I fall asleep at Len's?*

But then I realize that I'm in my own room. There's light coming through my windows, so I have the strange sensation that I fell asleep doing homework or something and now I'm waking up just as it's starting to get dark. But I'm wearing this old flannel shirt of my dad's that I usually sleep in, so that can't be right. Then I roll over and my clock tells me it is 7:15 a.m.

I can hear birds out on our lawn making a lot of noise. Jesus, they're loud. What are they, crows? Do they do this every day? I have no idea. I'm a snooze alarm kind of girl. I squint out the window at them, but I'm facing into the rising sun, so all I see are their silhouettes.

I haul myself out of bed and start rummaging around in my closet for something to wear. If I hurry, I can get out of here before my mom gets back from her early-morning gym workout. Our talk last night was enough for me. I'm in no rush for round two.

I fail the sniff test, but to expedite matters I skip the shower, and instead I just dump a few handfuls of water on my head and smear on some deodorant. I finger-comb some pomade into my hair, rake together two stubby ponytails, and brush my teeth. I find clean underwear, one of my bomber bras, a mint-green polka-dotted shirt, and a skirt I made by sewing seven vintage aprons together. I add bobby socks and my bowling shoes to complete the look, even though I will likely pay for this fashion choice in blisters.

In the kitchen, I make some toast, eat half of it, and leave a note perched on my dirty plate. It's a conscious choice, made to give my mom something to harp on so the focus of our next conversation will not be my personal life. She takes the bait every time.

I walk to work fast, even though my shoes hurt and I no longer have anything to look forward to there. That damned refrain chases me, taunting me with each step. Because I just can't seem to get him out of my head.

Miss-ing The Nail, miss-ing The Nail, miss-ing The Nail . . .

Gonna miss that Nail, miss-ing The Nail, miss-ing The Nail . . .

Because it is Friday, the line of Pickers is already there when I arrive at the store at a quarter of eight. Bill's face lights up when he sees me through the window in the door.

"Veronica, hey! What's shaking?" he asks, ushering me in with his usual greeting. If he knows that I saw him and Ginger in the stairwell, he's not letting on. Which, knowing Bill, means he can't know. Bill always lets on.

"Not a lot," I say reflexively. I start toward the stairs, but slower than usual. I kind of want to tell him about how things unraveled with Len and get his thoughts on what I should do. So I wait for Bill to try to engage me in conversation, as he does every day.

"Okay, catch you later," he says over his shoulder. The back of his shirt reads I GOT THIS WAY FROM BOWLING! I guess I finally convinced him that trying to talk to me on my way upstairs is futile. I stop on the second stair and wait another beat.

Nothing.

Finally, I turn and see Bill pushing the big flat broom across the floor, containing The Pile's spread.

"Actually," I hear myself say, "it's pretty dead upstairs. Not a lot of consigners this week."

"Hmmm?" asks Bill, looking surprised.

"I said, it's really quiet upstairs."

"Wow," says Bill. "Must be nice. We're getting massacree'd down here lately. I've never seen anything like it."

"Oh, yeah? Huh. That must be why Shirley has been making Lenny fill the chute with back stock."

"Shit, is she really?" Bill looks concerned. "Wow, I'd better talk to her about that."

"Yeah, well, I mean, she won't be doing it anymore. You know, right?" I say. "About Lenny?"

"Yeah, man. Totally sucks." He shakes his head. "I wouldn't wish that on anyone."

"What, getting fired?"

"Lenny got fired?!"

"Hello? You just said you knew."

"Not about that. I thought you were talking about his cancer coming back."

"His—what?"

Bill winces. "He told me not to tell anyone. But you said you knew, and I thought—"

"It's okay," I tell him. "I do know. I mean, I know he had cancer. I just didn't know he was sick again. When did this happen?"

Just then there's a banging on the door. I hear the Pickers chanting, "Eight o'clock, open up, eight o'clock, open up."

"These goddamned back-to-school hours are killing me," says Bill. "Look, I gotta let them in or they'll take the door down. Just stay here a minute, okay?"

He goes to the door and unlocks it. Cheering, the Pickers troop in, some of them high-fiving Bill as they pass him.

"Hey, Dominic!" says Bill, greeting a tiny man in green platform flip-flops and mirrored sunglasses. "Hi, Rosie . . . Ay, Luigi, what's shaking? Long time no see . . . Hey, Mac . . . Hi, Red . . . April . . . Mrs. Nunez . . . Yo, Willie . . ."

Eventually the parade subsides and Bill returns to where I'm standing.

"Sorry," he says.

"You know all their names?"

"Nah, not all," says Bill modestly. "But some of these guys have been coming here for years. They're like my family or something. Anyway . . ."

"Lenny," I remind him.

"Oh, right. Well, the thing is—oops, sorry."

A lady is standing next to the scale, her arms full of garments already. Bill takes the load from her, weighs it, and rings her up. As she's digging through her purse, Bill leans over and whispers to me, "This might take a while. Irma's fast to shop but slow to pay."

I nod, then wander over to the edge of the counter and rest my elbows on it. Just then I feel a tug on my skirt.

I turn around and there's one of the store cats. He's got a paw in the air, like one of those statues you see in Chinese restaurants. His gaze is fixed on one of the dangling strings of my apron-skirt.

"Rags . . . ," I say warningly. He lowers his paw. But as I turn back toward Bill, my skirt swings and I feel his paw snagging the dangling sash.

"Chester, behave," I hear someone say. I look and it is the guy with all the hats on his head. Today he's wearing no less than seven, including three baseball caps and a ski hat with a pom-pom on top. He wades through The Pile, the hat tower wobbling as he walks, and scoops up Rags in his arms.

"He's just a youngster, that's why he's so feisty," the hat man tells me.

"He is?"

"Yup."

"I thought his name was Rags," I say suspiciously.

"Nah, this here's Chester. His brother Calvin's over there." He points to The Pile, and sure enough, I see a gray tail twitching from underneath a ripped cotton dress I depped the day before. "And that there's the mama cat, Dolly." He indicates a cat sleeping on Bill's chair. "Rags is Dolly's pop, so he's the grandpa of the bunch. He's probably down to about two lives, I tell you, the way this place is." His eyes scan the room. "I don't see him around just now."

"How do you tell them apart?"

The hat man sticks out his lower lip and shrugs. "By looking, I guess."

"Hey, Red," says Bill, coming up behind me. "What's shaking, my man?"

The hat man whips off his hats, and to my surprise they all come off as one.

"Can't complain," he says to Bill.

"Red, this is Veronica. She works upstairs."

"Hi," I say.

"Pleasure to meet you," says Red, bowing low and sweeping the hat tower across his waist. "See, I keep 'em on with spit and Velcro," he claims, scratching the tufts of white bristly hair on the sides of his otherwise bald head.

"He's just being modest," says Bill. "Red here used to be a costume designer. He's a bit of a living legend."

Red laughs. "You're half right about that," he says. Turning to me, he asks, "So, tell me, you didn't find that there skirt in The Pile, did you?"

I look down, surprised by the question. "No," I say. "I mean, it's not even really a skirt. I got the aprons at the fleas, and I was bored one day so I just kind of sewed a bunch of them together."

"Turn around," commands Red. Slowly, I do. He nods appraisingly.

"Girl, you've got the eye," he tells me.

"Thanks," I say. It feels odd to be accepting a compliment from a man wearing a tower of hats (in August, no less), but I actually kind of mean it. "And, uh, thanks for rescuing me from the killer kitty."

Red grins. "Think nothing of it."

I follow Bill back to the counter. "Everybody's got a story here," he says, shaking his head and smiling. "You wouldn't believe some of the stuff I've seen down here. One day—"

"Wait, Bill? You were going to tell me about Lenny," I remind him.

"Oh, yeah," Bill says. "Right. Well, Lenny had cancer when he was a little kid."

"Yeah, I know that part."

"Oh, okay. So you know that's why he walks the way he does. His bones just never healed right after all the surgeries, or something. But other than that, he's been fine for a long time. And then, out of nowhere, his doctors think the cancer's back."

"Oh my God. Why?"

Bill looks worried. "I dunno. That's what he said they told him. He said he's got to go get some tests to find out for sure. He made me promise not to tell anyone. I wouldn't have said anything, except I thought you knew."

"I won't tell anyone."

"It's heavy, man," he says morosely. "I mean, that kid's been through enough, you know?"

There's a shout from The Pile and Bill looks around quickly. "Shit, The Pile's getting picked over worse than usual. Wait, can you hang out a second?"

I nod. Bill goes over to the button and yells, "Clear!" All the Pickers solemnly start to make their way out of The Pile. Bill pauses, as he always does, to make sure everyone is out of the way when he pushes the button.

It's a funny thing. I've heard the chute being emptied from up in Employees Only! hundreds of times, but I've probably only seen Bill do it once or twice. Hearing it from above, it always sounds sort of like a giant toilet flushing. I always picture the Pickers gathering around the edge of The Pile, holding their breath reverently, their eyes turned toward the heavens. Wishing that something wonderful, something unspeakably beautiful and rare, will fall from above. Something with the power to transform.

The image always makes me want to roll my eyes because I know only too well what ends up in The Pile. After all, I'm the one who fills the chute with the ripped, stained, hopelessly cast-off rags that no one would ever pay retail for.

You fools! I always want to yell down the chute. *This is Dollar-a-Pound, for God's sake. There is no magic here. No surprises. Only junk.*

But standing here alongside them, I look around and I notice something for the first time.

No one is looking up.

Instead, they are talking to each other. Laughing. Comparing their finds. Bill may claim that the Pickers fight over treasures, but that's not what I see. Instead, I see an old woman, wearing a plastic grocery bag on her head to protect hair set in curlers, offering a skirt she has found to a younger woman and pointing out that the hem is torn. I see Earl picking his teeth with one of his tattooed hands while an admiring fan shows him the design on her lower back. I see the man with the mirrored sunglasses dragging a chair across the room for a hugely pregnant lady. I see Red striding out of The Pile in his ridiculous tower of hats, leaning his head from side to side to make the pregnant lady's young daughter laugh.

It's about the clothes.

But it's not just about the clothes.

And then Bill pushes the button. In a great shushing rush, I hear, then see, the great downpour. It sounds completely different from below. More like sneakers getting bounced around in a dryer. Some of the clothes fall fast—presumably the heaviest items, like winter coats and shoes—and some things flutter gracefully, as if suspended by invisible wires. A stained, filmy nylon lace nightgown that I remember depping floats down. It is so light, it practically dances in mid-air. The little girl, her mother restraining her by her overall straps, raises both of her arms with glee at the sight of it.

And despite myself, I smile.

No surprises. Only junk.

But maybe just a little magic.

I know I should go upstairs.

And eventually, I will. But I suddenly realize that there's something I've always wanted to do.

Cautiously, I wade into The Pile with the Pickers. I take one step, then another, until I'm up to my knees in clothing. I take comfort in the fact that the Pickers seem absorbed in their task, so I do the same, examining this and that. I find some things I've seen before, others I haven't. I find seven unmatched shoes, four black and three white. I line them up next to The Pile so they look like the keys of a piano.

The little girl tries on the fluttering nightgown over her clothes. I bring her two mismatched shoes and she climbs into them, giggling and holding up big handfuls of her skirt as she clomps in place. Red wades over wearing a new hat on the very top of his tower. It has a broad brim with a small bouquet of plastic daisies pinned to it.

"Nice hat," I tell him.

"It certainly is," he agrees.

He looks down at the little girl, who demonstrates another clomp and giggles. Solemnly, Red removes his new hat and places it on the girl's head. She grins shyly and folds both sides of the hat against her ears.

"Well, I'd best be on my way," says Red. "Nice to meet you, Veronica," he tells me. "William!" he yells, waving to Bill.

"No hats today?" calls Bill. Red shakes his head and winks at the little girl. "Nope," he says.

"Oh well," says Bill. "Rule Number Four."

"You're so right, my brother," Red agrees. "Not to worry, it's all good. See you tomorrow."

His hat tower wobbling precariously, Red saunters out the door. I watch as the little girl giggles and twirls in her new flowered hat, the filmy skirt of the oversized nightgown billowing out. Her dance is one of pure joy, pure happiness, pure trust. There's a part of me that remembers what it was like to be like her and feel that way, but it has been such a long, long time.

And yet.

Without checking first to see if anyone is watching or might laugh, I do a little spin, too. Then I do it again, a little faster, my apron skirt fluttering lightly.

It feels so good I do it a third time.

A little while later, Bill wanders over, a bottle of seltzer in one hand.

"Rule Number Four?" I ask him.

"I didn't tell you about Rule Number Four?"

"No! What's Rule Number Four?"

Bill smiles. "Rule Number Four," he announces. "There's always more hats."

I give him a suspicious look. "Is that another Sacred Rule of The Pile that's about the clothes but not *just* about the clothes?"

"Nah," he says. He takes a long drink, then burps heartily. "There's just always a lot of hats here."

"Are there more Sacred Rules of The Pile?"

"You tell me," says Bill cryptically. "So now, where was I? Did I tell you the part about Lenny's cancer coming back?"

"Yeah, you did."

"Right. I thought I did. Now wait, did you say Lenny got fired?"

I cringe. How can I tell him what Ginger told me without having to discuss the fact that I saw him and Ginger making out in the stairwell?

"Can I tell you later?" I finally say, returning the wave of the little girl, who is reluctantly following her mother out the door. "There's actually someone I've gotta go talk to."

What I don't tell Bill is, there are actually several some-ones I need to talk to.

Starting with Shirley.

CHAPTER NINETEEN

I don't know why, but I sort of feel like when Bill pressed that button to empty the chute down on Dollar-a-Pound this morning, it dislodged something inside me, too. For the first time ever, standing there with the Pickers, of all people, I had this tiny hopeful feeling.

And now that I've felt it, I just can't shake it. It's like a stone that I've been carrying in my pocket, polishing and polishing it without even realizing. Like something that's been with me for a long time, but I've just never felt ready to whisper it to myself, much less say it out loud, until now.

Don't get me wrong. I'm still about the clothes.

I still love, love, love the clothes.

But no matter what diamonds in the rough my trips to the fleas or my hunts through the consignment bags might unearth, I suddenly know in my heart that the clothes alone just aren't going to do it for me anymore.

Maybe, as much as I loathe to admit it, I am just a tiny bit like my mom. Maybe I actually do need people.

Not all people.

But some people.

So I go talk to Shirley. We talk for quite a while, actually. Which turns my feelings into a decision.

And yet even though I've made my mind up, it hasn't quite sunk in. I haven't quite figured out how I'm going to get along after I leave Employees Only!

The rest of the morning passes quickly. By lunchtime, I almost go into withdrawal for my beloved iced mocha smoothies. But I'm trying to avoid Zoe and Ginger, so I stay put and pull out my secret weapon: a frozen diet entrée swiped from Mom's stash in our freezer.

Nonchalantly, I saunter over to the side of the floor where the Lunch Ladies are hunched over their plastic bowls. Several of them glance up at me as I pass. I look away and approach the makeshift kitchen set up at the far wall. There's a fridge, a double-burner hot plate, and a microwave oven that is currently in use, rotating something that smells delicious. Like Mexican food, only better. A Lunch Lady stands beside it, watching the timer count down. She wears a snug embroidered sleeveless tunic with a wide collar. She has mermans just like mine.

"Is it okay if I . . . ," I ask her, pointing at the microwave, then at my frozen meal.

"Okay," she answers.

"Okay. Thanks," I say.

"The fat acheeni s'baytah," she says.

"I . . . sorry?" *Did she just call me fat?*

The Lunch Lady points at my box, a stern look on her face. "Chicken Veracruz is okay. But the fettuccine Alfredo is much better."

I can't tell if she looks so serious because this is important information or because she's concentrating hard on her pronunciation. My dad once told me that most Broadway actors can only do two looks: constipated and relieved. The Lunch Lady looks decidedly constipated.

"Ohhh . . . I'll, uh, I'll have to try that one."

She smiles big, her face relaxing into relieved mode, clearly pleased to have shared this wisdom. So much so that she gets brave and asks something else.

"Where's you friend?" she says.

"My friend? Oh, which one? The tall one? Or the little one?" I pinch sections of my hair to suggest Ginger's hairstyle.

The Lunch Lady looks confused.

"The boy," she says. "Lenny?" She pronounces his name *Lay-nee*.

"Oh," I say, surprised that she has noticed me and Len spending time together. Even though it's not actually all that surprising: Employees Only! is one big open space, so the Lunch Ladies and I can see each other's every move. I just pay

so little attention to them that I assume they do the same. "He, um, he quit."

"Ohhh. Too bad. Nice boy."

"Yeah," I say, more sadly than I intend.

She nods sympathetically and pats my shoulder before returning to her sewing machine. I nuke my lunch and return to my side of the floor, tossing a quick, shy nod in her direction. How strange. My first actual conversation with a Lunch Lady is a hello and a goodbye all in one.

The Lunch Lady waves back, then hoists her mini-fan and crosses herself. I kind of shrug reflexively, silently accepting the gesture. Maybe she's praying for me, maybe not.

Bottom line is, I can probably use all the help I can get.

I spend the rest of the day in zombie sorting mode, cleaning out file cabinets and sorting through clothes that have languished on my Definitely Should Dep This rack for way too long. When I finish, I compose a note on the back of a blank consignment invoice receipt:

> Claire,
> If you're reading this, then you're back. Welcome back! I tried to leave everything pretty much the way you had it. Except for your spider plant. It died in July. Sorry! I had a great time working in consignment. I couldn't use the

computer without a password, so I
made a log book. It is on the desk.
You can call me if you have any
questions.
Veronica

I stick the note in an envelope and lick it shut. A little before five o'clock, I pack up my personal stuff. I mark the envelope with Claire's name and put it on my desk, dead center.
I weigh it down with a coffee can filled with pens and pairs of
scissors—the industrial fans have been running on a take-no-
prisoners setting all August, and I don't want to risk having
my note end up flying out the window or into the chute or
something.

Like I told her in the note, I'm leaving all of Claire's stuff
where it is: the grass skirt on the computer monitor, the bust-
of-Elvis lamp. Who knows if she's ever coming back? Maybe
someday she actually will come back. There's not much of my
stuff here: just a handful of weird knickknacks that Bill scav-
enged from The Pile and saved for me, a few extra pairs of
shoes, a mini-umbrella, and my purse. I pack most of it into a
shopping bag and shove the umbrella into my purse.

I flip through my final rack: a Greatest Hits of my consignment days. All the stuff I could not bring myself to send
downstairs. Many of the items I have sketched are there: the
blue sailor dress, a pale yellow silk dressing gown with a scal-
loped lace hem, a dogs-playing-poker Western shirt, Ginger's
favorite—the beaded flag dress—and the burgundy smoking
jacket I wore that night with Len.

As I'm perusing the rack, saying goodbye to my favorite garments, I hear a quiet voice say "Veronica?"

I turn, and there's Len.

"Hey . . ." I drop the sleeve of the smoking jacket, feeling self-conscious. "I was just—hi."

"Hi." His voice is flat. "I came by to see Violet. I'm thinking I should take her back, probably."

"Listen, Len, I can watch her."

"That's okay."

"Yeah, but what are you going to do?"

"I'll manage." His face is grim.

"Look, Len? Bill told me."

"Bill told you what?"

"About your cancer, you know, coming back. Don't be mad at him, okay? He thought I knew."

"Oh."

"I guess he's worried about you."

"Uh-huh."

"I am, too," I admit.

"I'm going to be fine."

"Okay."

"They need to run a bunch of tests, that's all."

"Sure, okay."

"Don't get all weird. See, this is why I didn't want to tell you about this in the first place. You were the first person who ever just treated me regular."

"I won't get all weird," I say.

"Look, I haven't had a very normal life so far, okay?"

"Yeah, well, me . . . ," I start to say.

Quickly, he puts his hand up. "Just let me say this," says Len. "The way I walk, that's from the cancer and all the operations I had to have. It's not from being in a car accident."

I nod.

"But there was a car accident. It happened when I was five, but I wasn't in the car. My mom was in the car. She had been drinking. A lot. She didn't die, but she crashed into another car and two people in that car did."

"Whoa."

"Yeah. Plus, she was completely trashed, and it was, like, her tenth deewee, so they locked her up for a really long time. And she got out after I was diagnosed, but she started drinking again and using drugs and stuff, so I just kept living with my grandmother."

"And your dad?"

"No idea. Never met him."

"Wow."

"Yeah. So my mom's been pretty much dead to me ever since then. But at the beginning of this summer, she got into a program and my grandmother went to stay with her and make sure she stayed straight. Which she did—barely. So now she's making all kinds of promises that if my grandma lets her come live with us, it will be okay."

"Oh."

"Which it probably won't, but I kind of need to give it the best shot possible. My mom and . . . everything. You know?"

"Sure," I say, nodding like *I've been there* but still reeling from these developments. *Cancer. Drunk driving. Car accident.*

Dead people. Jail. Drug treatment. More cancer. My problems suddenly seem extremely small and pathetic.

"I just want you to know I wasn't using you."

"I know," I tell him.

"I never wanted to lie to you. But then, after everything that happened with Dep, I wasn't sure I could trust you with all this. It just seemed, I dunno, easier this way. I'm sorry."

"Me, too," I say quickly. "I mean, I'm sorry, too. For . . ." My voice trails off as I think about the many ways in which I've mistreated Len.

"For everything," I finally say.

"It's okay," he says.

And it feels so good to hear him say it that I lean in and, for the first time ever, I kiss *him*.

His mouth stays firm.

"Veronica," he says, and—*oh God*—"I'm sorry."

"Oh. I . . ." *I'm such an idiot.*

"I just can't . . . do this."

"Okay, sure." *I can't breathe.* I feel a wave of tears rising up.

"I should probably take Violet back."

"No," I say, clinging to words to keep from bawling. "That's okay. I can watch her." Where, I don't know, since I'm taking my stuff home today. But I'm not exactly thinking clearly right now.

Len looks hugely relieved. "Can I see her?" he asks.

"Sure," I say. I remove the boot box lid. Len frowns.

"That's not really going to work as a long-term habitat."

"You think?"

 257

Len gently removes Violet and holds her to his chest, stroking her head and whispering to her. I feel a pang of longing, watching his tenderness with her. *Okay, this is ridiculous,* I tell myself. *I can't be jealous of a lizard.*

"You don't have to do this," he says when he finally puts her back.

"No problem," I say, as casually as I can muster.

Len goes to put the box lid back on and accidentally bumps into me. And then he hesitates for a second and he looks like he's going to say something. And I get this fluttery feeling like I did in the split second just before he kissed me that first time. *Maybe he's changed his mind. Maybe it's all going to be okay.*

But just then, the door to Employees Only! slams open, making me jump.

"Jesus," I say.

"Noooo . . . guess again," murmurs Zoe, grinning like a maniac.

Ginger, at her side, giggles nervously.

CHAPTER TWENTY

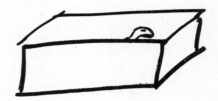

"Oh my God. Zoe, you scared me," I say.

Len steps away from me, looking uncomfortable.

Ginger is carrying a cardboard drink tray with three large coffee cups, and Zoe has a huge Mookie's bag. Zoe looks at me, then at Len, then at me again.

"I'm sorry, did we interrupt something?" asks Zoe, batting her eyes, all innocence.

"No," I say quickly.

"We just thought you might appreciate a little pick-me-up! And since the new assistant manager at the Mooks was *giving* things away, we figured, why not get enough to share with our good friend Vee?"

While she talks, Zoe walks over to the couch and deposits

herself onto it. Ginger goes over to my desk and sets the drinks down on it, then sits on my desk chair. I stand there uneasily.

"What's that smell?" asks Zoe.

"What smell?" says Ginger.

Zoe sniffs the air, then makes a face. "It smells like something died up here." She looks right at Len.

Ginger stifles a laugh.

Len's eyes narrow. Without a word, he turns and lurches off toward the freight elevator.

"Ta-ta!" yells Zoe, waving. "Bu-bye, Dead Boy."

"Hey, what's this?" asks Ginger, sliding the coffee can over and holding up the envelope marked *Claire*.

"It's nothing," I say.

Zoe raises an eyebrow, then jumps up and snatches it from Ginger. Without hesitating, she plucks a pair of scissors from the coffee can and snips off one end of the envelope. *Don't*, I plead silently.

"Hmmm . . . it looks like our dear friend Vee is quitting."

"What? Lemme see," demands Ginger, reaching for it.

Zoe holds the note out of Ginger's reach, her lips moving as she finishes reading it.

"Apparently, Vee here is leaving. Why is that, Vee, exactly?"

"Well, for one thing, I have school."

"Reeeeally?"

"Yeah. It, uh, starts in two weeks."

"*Interesting,*" says Zoe, doing her Shirley imitation. "Is that really why, Vee?" Her face contorts into an exaggerated

pout. "Or is it that you don't want to hang out with us anymore?"

"That's not it," I say.

"Or maybe you'd rather run off with your new *amour*? Muss-yer Dead Boy?"

"Don't call him that."

"Oh, I'm sorry! Do you call him something else? Isn't that sweet. Let's see. Maybe . . . 'King Cobra'? That's romantic. Or how about 'Komodo Dragon'—is that it? Or maybe . . ."

"Shut up," I say, my heart pounding.

"You know what I think, Ginger?" asks Zoe, her eyes beginning to flicker dangerously. "I think we've been had by Little Miss Two-Faced here."

"Zo," says Ginger in a warning tone.

"What? Come on, you know it's true. We were like fricking hostesses to her. We took her in, showed her the ropes, let her join our exclusive club. But meanwhile, she was always holding out on us."

"What are you talking about?" I ask, looking hard at Ginger.

"What am I talking about? Let's see. You're all, *'Oh, he's such a loser. Oh, he's so weird,'* when you're totally fucking banging the freak! You tell us, *'Gee, he's taking stuff! I wonder what he's up to?'* when you know exactly what he's up to, because you're his bitch! I mean, just look at this rack! You've been snagging all the best shit and hoarding it up here to send out with him."

"That's crap," I say.

"Hey, cut the shit," snaps Zoe.

"Look, Zoe," I try, taking a deep breath. "I know you don't believe me, but it's really, really not like you think it is. I'm not swiping clothing to resell it. Len's not swiping clothing and selling it. There's no big crime ring. No money. Nothing."

"Uh-huh," says Zoe, shooting a look at Ginger. "Sure. I suppose he's just taking things to start his own clothing line. *For lizards.*" She snorts with laughter.

I look at Ginger. *I fucking trusted you.*

Ginger looks away.

Zoe stalks over to the rack of all my favorites and grabs a handful of hangers. "Hmm, nice," she says, admiring the silk bed jacket. She turns to me. "Well, gee, if these clothes really aren't worth anything to you, I guess you won't mind if I get rid of them?"

She plucks two hangers, the dresses pirouetting from their wire gallows, and strides over to the chute. Before I can say a word, they're gone. Zoe tosses the hangers down, too, and goes back for more.

Back and forth she troops with my favorites, every one. I can tell she's waiting for a reaction, hoping each new twist of the knife will generate a cry for mercy. I keep silent, watching her with pure hatred, refusing to let her think she's won. *It's only clothes,* I tell myself. *Like Bill's Rule Number Four: There's always more hats.*

Zoe keeps on depping my treasures until only one item remains: the beaded flag dress.

"Not the flag dress!" says Ginger, making pleading puppy dog eyes at Zoe.

But Zoe's on fire and she can't stop. She's like this Greek

god in a cartoon they showed us at school once, Zeus standing at the top of the world emptying a big sack of lightning bolts one by one, then groping around the empty bag for more. She looks around eagerly.

"Where is it?" she asks.

I follow her gaze . . .

To the boot box on my desk.

"That's nothing," I say. "It's just an old box. There's no boots in it or anything." My words are reasonable, but they come out much too fast. I stand there, watching as Zoe studies me, then gets a whiff of my fear. And smiles.

"Oh, okay," she says.

Then she extends her long black pointer fingernail and slllloooowwwly lifts one corner of the box.

"Well, what have we here?" she says.

"Look, please," I say. "Just leave her alone, okay? She's my pet and she's sick, so I need to . . ."

"Who keeps a fricking alligator as a pet??!! Jesus!!" Zoe looks at me like I've sprouted an extra head or something.

"She's not an alligator," I say. "She's a blue-tongued skink. And she's got a rare bone condition." Suddenly, I sound a lot like Len.

"You," says Zoe accusingly, "are a freak. So's your boyfriend. And your fricking freak of a pet."

"Zoe, please. Don't hurt her," I beg.

Zoe laughs, long and loud.

"Don't hurt her," she says mockingly. "Or what?"

"Zoe, look, I was going to tell you . . ."

"Shut up!" she yells. "Don't bullshit a bullshitter. It's

fricking insulting. You weren't going to do shit if it meant crossing me. Dumb-ass."

She cocks her head, as if she's considering what she should do to me.

"I had you convinced I used to be a pathetic little fat girl like you. As fucking if." She shoots me a look like, *How dumb could you possibly be to believe that shit?* "The worst part is, I actually felt sorry for you and I went out of my way to help you. I can't fricking believe this is the thanks I get for all I've done for you."

All you've done for me? I think, blinking back the tears I cannot stop. *Lying to me? Pretending to be my friend? Oh, hey, how 'bout saying you'd take care of Len's snake, then getting it killed? I can't believe I trusted you.*

I look at Ginger, her eyes wide. *And you. You're just as bad. Maybe worse.*

"Awwww. Don't cwy," Zoe says through pouting lips. "I'm not going to hurt your pwecious widdo wizard."

"Thank you," I whisper, relieved.

"I'm just going to see how it likes going on a little ride down a nice long slide." She picks up the boot box and walks casually toward the chute.

"Zoe, no!" I yell.

I run over and grab hold of the box. "Please don't do this," I beg as we both struggle to keep our grip on the box. "Look, you can do whatever you want to me, but please don't take it out on Violet!"

"*Violet?*" Zoe smirks.

"That's her name," I say, holding on tight. "She's sick and

I've been trying to help her. Please don't put her in the chute. She might get injured or die, and I know you don't want that."

Zoe looks amused.

"Oh, that's rich," she says. "*You* know what *I* want?"

"Yeah," I say, trying to think of anything to stop her. "I do. I think maybe you're a little like me. You're afraid of getting hurt, so you put up your guard and push people away before they can hurt you."

"Look, you stupid cow," says Zoe, and with a yank she pulls the boot box out of my hands, causing me to fall backward onto the floor. She tosses it roughly onto a table, then stands towering over me. "I'm nothing like you. I'm not afraid of anything. But you—you're scared of your own fucking shadow! You can't get over with your shit around here so you're just gonna pack it in and run home to your mama, boo-hoo-hoo. Isn't that right, *Ve-ron-i-ca*?"

She hits all four syllables of my name like notes on a xylophone. Her message is clear: "Vee" is dead.

"I mean, aren't you, like, twelve or something?"

She stares me down, hard.

And for a second, I am the whimpering little fat girl she wants me to be. The girl I've never been able to figure out how *not* to be. The frustrated, bitter, beaned-in-the-butt, seduced-and-abandoned-by-so-called-friends, reduced-to-tears-by-a-stupid-game-of-"I-Never," who-needs-you-anyway girl. The girl hiding behind racks of mildewed clothing at the fleas, hiding in her room drawing decades-old dresses, hiding on Employees Only! for fuck's sake.

The girl I've been for fucking forever.

The girl I'm *never* going to be anymore.

"You're wrong," I whisper.

"What? Oh, I'm sorry! Are you eleven?"

"I'm fifteen," I say, picking myself up off the floor. "Fifteen and a half, actually. I don't steal. And I didn't quit."

"Oh, really?" says Zoe, laughing.

"I got promoted," I announce, trying to look calm and composed while my heart pounds out a drumbeat.

"Right. To what? Barnacle Bill's first mate?"

Zoe laughs so hard at her own joke that she misses the way Ginger's eyes flash. I'm tempted to say what comes into my head. *Actually, I think that position's already filled. Isn't it, Ginger?*

Instead, I coolly say, "Display designer. I'll be in charge of all the store windows and promotional displays."

"What? Bullshit."

"Yeah, well, ask Shirley."

"I thought you were still in *high school.*"

"I'm going to work after school, starting next month. Half the hours, twice the pay."

Zoe stares at me. Finally, she says in a dangerous voice, "So starting next month, you'll be working down on the *floor?* With us *Florons?*"

"With my real friends," I say, trying to sound convincing on the plural part, even though I'm pretty sure all I have left is Bill.

"Now, who would that be? Oh, of course! Barnacle Bill and Dead Boy *Drooling.*" She makes a zombie face.

"For your information, Bill is a good guy. And Len is a better friend than you'll ever have." *Better than I'll ever have again, too, in all likelihood.*

"Oh, lucky, lucky you!" she trills sarcastically. "But remember, sweetie. Your boyfriends don't stray far from The Pile. So you'd better watch your back. Because on The Real Deal, your fat ass is mine."

"I'm not afraid of you, Zoe," I tell her.

"You should be," she snarls.

And she's right. I should be afraid. I look at her and I see her mouth moving and that look on her reddening face and I feel the hot wall of her power.

But I don't hear her words. Instead, what I hear is a voice in my head that says, *Veronica, man? Close your eyes.* It sounds a lot like Bill's voice.

So I do. I close my eyes and just listen. But I don't hear words. Just . . . noise.

See? says the voice. *That's the shit talking.*

And it hits me. It's just like Bill said, like that song of his.

If you need somebody you can trust, trust yourself.

I don't need to trust Zoe anymore. Or Ginger.

There's only one person I need to trust.

Me.

And then I hear something else.

Not Zoe's voice.

Ginger's.

"Just . . . let it go, okay?" she is saying to Zoe.

267

I open my eyes and see that Zoe is not listening to her. Zoe is raging, exploding with anger and frustration.

"Let it go? Let it go?" she fumes. "Yeah, okay! You bet I'll let it go. Watch me let it go."

With no warning, Zoe stalks over and grabs the boot box from where she's left it. She grabs it and practically runs over to the chute. "I'm letting it go!" she yells, overturning the box. "See ya later, alligator!!!"

"No!" I yell, running with outstretched arms.

I don't make it in time.

But I do catch a glimpse of what falls from the box: a pink wisp of buttery soft flannel . . .

And a shoe.

Unfortunately, Zoe sees it, too.

"Where is it?" she demands, whirling around.

I stand there, my mouth open, saying nothing. I have no idea.

"Goddammit, where's the fucking lizard?!"

"Lizard?" says Ginger nervously. "What lizard?"

"Look, bitch. Give me the fucking lizard."

"I don't know what you're talking about."

Just then, Zoe spies Ginger's bag, her big hobo purse, next to my desk. She gives a knowing laugh, tosses the empty boot box aside, and strides over to it.

"Zo, what are you doing? Leave my bag alone."

Zoe ignores her, reaching in.

"Seriously, Zo, don't do that."

"Why not? You afraid I migh—augghhhhh!!!!"

Zoe's eyes suddenly bug out and she makes this horrible

noise somewhere between a scream and a gag. She shakes her arm violently, but the bag is stuck on it and won't come off. She backs up, still trying to knock the bag off, until she crashes into a wall. Then she twists her ankle in her thigh-high black vinyl boots. One ankle goes down; then her legs buckle and she completely slides down the wall, landing on her butt.

And her eyes close.

"Holy shit! Oh my God, oh my God. Zoe!!!" Ginger screams, horrified.

"She's gonna be okay," I tell her.

"What are you talking about? Look at her!"

"Actually, Veronica's right," calls a voice.

It is Len, standing quietly next to the freight elevator shaft. Hopefully, he's just come back from downstairs and has not watched everything that just happened.

Either way, I'm pretty glad to see him.

He hobbles over to us and awkwardly kneels down next to Zoe. He feels for a pulse. Then he unzips the purse the rest of the way and slides it off her arm . . .

Revealing Violet, with her jaws locked around Zoe's pointer finger. Her jaws unclench and clench repeatedly, like she did with the chopstick. Or like she's trying to chew Zoe's finger off.

"Oh my God," Ginger says again.

"Hold on," I say, as much to Violet as to Ginger. I slide my hand around her jaw and squeeze the hinge lightly. Her jaw extends and she releases her grip on Zoe's hand. I slide my other hand under Violet's belly and transfer her to Len, who wraps his T-shirt around her protectively.

"Is she . . ." Ginger gestures to Zoe, who is still out. "I mean, is she going to be okay?"

"Yeah, she'll be up in a few minutes," Len says. "The venom won't kill her, but it'll make her sick for a week or so."

"Venom?!"

Len shoots me a shy smile. "Just kidding," he says.

"Jesus," says Ginger. "You're sure? I mean, she really fucking bit her."

"All lizards bite," says Len. "Especially when they feel cornered. In their natural habitat, they're cave dwellers. They react pretty strongly when enemies enter their dens."

"Or purses," I add.

Len frowns. "In the wild, they don't have . . . ," he says; then a look crosses his face and I realize he just got my joke. "Oh, right. Or purses," he says.

I feel giddy and I almost laugh. The mighty Zoe, laid low by little old Violet. *Speak softly and carry a lizard in your purse.* Hey, maybe that should be Rule Number Five.

Just then, Zoe's eyes flutter and she mumbles, "I don' feel so good."

"I can't believe you did that," I tell Ginger. "Thanks."

"I can't either," says Ginger, making a face. "Now I'm really going to puke."

"You might want to take her to a doctor anyway," says Len, checking Zoe's pulse. "I mean, she's fine, but still."

Ginger nods and plays with a little stringy baby-blue tendril of her hair. She reaches out and touches my arm.

"Look, Veronica? I'm really sorry. I never should have told Zoe about Violet. You must totally hate me."

"Nooo," I say. "Okay, a little."

"I can't believe you didn't say anything, you know, about me and Bill," she mumbles. "I totally thought you were gonna . . ."

"I told you. I'm not like that."

Zoe twitches in her slumber. Ginger looks at her and groans. Finally, she says, "I guess I'll get Bill to bring his car around and we'll drag her out of here. Not that she'll appreciate it or anything."

"You're a better friend than she deserves," I tell her.

"Please. I suck," she says matter-of-factly.

"Yeah, that, too," I admit, and we both kind of chuckle.

"You should go," says Ginger. "When she really wakes up, she's going to be a fricking mess. You've dealt with enough of her shit for one day."

So I gather up my things. Len looks at me, surprised.

"You're leaving?" he asks.

"Yeah, kind of."

"For good?"

Hmm. Concern. This is a positive sign.

"No, just for a few weeks. I was thinking I might go visit my dad. You know, in New York?"

"But why are you taking all your things?"

"I'll tell you later. Can you do me a favor and carry some of this stuff downstairs for me?"

Len nods. He eases Violet back into the boot box, though her sleeping bag is, unfortunately, gone forever. Next to my desk is the almost empty Z-rack, formerly known as my Greatest Hits rack. Only one item hangs there now: the flag dress.

 271

I take it off the rack and bring it over to Ginger.

"Here," I tell her. "It's not really mine to give, but I really think you should have it."

Ginger holds up the dress, admiring the dangling rows of beads, rippling them like a row of dominoes. She lowers it and meets my eye.

"Thanks," she tells me. "That was pretty cool, the way you stood up to her."

"Yeah, brilliant move, I'm sure," I say.

"Don't worry. She'll have forgotten everything by next month."

"No, she won't."

Ginger grimaces. "Yeah, but come back anyway, okay?"

Len holds the freight elevator door open for me with his shoulder. I get in and hold the button for him, trying not to drop the boot box.

As the door is closing, I suddenly stick one foot out, blocking the door. I lean out of the freight elevator.

"Hey, Ginger," I call across the floor.

"Yeah?" she says warily.

"Good luck with . . ." *With what, exactly? Explaining to Zoe how exactly she came to be bitten by a lizard? Continuing to hide her relationship with Bill from Zoe? Finding the courage to ever tell Zoe what she really thinks about anything?*

"With everything," I finally say.

"Yeah, I'm gonna need it," says Ginger, staring at Zoe and shaking her head.

"Nice," Len says to me in his quiet, understated way.

"Thanks," I reply, my heart pounding.

He releases the button and the elevator door swings closed. We start to ride down in silence.

"I never . . . ," I start to say, but my voice trails off. *I never felt this way about anyone before. I never would have acted like such a jerk if I had realized how much I care about you. I never wanted things to end like this.*

". . . rode in the freight elevator before?" asks Len.

"Yeah," I say, gratefully.

"Well," says Len softly, "there's a first time for everything."

It turns out the door side of the freight elevator has a metal gate but no actual wall. So as we descend, we watch everything go by: Employees Only!, The Real Deal, and finally, our destination: Dollar-a-Pound. Len gets out first and holds the gate open for me.

The lights are all out, and Bill has already gone for the day. In the light filtering in from the small windows on one side, I see the hulking mass of The Pile. It looks like a giant slumbering spider, with sleeves and trousers sticking out in all directions like legs.

Tomorrow morning, as usual, the spider will wake up and Dollar-a-Pound will be in full swing. The Pickers will line up early and get right to work dissecting The Pile. I pause, imagining the Pickers' cries of astonished glee when, later in the morning, Bill yells "Clear!" and my prized possessions float down from the sky.

I feel panicky as it occurs to me that the Pickers may not recognize the value and intrinsic beauty of my hoarded treasures. They may step on these prizes as they would any other

rag in The Pile, or fight over them and rip them to shreds. I suddenly long for all the gems I spent the summer culling, all the prizes Zoe snatched and fed to the chute. I feel a strong desire to run to the button myself, right now, and empty the chute so I can rescue them myself. I imagine myself as a firefighter rushing into a burning building, dashing into The Pile to pluck my beloved garments and saving them from being trampled, destroyed, or—worst of all—ignored and unappreciated.

But the moment passes and I don't do it. Maybe I'll be walking down a street someday and I'll see a woman wearing that blue sailor dress and I'll smile to myself, remembering that once it was almost mine. And then I let it go. Why? Because dresses are dresses, and no matter how special, how perfect, how sublime, there will always be more dresses.

I think about how some Picker will find Violet's snuggle sack tomorrow and not have any idea what it's been through. I imagine the Picker considering it—trying it on like a sock, or an earwarmer maybe—and then noticing how breathtakingly, unspeakably soft it is. I picture the Picker pausing, closing his eyes and stroking the fabric across his cheek. In my mind, he looks exactly like Len did that first day when he touched the pajamas.

I smile at the thought.

So instead of rushing to the button that empties the chute, I stand by the cash register and the giant scale and I take one last look around.

Somehow, I know that when I come back, everything will

be different. And, also, everything will be the same. After all, this is The Store Caught in a Time Warp! I see Bill's seltzer bottle under the counter, waiting for him to come open up Dollar-a-Pound to another crowd, another day. There's also a pad of paper, so I scrawl a note and tape it to Bill's seltzer bottle.

> Thanks for everything.
> See you soon.
> Veronica
> P.S. Remind me to tell you Rule #5.

"Rule Number Five?" asks Len.

"I'll tell you later," I say.

"Okay, but look. Even though we're not together anymore," says Len, "no more secrets, no more lies. From now on."

"I promise." My heart beats fast.

We're not together anymore.

And yet, *From now on.*

"Okay," he says, a warning note still in his voice. Which makes me feel the need to get something off my chest.

"Look, there's something I never told you," I whisper.

"Oh, yeah?" he whispers back. "What?"

"I used to have a name for you."

"What do you mean?"

"I used to—forget it, it's stupid."

"Now you've got to tell me," he insists.

"I used to call you The Nail."

He frowns. "With Zoe and Ginger?"

"No! Just me."

"Oh."

"I told you, it's stupid."

"Sounds dangerous. I like it."

"Yeah, well, you're weird."

"I'm weird? Who's carrying a lizard in a shoebox?"

I can't help but smile.

"Hey, why are we whispering?" I whisper to him.

"I have no idea," Len whispers back.

It's late, so the store air-conditioning has to be off, but I feel a sudden rush of cool air whip through me, startling me and standing the hairs on my arms at attention. Instinctively, I squeeze Violet's boot box just a little bit tighter.

Len holds the front door open for me.

"What does it mean?" he asks me suddenly.

"What does what mean?"

" 'The Nail'? Why was I 'The Nail?' "

I look at Len and I tell him the truth.

"It's something I thought you were. But you're not."

"Huh?"

I smile and shrug. "You're just not."

And neither am I, I think to myself.

When we get outside, we stand there awkwardly for a moment. He takes my bag off his shoulder. It occurs to me that this is goodbye. He is just going to hand my bag to me, collect Violet, and limp off in the direction of his house, while I stand there watching him getting smaller and smaller.

But he doesn't. He shifts my bag to his other shoulder and just stands there with me.

Almost like maybe he's waiting for something.

And so I say, "Follow me."

And we set off together, my lead, his pace, into the still-too-warm air and the dwindling light of what is left of the day.

ACKNOWLEDGMENTS

I suppose I should start by thanking *you*. Seriously, there are a lot of books out there. Thanks!

I also owe a huge debt of gratitude to a lot of people who helped *Vintage Veronica* become a book, and I'll apologize in advance if I forget to mention any of them here.

I will always be indebted to H. Billy Greene, who taught me to wear what you like and do what you love. I also want to thank Adam Kendall for writing and singing "I Am the Nail," which has to be the stickiest song ever written. Thanks to Jane Rosenzweig, the students in her Harvard Extension School Advanced Fiction class, and the *Harvard Summer Review* for encouragement and, in the case of the *Review,* publication of an early short-story version of *Vintage Veronica,* entitled "Following The Nail."

Thanks to my cousin Lucy Oakley for wanting to hear more. To Liz Donovan, Brooke Fletcher, Chris Cassel, Bonnie Marsh, and all the people and cats of the Garment District, thank you for taking me in from day one and making me feel at home. To Jennifer Oko (and Roomful of Writers), thank you for riding the roller coaster with me and always saving me a seat.

Thanks to Charisma Ridgley and Ann Pope: devoted babysitters, readers, grown-ups (how is this possible?), and friends. To Elizabeth Shreve, Susan R. Shreve, and Tim Seldes, thank you for your incredible generosity and for essentially adopting me. To my phenomenal agent, Carrie Hannigan, thank you for tapping me—repeatedly—with your magic wand. To Liz Van Doren and Gretchen Hirsch, thanks for editorial insights along the way. To Nancy Hinkel and everyone at Knopf Books for Young Readers, especially my amazing editor, Erin Clarke, thank you for believing in Veronica and in me. Thanks to Melissa Nelson for making this book gorgeous, inside and out.

To my parents, Dan and Elly Perl, thank you for your unconditional love and unwavering support. Thanks to my aunt, Emily Perl Kingsley, who inspires me as a writer, as a collector, and in so many other ways. To the literary lions of Washington, D.C., especially Katy Kelly, Mary Kay Zuravleff, and, again, Susan R. Shreve, thanks for your friendship as well as for feeding me lunch (Children's Book Guild) and dinner (D.C. Women Writers). Thanks to the Virginia Center for the Creative Arts for supporting my work. And major thanks to my family and friends for cheering me on every step of the way. I really couldn't have done it without you guys.

And finally, thanks to the thrifts and fleas—the Garment District, Thrift City USA, Old Gold, the Dead Mall, the 26th Street Flea Market, Lambertville, and the Georgetown Flea Market, to name but a few—and the people who love them and keep them alive.